CATCHING TI

To   Parsons is the author of *Man and Boy*, winner of the
B   of the Year prize. His subsequent novels – *One For My
B(Man and Wife*, *The Family Way*, *Stories We Could Tell*, *My
F   rite Wife*, *Starting Over* and *Men from the Boys* – were all
      llers. He has written a Quick Read for World Book Day
      pport emergent readers, *Beyond the Bounty*, and has also
s   a week as Heathrow's writer-in-residence. *Departures*,
      irst collection of short stories, is the result.

Praise for *Tony Parsons*

'I   s a remarkable novel, compellingly told'   *Mirror*

' ony Parsons gets inside the heads and hearts of modern
r n'   *The Times*

' unny, serious, tender and honest . . . Tony Parsons is writing
   out the genuine dilemmas of modern life'   *Sunday Express*

   arsons has taken as his specialist subject contemporary
   notional issues which almost every other male writer has
   ored'   *Guardian*

   Vith an intelligent dry humour, Parsons manages to astutely
   it right to the heart of family life'   *Woman and Home*

   As usual life gets worse before it gets better, making for exactly
   he sort of cathartic emotional rollercoaster read we've come
   to expect from Parsons'   *Glamour*

'Parsons' storytelling is superb and in his depiction of the
complex father/son relationship makes this a funny, insightful
and unforgettable book'   *Si*

By the same author

Man and Boy
One For My Baby
Man and Wife
The Family Way
Stories We Could Tell
My Favourite Wife
Starting Over
Men from the Boys

Tony Parsons on Life, Death and Breakfast (non-fiction)

Beyond the Bounty (Quick Read)
Departures – Seven stories from Heathrow (short stories)

TONY PARSONS

Catching the Sun

HARPER

This novel is entirely a work of fiction.
The names, characters and incidents portrayed in it are
the work of the author's imagination. Any resemblance to
actual persons, living or dead, events or localities is
entirely coincidental.

Harper
An imprint of HarperCollins*Publishers*
77–85 Fulham Palace Road,
Hammersmith, London W6 8JB

www.harpercollins.co.uk

This paperback edition 2012
1

First published in Great Britain by
HarperCollins*Publishers* 2012

A catalogue record for this book
is available from the British Library

ISBN: 978-0-00-732781-2

Set in Meridien by Palimpsest Book Production Limited
Falkirk, Stirlingshire
Printed and bound in Great Britain by
Clays Ltd, St Ives plc

For Yuriko and Jasmine
In sunshine and in shadow

Author's Note

This book is a work of fiction. But Hat Nai Yang – Nai Yang beach – is exactly where I have placed it, in the secluded northern tip of the island of Phuket on the Andaman coast of southern Thailand.

This book could not have been written without the kindness and generosity of the inhabitants of Nai Yang, who by showing me their beach helped me to understand and love their island and their country far better than I did before. But the characters in this book are all products of the imagination. The story is invented.

Only the beach is real.

'. . . it was now too late and too far to go back, and I went on. And the mists had all solemnly risen now, and the world lay spread before me.'

Charles Dickens, *Great Expectations*

'Do good – get good. Do bad – get bad.'

Thai proverb

PART ONE

Swimming With Elephants

1

On the first day we watched the elephants come from the sea.

'Look!' Keeva cried. 'Look at the sea!'

I sat up but I could see nothing. Just my daughter – Keeva, nine years old, stick thin, pointing out at a sea so calm it looked like a lake made of glass.

Tess, my wife, stirred beside me and sat up. She had been sleeping, worn out by a night in the air and coming seven thousand miles. We both watched Keeva, down where the sand met the water, excitedly waving her arms in the air.

I could actually see the heat. We were on the beach at Nai Yang, just after breakfast, and the air was already starting to shimmer and bend. I thought – If it's this hot so early in the day, what will it be like later?

Keeva was jumping up and down by now.

'Oh!' she cried. 'You *must* see it! Oh, oh, oh!'

Our boy, Rory, was between me and Tess, on his stomach, a wet and battered copy of *My Family and Other Animals* on his lap. He looked up at his twin sister, adjusting his glasses, impatiently shaking his head. Then his jaw dropped open.

'Oh,' he gasped.

Tess laughed, and stood up, brushing the sand from her legs, and all the exhaustion of the journey seemed to vanish with her smile.

'Can't you see them?' she asked me, taking Rory by the hand as they began walking down to the sea.

Then it was suddenly there for me too, this thing poking out of the water, a gnarled tube moving towards the shore. It looked like some prehistoric snorkel. Then there was another one. Then two more. All these prehistoric snorkels, steadily moving towards Hat Nai Yang. And always getting bigger.

Everyone on the beach was looking out to sea now, and there was a collective gasp as the head of the first elephant broke the surface, its huge eyes blinking, the mighty head nodding, the beads of water flying from the ears. And then another. Then an entire family of elephants was marching out of the water, their mighty grey bulks rising out of the sea like gods from the deep. I saw the men on their backs, the mahouts, lean and brown and grinning, steering with their bare feet pressed behind the ears of the great beasts.

But really all we saw were the elephants coming out of the empty sea.

'Wow,' said Tess. 'How did they do that, Tom?'

I shook my head. 'I don't know.'

I looked down the great sandy sweep of Hat Nai Yang. The beach was a perfect bow shape, and I guessed that somewhere beyond the curve in the bay there was a secluded spot where the mahouts slipped into the water to surprise the people further down the beach. But watching the elephants come out of the sea still seemed like more than a clever trick.

It felt like magic.

Keeva backed away from the elephants. They were out of the sea now, their giant feet contracting as they trod on the soft sand of Hat Nai Yang. She came running back to us.

4

'Elephants can *swim*?' Keeva said. 'Elephants can *swim*, Daddy?'

'Elephants are good swimmers,' Rory said, blinking behind his glasses. 'Like all mammals. Apart from apes and humans. They have to be taught to swim. The apes and the human do.'

His sister snorted with derision. 'I swim good.'

Rory's eyes never left the elephants. 'But you had to be taught, didn't you? And the elephants just *know*.'

Rory took my hand and we stood watching as Tess and Keeva walked down to the crowd that had gathered around the elephants.

There were four of the big beautiful brutes, being patted and petted and cooed over by the people on the beach. The bird-like chatter of Thai filled the air. It was a Sunday and Hat Nai Yang was popular with locals at the weekend. We were the only foreigners on the beach.

'Looks like a family,' Rory said.

'Four of them,' I said, smiling down at him. 'Same as us.'

But his face was serious. He peered at the elephants and the blaze of the early morning sun turned his glasses into discs of gold.

'They're very floaty,' he said thoughtfully. He looked up at me. 'What do you call it? When something is very floaty?'

I thought about it. But he was faster than me.

'Buoyant,' Rory said. 'Elephants are very buoyant mammals.'

We watched the crowd with the elephants. A young Thai woman in an old-fashioned swimsuit was lying on her belly and one of the elephants was softly patting her on the back and legs with one of its mammoth feet. The monster paw lingered over her buttocks, and seemed to think about it. The crowd roared with laughter.

'She Yum-Yum,' one of the elephant handlers shouted to

me. This mahout, the one who had some English, was by far the oldest. They looked like a father and his three sons, and they all had lean, stringy bodies. Ropey muscles, bulging veins. Their skin was almost black from the sun. 'Yum-Yum give massage,' the old man called.

It did look like a massage. We watched the largest elephant carefully wrap its trunk around Keeva and lift her clean off the sand. She shouted with delight.

'You want to do that?' I asked Rory.

He shook his head. 'They're not meant to be clowns,' he said. 'Elephants are working animals.'

'Oh, come on, Rory,' I said.

'They're not here to entertain us,' he said. 'For some sort of show. Some sort of circus. They carried teak. Maybe these ones. Maybe these were the ones who carried the teak. Up in the mountains. Elephants are good in mountains.'

'But this is work too,' I said. 'Maybe they prefer to do this than carry piles of wood around all day.'

He was not convinced.

'Elephants are strong,' he said. 'Elephants are smart.' He looked up at me through his glasses. 'Now they have to muck about with Keeva, who didn't even know that elephants can swim.'

I felt a flicker of irritation. Silently we watched the elephants moving into the sea. There were children on their backs. Keeva was on the largest elephant, gripping its ears and laughing as it splashed into the water.

We watched the elephants gently crashing through the tiny waves that lapped the shore at Hat Nai Yang. Tess was smiling as she took a photograph of Keeva. The elephants were mugging for the cameras now. The one that my daughter was on dipped under the water and then surfaced. She gasped, eyes wide, trying to find some air before she could even think about laughing.

'But they're beautiful, aren't they?' I said, mostly to myself. 'They're beautiful.'

I wiped my fingers across my forehead. The sun was getting hotter.

When the sun was setting over the looking-glass sea, we found a small strip of seafood restaurants on the beach at Nai Yang.

We walked past them on the dirt road that ran by the beach, and we had no idea which one to choose. They all blurred into each other, a jumble of tables and chairs on the sand, candlelight flickering on the tables as night came quickly in, and they all had the day's catch displayed at the beach entrance, fresh fish glistening in deep boxes of ice.

They were not much more than barns with no front and no back, straddling the road and the beach, and they all had curved wooden entrances wrapped with palm leaves. The doorways were just token gestures. There was nothing either side of them, and you could walk straight into any one of these places from the road or the beach or even the sea.

'This one,' Tess said.

The Almost World Famous Seafood Grill, a sign said in English.

The owner had strung fairy lights in the casuarina trees that rose between the tables. We stood there watching the lights twinkle green and red and blue, starting to feel the jet lag kick in, when an old Thai woman came out of the kitchen and took the children by the hand.

'I'm Mrs Botan,' she said. 'Come with me, please.'

We watched the children go off with her, passing through the archway, also wrapped in fairy lights, and down the beach to a table at the edge of the sea. Tess and I looked at each other for a moment and then followed.

7

Mrs Botan parked us at our table and disappeared. We kicked off our shoes and wiggled our toes in sand that was more white than gold. The sun went down blood red and very quickly, and the green hill that rose over Nai Yang grew dark above the glassy bay.

I had never seen a sea so peaceful. It barely rippled when it touched the shore. There were no banana boats or jet skis out in the bay, just the longtails of the fishermen, thin and wooden and curved, like one-man Viking ships. They all had a single parking light, green or blue, and the lights nodded in the warm night air.

Without being asked, the old woman – Mrs Botan – came back with bottled water for the children and Singha beer for us. Then a waiter who was about eleven years old started bringing the food. An omelette stuffed with mussels. Giant barbecued prawns in sweet chilli sauce. A fish and vegetable curry. A huge plate of steaming rice.

Tess and Keeva began to tuck in. But Rory and I exchanged a look. I think we both felt overwhelmed.

'And some bread,' I told our child waiter.

The boy was startled. He stared at me for a while, looking worried, and then he raced off to fetch Mrs Botan.

'Some bread, please,' I asked her.

Mrs Botan furrowed her brow thoughtfully. She returned to the kitchen and I could hear excited voices. The clash of pans. Eventually she returned with a plate. And on the plate there were four thin slices of white bread.

'Some bed,' she said, and then she smiled, and gently patted the arms of my son and my daughter.

'Your bread, sir,' Tess said, reaching for a prawn the size of a lobster.

The bread was white and processed and at some point, although perhaps not recently, it had been purchased in a supermarket. Surrounded by the endless bounty of the

Andaman Sea, the store-bought white bread looked like a rebuke.

Mrs Botan came back to make sure we were all right and to fuss over the children. Keeva preened and beamed, all poise and charm, but Rory was shifty and self-conscious, as if he thought himself unworthy of all the attention.

'Enjoy your holiday,' Mrs Botan said.

'Oh, it's not a holiday,' Tess said, and she smiled at me.

I smiled back. No, it wasn't a holiday.

It was work that had brought us to Phuket. We were here because of my new job and everything that came with it.

A new life. A better life. The chance to try again.

Tess did not say any of that to the owner of the Almost World Famous Seafood Grill. You can't say any of that to someone you have just met, even if they are as nice as Mrs Botan.

But Tess smiled at me on Hat Nai Yang with the fairy lights glinting in the trees behind her, and the children ready for their beds, and the bone-white moonlight washing across the looking-glass sea, and it was all there in her smile.

2

I stood at the window waiting for the rain to stop. I looked at my watch and wondered how much longer it could last. The roads here scared me when it rained.

Keeva came and stood beside me and I put an arm around her shoulder. She was still warm from her bed.

'It rains in Thailand?' she said.

I heard Tess laugh at the table behind us. 'It rains a lot in Thailand,' she said. 'Don't you remember when we came here when you were little? How hard it rained?'

'The day we fed the elephants,' Rory said.

Keeva shook her head. 'I remember the elephants,' she said.

We had arrived on Phuket at the start of the long rains, although what I had seen of the weather forecasting on the island was so vague as to be useless. The storms often announced themselves, the sky flashing electric white, and then nothing happened, or it was happening on another part of the island, or out to sea. But when the rains fell on you the sky was full of water, warm hard rain that immediately soaked you to the skin, and all you could do was run for cover and wait.

Through the trees and out on the sea, I could see the stately progress of a longtail boat. As it turned to shore, the two-stroke engine lifted from the water, and the long metal pole that held it was secured in the air by twine. The solitary figure on board began pulling fishing nets from the bottom of the boat, and tossed them on the beach. Even from this distance you could see them moving with life.

The house we were living in was a villa in Nai Yang, on the green hill that sits high above the beach. It was one of two small houses that stood at the end of a dirt road. They both had double-gabled roofs, the typically Thai roof that looks as if it has a smaller version of itself on top, like a lovely echo. The only way to tell the two houses apart was that one of them had a red satellite dish on the roof. To the great disappointment of my children, that was our neighbour's house.

Our neighbour was also our landlord – a fit-looking, elderly man with a face that seemed more Chinese than Thai. I had only met him once, when I collected the key on the first day, but I could see him at the window of the house next door now, watching the rain. He rented our place to Wild Palm, the property company where I worked as a driver.

Wild Palm staff were scattered across the island, but everyone else was a lot further south, around Phuket town and Ko Surin Tao and Ko Patong, close to the Phuket of travel brochures and dreams. But where we were, Nai Yang, was old Phuket.

This far north, surrounded by plantations of rubber and pineapple, forty years of tourism were wiped away and you could feel the centuries recede to when Phuket had been one of the world's great trading posts.

It took thirty minutes to walk down the green hill to the beach, and yet the sea felt very close. You could hear it breathing in the distance against the bow-shaped beach of Hat Nai Yang and when the rain stopped and the sun broke through, the Andaman glittered blue and gold through the casuarina trees.

This was not a place to come for a holiday. It was inland, with a different, rougher kind of beauty, thick forest that you could hear dripping when it rained, and the abandoned tin mines that dotted the landscape were a reminder that this had always been a place of sweat and toil and hard graft. This old Phuket was a place you came to look for a better life. A place to work.

I looked at my watch and decided I couldn't wait any longer, whatever the rain decided to do. It was only my second week on the job and I wasn't going to let a bit of rotten weather make me late.

As Keeva and Rory carried books to the kitchen table, preparing for their lessons, Tess came across and gave my arms a quick squeeze. I nodded because I knew she was telling me good luck, she was telling me to be careful, she was telling me that she would be thinking of me.

I kissed her lightly on the lips and went to the porch. Our neighbour was still at his window and his wife had joined him. She smiled and waved and I recognized her immediately as the owner of the Almost World Famous Seafood Grill. Of course. The landlord's name was Botan too. Mr and Mrs Botan. Mrs Botan gave me an encouraging nod as I ran through the rain to a shed by the side of our house, skidding slightly on the rain-slick dirt. Mr Botan watched me and looked unimpressed.

There was an old motorbike in the shed. A 500cc Royal Enfield, made in India, the blue paint worn down to silver metal by the years and unknown riders, its frame freckled with rust. I wheeled it outside and looked up at Tess and Rory and Keeva standing on the porch, the children holding their books, the three of them looking from me to the sky. The rain seemed to be slowing down a touch, but I wondered if that was just my imagination.

I kicked the bike into life and at that moment the rain stopped dead and the sun burst through – dazzling, impossible sunshine so bright that it seemed to have a different quality to any sunshine I had ever known. Tess laughed and shook her head and held out her hands palm up as if to say, *See how lucky we are?*

Then, waved off by my family and watched by our curious, slightly disbelieving neighbours, I rode the Royal Enfield very carefully down the yellow-dirt-track road that had been darkened to a dirty gold by the rain, and I went to work.

The Royal Enfield made you sit upright, like a man from the past, and I still wasn't used to it.

But as I rode to the airport, the sweep of Hat Nai Yang on my left, and the warm air full of the smells from the shacks cooking barbecued seafood on the beach, I felt Phuket wrap itself around me, and I began to feel better.

I looked out at the longtails moored on the bay, still surprised that so much of island life took place on the water, and when I turned back I saw a motorbike hurtling towards me on the wrong side of the road.

There were two young women on it, their black hair flying, their eyes hidden behind shades. The one riding pillion was sitting side-saddle, her flip-flops dangling at the end of her thin legs, smoking a cigarette, and the one who was meant to be riding the motorbike seemed to be reading a message on her phone.

I cried out and swerved and just missed them, smelling the stink of a two-stroke engine as we passed each other by inches and I fought for control of the Royal Enfield on the wet road. The motorbike rider had not even looked up. But her passenger turned and gave me a lazy smile, her teeth bone white against her shining brown face.

As I looked back, she *wai*-ed me.

Still smiling, still hurtling down the road, she put her hands together close to her chest and lowered her head, the sheets of black hair tumbling forward, whipping wildly in the wind. Her friend was still busy riding the motorbike and now seemed to be replying to the message. But the girl on the back gave me a *wai*.

In the short time we had been on the island, I had seen the classic Thai gesture every day and everywhere. The *wai*. I was still trying to understand it, but I didn't think I ever would because the *wai* seemed to say so much.

The *wai* was respect. It said thank you. It said hello. It said goodbye. It said very nice to meet you.

It said – Whoops! Really sorry about nearly killing you there.

And whatever it was saying, the *wai* always looked like a little prayer.

The sign I held at Phuket airport said WILD PALM PROPERTIES in the top corner, with a picture of two sleepy palm trees, and then a name and a city that blurred into one. MR JIM BAXTER MELBOURNE. Standing at the airport with a sign in my hands was about the only thing that did not feel new to me, because I had done the same thing in England.

You hold your sign and you look at the crowds but you never really find them. They always find you. I watched the crowds pouring out of arrivals until a tired-looking man in his fifties with thinning fair hair was coming towards me.

'I'm Baxter,' he said, and I took his bags. There wasn't much for someone who had come all the way from Australia.

As we walked to the car park I made some friendly noises

about the flight but he just grunted, clearly not interested in small talk, so I kept my mouth shut. He seemed worn out, and it was more than the sleep-deprived dehydration of a long haul flight. He only really perked up when we arrived at the Royal Enfield.

'Bloody hell,' he said. 'Wild Palm can't send a car? All the business I put his way, and your boss can't spring for a car?'

I smiled reassuringly. 'Mr Baxter, at this time of day the bike is the quickest way to get you to our destination.' I nodded and smiled some more. 'And you're perfectly safe.'

That wasn't strictly true. Most of the foreigners who die in Thailand are either killed on motorbikes or after taking fake Viagra. It's all that sunshine.

It does something to the head.

As we drove south, the other riders swarmed around us. Sharing food. Checking their email. Gossiping. Admiring babies. Calling mum. And all of it at sixty miles an hour. Baxter clung to my waist as the island whipped by.

We rode past walled villas and tin shacks, mosques and temples, scraps of land for sale and the lush spikes of the pineapple groves, the thick green forest of Phuket's interior always rising above us.

On the back roads the rubber plantations went on forever – tall thin trees in lines that were so alike I realized that they could hypnotize you and tear your eyes from the road ahead if you let them. On the main roads there were giant billboards with men in uniform, advertising something unknown, smiling and saluting, soldiers where the celebrities should be.

I watched for the landmark I had been told to look out for – the big roundabout at Thalang where dark, life-sized statues of two young women stood on a marble plinth in the middle of the busy junction.

I turned left at the statues and then took a right on to a side road where a Muslim girl who was about nine years old, the same age as Keeva and Rory, bumped solemnly towards us on her motorbike, her eyes unblinking above her veil.

As the warm air touched the sweat on my face, I felt Baxter clinging to me even tighter.

I knew exactly how he felt.

It was all new to me, too.

Farren's home came out of nowhere.

The road stuttered out into almost nothing, just this hard-packed dirt track surrounded by mangroves, making me think I must have taken a wrong turn.

Then it appeared. A development of modern houses that had been carved out of the mangrove swamp. You could see the bay beyond, and the boats in their berths at the yacht club.

We paused at the security barrier and now Baxter felt like talking.

'Farren has done all right for himself,' he said. 'Your boss.' I could feel his breath on the back of my neck. 'Known him long, have you?' he said.

I nodded my thanks to the security guard as the barrier came up.

'Not long,' I said, and it sounded strange – that I would be here on the far side of the world working for a man who I had known for just a few months. But Farren had found me in London when I was at a low and feeling that all the best times were behind me. He had seen some point to me when I was struggling to see it myself. Most important of all, when I had no work, Farren had offered me a job. 'Long enough,' I said.

I parked the bike in the car park and we started up the

path towards the house. A pale green snake, eighteen inches long, slithered along beside me. Its head was livid red, as if it was enraged about something. I kept an eye on it. But it got no closer, and it got no further away. It was as if we were out for a stroll together. Then at the last moment, at the end of the mangroves, it slipped back into the trees.

Before I rang the bell, Farren's man answered the door. Pirin. A short, heavy-set Thai, dark as one of the elephant mahouts. He led us inside. I had only been here a handful of times, and the beauty of Farren's home took my breath away.

It was full of glass and air and space. But it was Thai. Handwoven rugs on gleaming hardwood floors. Claw-foot sofas and chairs carved from more hardwood. That sense of abundance, as though the world would never run out. Beyond the glass wall of the living room there was an infinity pool that seemed suspended in space. It hung above the bay like a good dream.

Farren rose from the water, his body tanned and hard, and as Pirin draped a white towel around his broad shoulders, he came towards us smiling with all his white teeth.

'I want my money back,' Baxter said.

The Australian was an old guy, worn out from the plane, stiff and creaky from the ride on my motorbike. His strong days were all behind him.

But once he had his hands around Farren's throat, it took Pirin and me quite a while to pull him off.

3

I walked from Farren's home back down to the security gate, pausing to let a flock of two-stroke bikes pass by – all the cleaners and cooks and maids coming to work, two or three of them perched on some of the bikes – and I tasted the diesel of their little machines on the back of my throat.

I watched the tribe of helpers hurrying to their work in the big white houses and it seemed strange to me, like something from a hundred years ago, a world divided into people who were servants and people who were served.

I headed down a track through the mangroves that eventually led to the bay until I came to a single-storey building with blacked-out windows. It looked like an abandoned barracks at an army base. But this was the heart of Wild Palm, and as soon as I opened the door I was hit by a barrage of noise.

A long table, covered with phones, computer screens and half-eaten food, surrounded by a dozen men and women – mostly men – all of them dressed for the beach, all of them speaking urgently into handsets – cajoling, pleading, bullying, laughing, taunting and selling – always selling. None of them were over thirty. All of them were talking English but the accents were from the US and the UK and South Africa and Australia. I walked to the far end of the room to the water cooler. Some eyes flicked my way, but they all ignored me.

I sipped from a polystyrene cup, and nodded at a young Englishman called Jesse. He was very white – his skin, his cropped hair. For someone living in the tropics, he looked as though he had never been touched by the sun. He was wearing a baggy pair of Muay Thai shorts and nothing else. He cradled the phone between his neck and shoulder as he doused a bowl of noodles in sweet chilli sauce.

'Yeah, yeah,' he was saying, the accent from the north of England. 'I'm at Heathrow. Just checking into my flight for Thailand. Excuse me a second,' he said into the phone, and then he stared at me, the pale eyes wide, as if I was someone else, in some other place. 'Seat 1K?' he said. 'Oh, that will be fine. The vegetarian meal, please . . .' The eyes flicked away, and I noticed that there were three watches on his thick white arm, all of them set to a different time zone. 'Sorry about this, John,' he said into the phone, and the eyes were on me again. 'Do you have my Gold Executive Club Number?' A pause. I sipped my water, trying to fit the words he was saying to the place he was in. But I saw that was impossible. 'Oh, it's in the system already?' he said, eyes wide with surprise. 'Perfect. Sorry, John – the hassle of modern travel, eh? What's that?' A burst of mad laughter. 'Yeah, you're right there – at least I'm in First Class.' He covered the phone with his hand. 'Don't you have anything to do?'

'Getting you,' I said. 'Bringing you to the house. That's what I've got to do.'

'Where were we?' he said into the phone, raising five fingers to say he would be right with me. 'As I say, I'm leaving London right now and coming to Thailand. I am going to be there with my boss, Mr Farren, for forty-eight hours. And there's a brief window of opportunity – a *brief* window – for a serious investor such as yourself who was smart enough to retire to Phuket with his lovely young Thai wife. A high-yield investment programme. New beach-front apartments in Hat Nai Han. You got it – just south of Hat Kata and Hat Karon. I shouldn't really be telling you this . . .'

I watched him over the rim of my polystyrene cup. His pale features creased with concentration. There was a script on the table in front of him. But Jesse did not need it.

'Phuket has one of the fastest-growing property markets in the world,' he said, his voice lower now. 'The cost of living is low but rental returns are high. You retired to the most prosperous province in Thailand.' He paused dramatically. 'When the other Asian Tigers were mewing for mercy, on Phuket you were still roaring . . . on Phuket you have muscles on your muscles . . . Phuket me love you long time . . . Phuket me love you too too much . . . Phuket your only problem this side of the grave is wealth management . . . on Phuket you will live forever in the lap of luxury and the gods will get down on their knees and bow before their master . . .' He winked at me. 'Listen, we're getting ready for take-off,' he said. 'I am going to have to turn off my BlackBerry now. Oh, glass of champagne, please! No nuts! Do you have the extra-large sleeper suit? Look, I'll call you when I land, John. A beer at the Sunset Bar in the Chedi? Sounds good.'

He hung up and stood up, and I saw his gaudy Muay Thai shorts. The first time we met he had told me that he came to Phuket for the martial arts, that there were serious Muay Thai training camps all over the island and any day now he was going to cut back on the Tiger beer and get back in training.

We walked up to the house together.

20

'What's it like in First Class?' I asked him, still somehow believing that what he said on the phone had some roots in reality.

Jesse adjusted his Muay Thai shorts, and his blue eyes got a faraway look. 'I reckon it rocks, don't you?' he said.

I nodded towards the house. 'The Aussie I picked up at the airport,' I said. 'Baxter. He doesn't seem very happy.'

Jesse laughed at that.

'Farren will sort him out,' he said.

We were on Bangla Road, the great gaudy strip of Patong, and there was a gibbon in a cowboy hat outside the bar.

'Hello, sexy man,' one of the girls said to Baxter – fifty-something, fifteen stone, pale and shaky from the long day – and the gibbon bared its teeth and had a good old laugh at that.

I looked up at the cracked neon sign above the bar. The gibbon in the Stetson followed my eyes. The sign said NO NAME BAR. I looked at the gibbon – the endless limbs, the dark triangle of its face, and eyes so black they seemed to carry the night inside them – and the creature examined its fingernails, massively bored. I don't think I had ever seen a gibbon in my life before. But somehow a gibbon in a Stetson outside the No Name Bar did not look as strange as it should have.

Bangla Road was a bedlam of bars. They all played their own music, and the songs and the bars and the girls all seemed to melt into one another, and drain each other of meaning. There were bars down the side alleys, bars up a flight of stairs that you could see from the street if you craned your neck, and what looked like giant bars the size of supermarkets until you went inside and realized that the place was actually made up of countless tiny bars, all identical apart from the different songs, where girls hung on poles as if they were on a tube train, or played Connect Four at the bar with customers, or yawned on a bar stool, staring into the wintry glow of their phones.

Bangla Road had a kind of debauched innocence about it because the street was a tourist sight, and entire families from Australia or Europe wandered the strip, gawping at the chaos, soaking up the famous naughty Thailand night. But more than anything, Bangla Road was a place to do business.

'Is this the place?' Baxter said, staring beyond the gibbon and the girls at the dark howling interior of the bar. He turned to Farren, who had a protective arm around the Australian's shoulders. 'What was the name of those two girls I was with last time?' he asked.

Farren patted Baxter reassuringly on the back.

'Number 31 and number 63,' Farren said. 'Lovely girls.'

They went inside. Jesse and I stood on the street, staring at the gibbon. It had a soft brown coat with a white trim of fur around its face. I stared again at the eyes. They were totally round. Moist and black and bottomless. It hopped on a stool between the two girls and examined its fingernails.

'Body massage?' one of the girls said to me. 'Hand massage?'

She touched my arm and I pulled away.

'Why would I want my hand massaged?' I said.

Jesse laughed. 'Forgive my friend, ladies. He is fresh off the banana boat. You haven't quite got the hang of it yet, have you, Tom? They don't massage your hand or your body. They massage you *with* their hand or *with* their body.' The gibbon chuckled at my dumb mistake. I shot it a filthy look. 'Slip them a few extra baht and they'll even wash behind your ears,' Jesse said. 'Come on.'

We went inside the bar. Farren and Baxter were talking at a table. We joined them. A round of Singha beers appeared in front of us. Farren signed the chit, not taking his eyes off the Australian.

'I just want my money back,' Baxter was saying, much calmer now, encouraged by Farren's thoughtful nodding. 'My wife says that foreigners can't buy land in Thailand. She says it's illegal.'

Farren took a cheque out of his back pocket and gave it to Baxter. The Aussie put on his reading glasses, peered at it in the darkness. And smiled at Farren. The two men laughed and Farren clapped him on his back.

'Jesse,' a girl said. She was holding a Connect Four board and despite the fact that she was dressed as a cowgirl in a mini-skirt she looked like a kid asking another kid if he fancied a game.

'Legend has it that all these girls are grand masters of the game they call Connect Four,' Jesse said, rising from his seat. 'We shall see.'

A girl sprayed my bare arms with Sketolene mosquito spray.

'What did you do that for?' I asked, recoiling at the stink.

'Nuts are not available,' she said, as if that was any kind of answer.

'Your wife is quite right,' Farren was saying to Baxter. 'Under Thai law, foreigners are not allowed to own land. However, foreigners can own a building, a leasehold of up to thirty years, or a unit in a registered condominium.' He leaned back and sighed with contentment. The Singha beer in his fist was beaded with sweat. Here I am, his body language said. Exactly where I ought to be. And only a coward or a fool would not choose to join me.

'Foreigners can't own land in Thailand,' Farren repeated. 'But foreigners are allowed to have a licence to print money. You can lease land for a period of thirty years and have the right to renew a further two times, giving a total of ninety years. How long you planning to live for, Mr Baxter? Just kidding. Or, even better, you can set up a Thai company that you control and which is allowed to purchase land totally legally.' A girl tried to perch on his lap but he declined with a polite smile and she disappeared into the darkness of the No Name Bar.

'But if your wife has doubts,' Farren said to Baxter, 'then let's have some *sanuk* and you can go home with your money. You know *sanuk*? It is a very Thai concept. A lot of *farang* think it means fun but *sanuk* is far more than that. It means finding pleasure in everything you do. Finding pleasure in all things. It's not hedonism. It's a philosophy, a credo, a way of life.'

The two men clinked glasses. I went to the bar and watched Jesse playing Connect Four. He was playing with a different girl now. The prettiest girl in the place, who wore jeans and a T-shirt and served behind the bar. They had already gathered an audience. Every time it was her turn, the girl slammed small blue discs into the slots on the board. Jesse laughed, shook his head.

'The reason they always win is because they are allowed to set the pace,' he told me, dropping a red disc into a slot with slow deliberation. 'And you have to play at your own pace, not theirs,' Jesse said.

The gibbon hopped up on to the bar and straightened the rim of its Stetson. It seemed fascinated by Jesse's ground-breaking Connect Four technique. Girls climbed on bar stools to get a better look at the action. It was like watching James Bond blowing them away at baccarat at a casino in Monte Carlo.

The wall behind them was covered in photographs and I wandered over to it. I didn't see any of the faces in the bar in the photographs. These were all the girls who had worked here in the past, and the men who they had known.

Everybody was gone now. Years of thin women with smiling faces and the men, older and whiter and drunker, all mugging for the cameras, all seeming to have the night of their lives. I wondered what had happened to them, all those girls and all those men, and if they missed the Bangla Road and the gibbon in the cowboy hat. Although I guessed it must have been a different gibbon back then.

A roar from the bar. Jesse had won again. Now a small stout woman in her forties was rolling up her sleeves and taking her seat opposite Jesse.

'Oh no,' Jesse laughed, his pale face shining like the moon in that unlit bar. 'Secret weapon. They're wheeling out the mamma-san.'

'I beat you,' the mamma-san said, with no trace of humour in it. 'I beat you good, white boy. Oh – such a white boy, you are, I never saw such a white boy.'

The mamma-san reached for Jesse's face and took a fistful of his ghostly flesh in one of her small brown hands. The No Name Bar girls laughed with appreciation.

'Want a bet?' Jesse said.

'Yes, I want bet,' the mamma-san said, and the girls all cheered.

Jesse rolled his eyes.

'But what do you have that I could possibly want?' he said, and the gibbon's mouth stretched in a huge and mirthless smile.

When I went back to the table Baxter was entwined with girls. Their thin brown limbs snaked around his waist, his neck, his khaki shorts. The girls chatted among themselves, examined their nails, and stared into the glow of their phones while absent-mindedly rubbing his old didgeridoo. And now it was Baxter who had his cheque book at the ready. A girl approached Farren but he held up his hand. He had lovely manners. She shrugged, smiled and walked away.

'Explain one more time,' the Australian said. 'About setting up a Thai company that I control.'

The thing I was realizing about that Phuket, the Phuket of bars and beer and girls – the hundreds of bars, the thousands of girls, the ocean of cold Thai beer – was that it offered more than anyone could ever possibly want or need. And although, as Jesse said, I was fresh off the banana boat, even I had already worked out that they were not really selling sex on the Bangla Road.

They were selling dreams.

'Come on, mate,' Jesse shouted. 'We're going home.'

I looked up but he wasn't talking to me. Jesse slid from his stool and took the hand of the gibbon.

The creature adjusted its cowboy hat and fell into step beside him, its free arm trailing, and there was much wailing and moaning among the bar girls as the pair of them disappeared through the curtain that covered the door.

The mamma-san spoke sharply to the girls. You didn't need any Thai to know she was telling them that Jesse had won the gibbon fair and square and they should get back to work. One of the girls wiped her eyes with her fingers and started packing away the Connect Four. I headed for the door.

Out on the street Jesse and the gibbon were already settled in the back of a *tuk-tuk*. The gibbon stared straight ahead with its depthless black eyes, unsentimental about leaving its place of work, although holding on to its hat as if fearing it might blow away on the ride home. I called Jesse's name but he didn't hear me, and the *tuk-tuk* puttered off down the Bangla Road, trailing smoke.

Back inside the bar Farren and Baxter were shaking hands.

'We're going to clean up!' Baxter bawled over the song they were playing and when he stood up to embrace Farren his sturdy legs overturned a table of glass and beer and overpriced fruit juice.

26

It was 'Highway To Hell' by AC/DC.

I recognized it now.

It felt very early when I left them to it in the bar, but by the time I got back to Nai Yang it seemed very late, as though everyone around here had gone to sleep hours ago.

The lights were off in the Botans' house. In our place there was a light left on for me. I wheeled the Royal Enfield into the shed as quietly as I could and stood there in the moonlight, smelling the clean air, just a hint of sulphur from the mangroves, and hearing the insect-drone of the traffic.

Our house was still unfamiliar to me and in the darkness I held out a hand to guide myself, the hard wood of the wall panels cool and smooth and somehow comforting against the palm of my hand. In the bedroom I undressed quickly in the darkness. When I curled up against Tess she murmured and pressed herself against me and I buried my face in her hair.

'Good day?' I said softly.

'They're all good days,' said Tess. 'How about you? Is everyone really friendly? Did you meet anyone you like?'

'There's an English kid called Jesse. He's full of himself but I like him.'

I didn't tell her about the gibbon and I didn't tell her about the Australian who tried to strangle my boss and I didn't tell her about the little Muslim girl on a motorbike. Because I wanted it to be true – for all of the days to be good days. But it felt like there was a lot I couldn't tell Tess if I wanted her to keep her smile. And I wanted that more than anything.

'You need to talk to Farren about our visas,' she said, more asleep than awake now. 'Your work permit. All of the paperwork. We need to get that sorted.'

'Tess?'

27

'What?'

'Nothing. Close your eyes, angel.'

Soon I felt her slip into sleep but I stayed awake for a long time, curled up against her, my face in her hair, listening to the distant buzz of the motorbikes out there in the wide wild night.

4

The pick-up truck woke me just after dawn.

I could hear the diesel engine rumbling right outside our bedroom window as it slowly backed up our narrow road.

'Somebody must have the wrong place,' I told Tess, pulling on my jeans.

I went out on the porch. The open back of the pick-up truck was piled impossibly high with pallets of plastic bottles of water. The pallets were stacked higher than the cabin. It was one of those sights you saw all the time in Phuket – loads that seemed to violate every law, especially the one about gravity. The driver's face frowned with concentration as he carefully reversed past a banana tree.

Mr and Mrs Botan came out to watch. I looked at them and smiled, hoping they would take responsibility for the delivery. But Mrs Botan just shouted something at the driver. She seemed to be telling him to be more careful with our banana tree. Some of the thick leaves, still shiny with rain, had already been ripped off by the truck and littered the road.

Tess came out of the house, tucking a T-shirt into her shorts. The driver seemed to know her. He leaned out of his window, holding out an invoice, tapping it for a signature.

'Not this much!' she said, shaking her head at the mountain of mineral water, and I heard the sharp tone of the teacher she was back in England. 'I didn't order this much!'

The water came in cellophane-wrapped six-packs – big bottles, 1.5 litres, with a dozen of the big six-packs on every cardboard pallet, and another layer of cellophane over that, and too many of the pallets to count.

'Reckon we've got enough water, Tess?' I smiled, and she shot me a look before ripping the invoice from the driver's hands. He was talking in Thai, very insistent now, and Tess was standing up to him, staring hard at the paperwork. 'But I can't read this,' she said. 'It's all in Thai.'

Rory and Keeva came slowly out of the house, still in their pyjamas, still rumpled and sleepy from bed. We all stared at the pick-up truck.

'I wanted a twenty of the six-packs,' Tess was telling the driver. 'Not all these – what do you call them?'

'Pallets,' I said.

It was getting heated. Mr and Mrs Botan came over to help, or perhaps just to get a better view. The old man looked at the invoice and nodded thoughtfully.

'He is right,' Mr Botan said. 'You ordered a lot of water.'

Mrs Botan was more concerned about Tess.

'*Jai yen*,' she told Tess. '*Jai yen*. Keep a cool heart.'

Tess and I looked at each other. We had never heard of *jai yen* before. We had not heard the words or the concept. Where we came from, great importance was placed on being warm-hearted. But in Thailand they believed in the opposite. They believed in *jai yen*. Mrs Botan took Tess by the hand and gently stroked her arm, smiling as she taught her about the benefits of a cool heart.

'All right,' Tess said, and she nodded curtly at the driver. 'My mistake. Sorry.'

'Good,' Mrs Botan said.

30

We kept the water. We kept a cool heart. The neighbours and the driver, all smiles now, helped us to unload it. I moved the motorbike out of the way and we stored it in the shed that passed for a garage.

'*Mai pen rai*,' the old lady told Tess. 'Never mind. The water will keep. Never mind, never mind.'

When the water was unloaded, Tess and Mrs Botan and the children went inside our neighbours' house for breakfast while I stood outside with Mr Botan as he smoked a cigarette. You could tell that he wasn't allowed to do it in their house. The sky rumbled and cracked somewhere out to sea. You could see the storm clouds gather and the lightning flash.

'Will it rain again soon?' I asked him.

Mr Botan considered the sky. He took a long pull on his cigarette.

'It hasn't rained since yesterday,' he said.

I digested this information, and wondered what it could possibly mean. We watched the sky in silence for a while.

'How long do you stay?' Mr Botan asked.

'What?' I said, shocked by the question. Wild Palm had a year's lease on our little villa, and Farren had told me with a smile that Mr Botan had insisted on half of the money in advance. But I knew my neighbour was not asking me about leases or rent money.

'I wonder how long you stay,' Mr Botan said, and it didn't sound so much like a question now, more of a reflection.

'Well, we're staying,' I said. 'We have no plans to go back to England. There's nothing for us there.'

I said it with great conviction, but Mr Botan did not look persuaded. He smiled with a bashful courtesy, as if he had heard it all before, and examined his roll-up with great interest.

I live here, I thought. *This is my home now.*

But I remembered Baxter's hands on Farren's throat, and the lies that Jesse had told so easily on the phone, and the lie that I had been forced into myself the moment our plane touched down and they had asked me about the purpose of my visit, and so I did not dare to say it aloud.

'Your boss,' he said.

'Farren,' I said.

'Many men like him in Thailand.'

'Businessmen,' I said. 'Many foreign businessmen?'

'England rich country,' Mr Botan said. 'Thailand poor country.'

I laughed and nodded.

'But there are plenty of poor people in England,' I said. 'I was one of them.'

'Ah,' said Mr Botan, smiling shyly at the sky, as if we had gone too far. 'Ah.'

Mr and Mrs Botan. Our neighbours lived from the sea. He caught fish on his longtail and she cleaned it, cooked it and served it on the beach at the Almost World Famous Seafood Grill. He wore the baggy trousers of the Thai fisherman and she was usually dressed in a white apron, as if she was coming straight from a kitchen or soon returning to one. Their lives centred on the few miles of sea and land around Hat Nai Yang, and right from the start they wanted us to see its secret beauty.

'Many bad people come to our area at this time of the year,' Mr Botan told Tess the day after the mountain of water had arrived. He rubbed his hard old hands with anxiety. 'They take great advantage of poor stupid *farang*,' he said. 'Make easy money from the foreigners. Sell them shells. Leaky boat rides. Massage.' He shot me a meaningful man-to-man look, and lowered his voice to an embarrassed whisper. 'Love pills,' he murmured.

32

Tess looked up from the rucksack she was packing.

'Oh, I'm sure we'll be fine,' she said with a smile. 'Everybody seems very kind.'

Mr Botan was unconvinced. He had taken it upon himself to protect us from the venal side of Phuket and insisted on accompanying us on our trip to see the turtles lay their eggs.

Rory looked up from his collapsing copy of *Traveller's Wildlife Guide*.

'This is so cool,' he said excitedly. 'During mating rituals, the male turtle swims backwards in front of the female while stroking her face with his clawed foot. When he is ready to mate, he climbs on to the female's shell and grips the rim with all four feet.'

Tess smiled at him. 'You're so clever,' she said.

Rory was too young to know anything about sex. But he knew everything there was to know about mating habits.

It seemed like a miracle that, of all the beaches on the island, the turtles came to lay their eggs on our beach. But Hat Nai Yang was one of the most secluded beaches on the island, visited mostly by locals and only at the weekend, when they spent the day in the shallow waters and the night eating in places like the Almost World Famous Seafood Grill. Those turtles knew what they were doing.

When we got to the northern tip of Hat Nai Yang just as the sun was fading, the beach was deserted. It was Sunday, my day off, but it was that dead part of the day when the swimming was over and the eating had yet to begin. No people. No turtles. We sat on the sand staring out at the empty sea.

'So basically turtles are like big tortoises, right?' said Keeva.

Rory looked at his sister as if she was raving mad. 'No,' he said. 'Basically not. They live in the open ocean and the female only comes to shore to lay her eggs. Tortoises are more like – I don't know – hamsters. Tortoises live in your back garden. Turtles live in the sea.'

'Well,' Keeva said. 'Looks like they're staying in the sea.'

She picked up a red plastic frisbee and wandered down to the water. Rory pushed his glasses up his nose and anxiously watched the sea.

'It's November and they lay their eggs from now to May,' he said. 'But they're dying out.' He watched his sister throwing the frisbee in the air and catching it as she let the almost non-existent waves lap her toes. 'No loggerhead turtles for fifteen years,' he muttered to himself. 'They're all endangered, or already dead, maybe even extinct.'

Tess touched his back.

'One day we'll see the turtles,' she promised. 'One day soon. We'll keep watching, okay?'

Rory nodded and went down to join his sister. Mr Botan checked his watch, as if he had specifically told the turtles to be at Hat Nai Yang at this time and place.

The children played with the frisbee on the edge of the sea until Keeva got bored and came back complaining of hunger. Her brother followed her and we ate our picnic – Pahd Thai from the Almost World Famous Seafood Grill. The light had almost gone and we were packing up to go home when we saw the turtle.

It was already out of the water and hauling itself across the smooth white sand, looking like the most exhausted thing on the planet. Its head looked a thousand years old and there were tears streaming from its depthless black eyes.

'Daddy,' Keeva said, stricken. 'She's crying.'

'No,' Mr Botan said.

'That's the salt gland,' Rory said, trembling with excitement. 'It helps the turtle to maintain a healthy water balance when it's on dry land. Don't worry, Keeva.'

Mr Botan nodded. 'Not sad. Not upset.' His Chinese face

grinned. 'Very happy day,' he said, genuinely delighted at the sight of the turtle, and not for our sake. 'Very good luck,' he said. 'Very good luck for Thai people.' He pointed an instructive finger. 'They are the universe,' he said. 'The top of the shell is the sky. The bottom of the shell is the earth.'

We watched the turtle for a while and then we saw the boat. A rough canoe, no engine, containing three shadowy figures. It was difficult to see them in the dying light, but they were coming to land where the turtle must have crawled from the sea.

Mr Botan watched them suspiciously.

'They are not Thai,' he said. 'They are *chao ley*. They stay close to the shore during the long rains.'

'Fishermen?' said Tess.

He laughed shortly.

'They do a little fishing, but they are not fishermen,' he said. 'They look on the beach for anything they can eat or sell or use.' He spat on the sand. 'Look at their boat!'

As they landed on the beach we could see that it was a canoe that seemed to have been carved out of some ancient tree. 'No engine!' Mr Botan snorted. All the longtails had two-stroke diesel engines. He considered a dugout canoe to be a relic of the Stone Age.

'They live on the island?' Tess said.

'A few,' Mr Botan said. 'Down south. All the way down south. On Hat Rawai. They approach tourists with their rubbish. There are others on Ko Surin and Ko Boht. They have *Kabang*. House boat. Or shacks. They move around the sea.'

'Gypsies,' I said. 'Sea gypsies.'

'Thieves,' said Mr Botan. 'Beggars. Tramps. Some *chao ley* are not so bad. Almost like Thai. Almost. They get registered. We call them *Mai Thai* – new Thai. But these are *moken*. Like *oken* – sea water. Same name, almost. They don't even want to be Thai, these *moken*.' He clearly took it personally. 'Anyway,' he said, looking back at the turtle. 'They are more Burmese than Thai. Anyway. *Mai pen rai.* Never mind, never mind.'

The rough boat was being dragged out of the water. There was a man and two children. A girl in her mid-teens and a younger boy who, now I looked at him again, was more like a tiny man than a child. He was not tall but he was broad and the way he moved as he dragged the canoe further up the sand suggested the kind of workhorse strength that you only get from years of manual labour.

I looked at Rory and Keeva with the turtle. They were keeping a deferential distance as the turtle started to dig into the sand, moving its flipper-like feet to dig a hole.

As the feet fluttered in the sand, it didn't look like very effective digging. But a hole somehow began to appear, and the head and shell of the turtle became covered in sand, giving it a carefree, oh-I-do-like-to-be-beside-the-seaside air.

The sea gypsies, the *chao ley*, were slowly coming up the beach towards the turtle. They were different from any Thais that I had ever seen – shorter, stockier and darker, and yet their hair was streaked with gold, as if they had just emerged from a fancy hairdressing salon rather than the Andaman Sea.

They stopped some distance from the turtle, kicking their bare feet in the sand, not looking at us, and now ignoring the turtle. At first I thought they were beachcombing. But they were waiting.

Mr Botan watched them with mounting anger. To us they were colourful travelling folk. To him they were a bunch of thieving, peg-selling pikeys.

'Look!' Rory cried.

The turtle had begun to lay its eggs. We edged closer and so did the *chao ley*.

'These sea beggars,' Mr Botan said to me. 'They follow the turtle. They know she will lay her eggs.'

Rory's eyes were pleading. 'They're not going to hurt her, are they?'

I stared at the *chao ley*. They didn't seem as though they were going to give her a saucer of milk. The three of them were watching the turtle now. The tough-looking little boy. The girl, who was perhaps sixteen. And the old man. Watching the eggs emerge. If their skin had been one shade darker then it would have been black.

The turtle laid five eggs and then seemed spent. Keeva was disappointed.

'Is that it?' she said. 'Is that all the eggs? I thought there would be – I don't know – millions.'

But Rory was in a fever. I really believe it was the best day of his life.

'They don't lay many eggs in Phuket,' he said to his sister, patient but breathless, grateful for seeing this vision. 'Because it's warm all year round, see? So they don't have to worry about the weather. But the eggs are left unprotected. They're small and soft. The eggs are. Predators eat them up. Rats. Lizards.' He looked at the *chao ley*. 'People.'

The turtle was dragging itself back to the sea. The old *chao ley* passed it and walked swiftly to the eggs. He picked one up, examined it briefly, and started back to his boat.

'I can't believe that's legal,' Tess said.

Mr Botan spoke harshly to the *chao ley* and began following him.

Hefting the egg, the old man gave him a mouthful back.

Mr Botan stopped, shaking his head. 'He says he only takes one, out of respect for the mother. But he says the rats will eat the rest anyway.'

Rory whimpered. Tess looked at me, as if I might somehow rescue our day out. But all I could do was shrug. I wasn't going to get in a punch-up with some old sea gypsy over a turtle's egg.

'Sounds sort of reasonable,' I said.

Rory walked warily to the sea turtle, his shoulders sunk with anguish. We all followed him. The tough-looking *chao ley* boy was squatting on his haunches watching the turtle as it crawled and clawed its way to the sea. He ran one curious hand across the turtle's rock-like shell.

Rory began hyperventilating.

'He shouldn't touch it,' Rory said. 'Excuse me? Oh, excuse me? You shouldn't touch it. I don't think he speaks English. Tell him not to touch it.'

But the young sea gypsy was already up and off towards their boat, pausing only to scoop up the frisbee that our children had discarded in the sand. He looked at it as if it was a shell, and wandered down to the shore, idly tapping it against his thigh.

'Hey,' Keeva called, going after him. 'That's not your frisbee.'

The boy turned to face Keeva. She held out her hand and he took a step back, holding the frisbee above his head, although he was a couple of inches shorter than her.

Then Tess was there.

'Do you speak English?' she asked with a friendly smile, and in that simple question you could see that she had been a great teacher.

She had been sick of the school at the end – the lack of discipline, the lack of ambition, the parents who owned more tattoos than books. But the way she looked at that hard little child who was stealing our frisbee made me see that she had loved her job once, and maybe missed it more than she let on.

The boy looked at Tess with his fierce feral eyes.

'I am an engineer,' he announced, his voice thin and

reedy. 'I am from Germany. I am from Australia. What time is the train to Chiang Mai? Is there anything cheaper? I want something cheaper. I am a student. I am an engineer. I am Mr Smith. I am Mr Honda from Tokyo bank. Take me to a doctor. My stomach is bad.'

Tess clapped her hands and laughed.

'That's very, very good,' she said. 'What's your name?'

But he stared at us silently, bitterly, and it was his big sister calling to him from the boat where she waited with the old man who revealed his name.

'*Chatree!*' she called. '*Chatree!*'

'Look, you can play with us if you want,' Keeva told him. 'But taking something that doesn't belong to you is basically not cool.'

But the boy had no time for play.

He ran off to join his family. They were getting back in the boat, the man wrapping the egg in some sort of filthy blanket.

I picked up the red plastic frisbee as they pushed off. The turtle swiftly disappeared below the waves, but we watched the canoe for a while longer, the three dark figures bobbing up and down on the empty sea until they were round the bay and out of sight.

'They wander still,' said Mr Botan, making it sound as if it had always been that way in the past, and it would be that way forever.

5

We walked back up the green hill to home and every step of the way the sound of Rory's crying mixed with the evening sigh of the sea.

'Stop crying,' I told him, and it came out far too harsh, but tears in my family always filled me with a wild panic.

Keeva threw a thin protective arm around her brother's shoulders.

'Crying doesn't change anything,' I said, more gently now, although I knew the damage had been done.

'I can't help it,' he gulped. 'I know it doesn't do any good. I know that. But I can't stop.'

'Why do you cry?' asked Mr Botan.

He did not know Rory like the rest of us. We knew exactly why he was crying.

'The egg,' Rory said, a tear running down one lens of his glasses. 'The mother. The baby.'

Tess looked at me and something passed between us.

'Why don't you boys go to see Daddy's friend?' she said, putting an arm around Rory, now smothered in the limbs of his sister and mother. 'The one with the – what is it?'

40

Rory's wet eyes were wide. 'The gibbon?' he gasped. 'The man with the gibbon?'

'That will cheer you up,' Tess predicted, and while I got the Royal Enfield out of the shed, she dried his eyes, wiped his nose and strapped him into a crash helmet.

Jesse was standing outside the front door of his apartment. His shirt was ripped open and his pale features were slick with sweat. There were fresh scratches on his forehead. He stared at Rory and me, as if trying to place us.

'Yes?' he croaked.

I was silent for a moment.

'This is my boy,' I told him. I waited. Nothing happened. 'You said we could come round,' I reminded him.

Jesse looked at us wildly.

'To meet the gibbon,' Rory added, his eyes blinking behind the glasses. He chewed his bottom lip. I had never seen him so excited.

Behind the shut door we heard the sound of things being smashed.

'Ah,' said Jesse, attempting to smile at Rory. 'Of course. Your little boy. The nature lover. The lad who likes monkeys.'

I looked down at my son and watched his mouth tighten.

'Gibbons are not monkeys,' he said quietly, then shot me a look – *Who is this fool?* 'Gibbons are the fastest and most agile of all tree-dwelling mammals.'

The sound of breaking glass came from within the flat.

'Yeah, well,' Jesse said, passing a hand through his sweat-soaked white hair. 'Travis – my tree-dwelling mammal – is having a bad day.' Furniture crashed against the door and we all jumped back. Down the hall a neighbour stuck her head out of her door. A woman in her forties, Thai, frowning at the crowd of foreigners standing outside the noisy apartment. 'Fine, all fine, all under control,' Jesse laughed. 'Sorry about the noise, we'll keep it down.'

The neighbour went back inside shaking her head and no doubt muttering about bloody foreigners.

'If it's inconvenient . . .' I said.

My son glared at me – *Don't say that to him.* Amazing how much your child can communicate without saying a word.

'It's actually really inconvenient,' Jesse said. 'Maybe you boys could come back some other time.'

Sounds from inside the flat, although further away from the door. Crash. Bang. A distant screech.

'How old is Travis?' Rory asked.

Jesse shook his head. 'Five, they said in the bar. I got him in a bar. Rescued him, sort of. From a life of depravity. Five or six.'

'That's not a bad day,' my son said. He sighed with the kind of weariness that only a nine-year-old can call upon. 'That's sexual maturity.'

Jesse laughed. I had to smile.

'What do you know about sexual maturity?' Jesse said.

Rory narrowed his eyes. 'What do you know about gibbons?' he said.

It was all silent inside the apartment now. I took my son's hand but he pulled away.

'But I want to see him,' Rory said. He looked up at me. 'Can we see him?' He looked at Jesse. 'Please, sir, may we see your gibbon?'

Jesse listened at the door. Nothing. 'He'll take your eyes out, kid,' Jesse said. 'He's gone buck wild in there.'

'That's just sexual maturity,' my son said. 'They get to that age – five or six in gibbons – and they want to mate with you or fight with you.'

'Sounds like chucking-out time on a Saturday night,' Jesse said. We both looked at Rory for a moment, wondering what to do next. Then my son opened the door and we went inside.

It was a single guy's flat above Hat Surin and it was a mess. An even bigger mess than usual, no doubt. There were smashed plates all along the hall. A stain on the wall. Some kind of food smeared across the ceiling.

'Excuse the mess,' Jesse said.

The gibbon – Travis – was in the kitchen, having a beer. He squatted by the sink, glugging down a can of Singha, staring thoughtfully around the little room with those huge black eyes.

'He likes his brew, does old Travis,' said Jesse, and laughed shortly. 'He likes a beer at the end of a long hard day of scratching his arse and smashing up my flat.'

'No,' said Rory, and I didn't need to look at him to know how hard he was trying not to cry. 'He has just forgotten,' he said. 'He's just forgotten, that's all.'

Travis looked at us out of the corner of his eyes, and I was suddenly very scared of him, and thought how stupid I was to bring my boy in here.

'Forgotten what?' Jesse said.

'Forgotten that he's a gibbon,' Rory said. 'He just doesn't know he's a gibbon any more. Can't you see? He doesn't understand how to act like a gibbon. Somebody probably stole him from his family when he was a baby.'

The three of us watched Travis slurping his Singha.

'A beach photographer had him on Hat Patong,' Jesse said. 'Then they got him for the bar.' We watched the gibbon contemplate his soft brown fur, pick an insect from it, pop it into his mouth. 'But I don't know where the photographer got him from,' Jesse said.

The pink cowboy hat was gone, but Travis still looked like a creature of the No Name Bar, like something from the Bangla Road night. He rolled his shoulders and contemplated

43

his beer and narrowed his eyes, as if sizing up his opportunities, as if ready for action.

'They shouldn't keep an animal like him in a bar,' Rory said. 'That's so wrong. They shouldn't keep any kind of animal in a bar. They do it for fun and it's so wrong.'

I looked at my son but I heard my wife. Rory had the clear-eyed goodness of Tess about him. Both of them could look at something and tell you if it was right or wrong, even if you hadn't asked. I loved them for it, though it frightened me.

The gibbon stared at us, as if suddenly aware of our presence.

'Settle down now, Travis,' Jesse said. 'We've got guests.'

Travis had soft brown fur with a snow-white trim around his black face. He had those perfectly round eyes, moist and black and bottomless. They seemed full of what I can only describe as pain.

Jesse picked up an open packet of cheese puffs and held them out to Travis. The gibbon snatched them from his hand and began stuffing them into his mouth. Flecks of orangey-yellow cheese puffs sprayed out of either side.

'He loves his Cheesy-Wheezy Puff-Puffs,' Jesse said quietly. 'They always calm him down.'

Rory did not take his eyes from the gibbon by the sink.

'Gibbons eat some insects and small animals such as tree lizards, ants, beetles, butterflies, crickets, stick insects, maggots, Asian leaf mantis,' my son said. 'Things that gibbons don't eat include Cheesy-Wheezy Puff-Puffs.'

Travis wiped his mouth on the back of his arm and picked up a bread knife. With one bound and then another he was across the kitchen and in our faces. His teeth were bared. The knife was in his hand and the knife was at Jesse's throat.

Then Rory reached out and placed his hand lightly on the gibbon's arm.

44

The gibbon froze.

He stared with shock at the small dimpled hand of the child resting on the brown fur of his left arm, just below the elbow. For a long time, neither of them moved. Then the gibbon pulled away, totally subdued, moving very slowly and very gently as if afraid a sudden movement would disturb my son. None of us moved. But the gibbon hopped across back to the sink where he paused to examine the nails of his fingers.

'Where the bloody hell did you learn to do that?' Jesse asked my son.

Rory did not bother to reply but I already knew the answer. He had read it in a book.

'I keep thinking we're going to be struck down,' Jesse said, looking at me.

'What?' I said, wrapping my son in my arms.

'I keep thinking that some lightning bolt is going to strike us,' Jesse said. 'To punish us for the way we live here. For the lies we tell. For the rules we break. For the things we do.'

'Shut up, Jesse,' I told him, annoyed. 'This is crazy talk.'

'I know I'm stupid,' Jesse said, looking at Rory now. 'I know I did a bad thing bringing him here. A stupid thing. But he was drinking beer till he puked in the bar and he didn't like the flashing lights and they had filed down his teeth and they were giving him stuff to make him stay awake until closing time. And he doesn't like being made to wear a hat.' Jesse hung his head. 'And I thought it would be a bit of company.'

'No,' my son said, and he placed a hand on Jesse's arm, as he had on the arm of the gibbon. 'You think you did a bad thing.' He smiled up at us and for a second it was as if he was the grown-up. 'But don't worry,' Rory said. 'I think you found him just in time.'

6

Up in the ring, Jesse was in trouble.

He was limping, and his mouth was twisted with pain, a thin stripe of blood on his lower lip.

He towered over the small Thai youth in front of him but every time Jesse stepped forward, the Thai kicked him with his shin. Always the same kick. The gleaming thin brown shin lashed out hard and high on Jesse's plump milky thigh, and the pain in my friend's face registered as clearly as if he had been given an electric shock.

Farren leaned into me and shouted something in my ear, but I didn't get a word of it. Near midnight the noise in a Muay Thai stadium is deafening. There's a live band, tucked up somewhere high in the rafters, so hidden that they could be some kind of mad radio, and as the night goes on they build in intensity, their pipes, drums and cymbals – you notice the *clash-clash-clash* of the cymbals most of all – sounding like a commentator who has lost control, echoing and encouraging and urging on the violence in the ring. I had never heard such a racket. Farren had to put his arm around my shoulder and pull me closer to make himself heard.

'Look at that,' he shouted. 'There's the reason why the Thais were never colonized – right there. There's the reason why, out of all the nations of Asia, only the Thais were never ruled by the white man from the big bad West. Because they have a mean streak.'

Directly above us, Jesse reeled on the ropes, the sweat flying from his body. The Thai kid seemed to be moving in for the kill. I found that I was shouting Jesse's name. It did no good.

On the other side of Farren, I saw the Russian jump up and laugh. I had driven him from the Amanpuri resort in Surin all the way south to the stadium in Chalong, his big meaty arms wrapped around my waist all the way. The Amanpuri was the most exclusive hotel on the island but, unlike a lot of clients I was sent to pick up, the Russian didn't complain about being picked up by bike.

Farren often did business at night. Phuket had two seasons – wet and dry – but the heat was always with us, and in the day it could kill you. So business was often conducted in the cooler, darker hours, when it was easier to work, and think, and sell, and dream.

'A mean streak,' Farren repeated. 'A lovely people who are capable of extreme cruelty if you push the wrong button. Just like the Brits.'

It wasn't a criticism.

'Come on, Jesse!' Farren laughed. 'Murder the little bastard!'

Leaning against the ropes on the far side of the ring, Jesse gamely motioned for his opponent to come forward, and he did, the Thai kicking him high on the thigh again, and then again, and then again. Three kicks that blurred into one kick and seemed to shrivel something in my lower stomach.

Farren turned away and clinked beer cans with the Russian, who seemed to be having a rare old time. We were in the VIP section. There were only a dozen seats in there, but if you were in the VIP section they put a rope around your little area, and gave you a plastic bag that contained two cans of Tiger beer. I took a nervous swig of the can I was holding.

Jesse lunged forward, hunched down and fists flying, one last desperate try at getting past the kicks that were crippling him. But the Thai lifted one knee and it met Jesse flush on the chin and he dropped into the arms of the referee who hugged him like a loving parent and waved it all off. I felt a sickened relief that it was all over.

The little Thai did a series of perfect, joyous backflips, and his bare feet cracked against the well-worn canvas of the Muay Thai ring like pistol shots.

Pirin, Farren's Thai, was in the corner and he looked at me now and nodded, but the band had stopped playing and there was a brief moment for talking normally.

'All good with you and the family, Tom?' Farren said, and something must have passed across my face because he leaned in and poked his finger against my chest. 'We're going to get you that car,' he said, and I could smell the Tiger beer on his breath. 'That old bike is not good enough for you.'

This was the chance I had been waiting for.

'I like the bike,' I said. 'I can fix it up.' I hesitated for just a second. I had been thinking about this for a while. 'But it's my visa,' I said. 'It's a tourist visa. I appreciate everything you've done for me – I really do – but I want to be legal.'

I shook my head, not knowing what else to say. That was it really. I wanted to work. I was happy to work. But I wanted to be legitimate. And Tess wanted it for me too.

'But everyone comes in on a tourist visa,' Farren said. He clapped me on the back and it was a good feeling. 'We'll sort out the paperwork later,' he told me. 'We're not going to let the little men stop us with their bloody paperwork, are we?'

'No,' I said, smiling back at him, and enormously relieved even though nothing had changed. 'No. We're not.'

I climbed into the ring where Pirin was nursing Jesse. 'Always the same in *moo-ay tai*,' Pirin said, and it sounded strange to hear the national sport of Thailand pronounced with a Thai accent. 'Kick loses to punch. Punch loses to knee. Knee loses to elbow. Elbow loses to kick.' We helped Jesse to his feet. He could just about stand, although his pale blue eyes scared me. They didn't seem to be looking at anything. 'And Jesse loses to everyone!' Pirin laughed, and slapped him on the back.

Jesse looked at us. 'What happened?' he said.

'*Cha-na nork*,' said Pirin. 'Knockout. But you fought bravely. There's no shame. Be proud of your heart.'

'No,' Jesse said. 'I mean, what happened to me? I used to be quite good at all this.' He looked at me, bleary with sadness as much as anything else. 'I really did. Quite good, I was.'

'I know,' I said. 'I saw your fights. You showed me the DVD, remember?'

'You saw my DVD?'

We gently helped him between the ropes and into a chair in the little VIP section. There was a backstage area by the toilets where the fighters prepared and got patched up and exchanged equipment – a surprising amount of sharing went on – but Jesse did not look ready for the long walk to the toilets.

Farren was making his pitch to the Russian.

'A foreign buyer in Thailand needs to bring in one hundred per cent of the purchase price in foreign currency,' he said. 'We can help you with your FETF – that's the Foreign Exchange Transaction Form you need for the Land

Department. Then Wild Palm helps you to set up a Thai company that legally owns the land. A Thai company that *you* control. You are allowed to own up to forty-nine per cent of the shares.'

Then there was what they called the money pause.

Farren was silent, staring at the Russian, giving him the chance to ask the obvious question – *But how do I control a company if I own less than half of it?*

The Russian did not ask the question.

They never did.

Jesse sat with his head between his legs and Pirin and I stepped aside to allow two Thai fighters to enter the ring. Their bodies shone and dazzled under the lights and although I had taken it for sweat, I saw now that they were oiled. There were curved rope bandanas around their foreheads, and thin coloured scarves around their biceps. They both circled the ring, lightly touching its ropes.

'Keeping out evil spirits,' Jesse said, and I looked at him, expecting to see mockery in his face. But his eyes, closing as I looked at them from the beating he had taken, were misty with belief.

The two Muay Thai fighters got down on their knees and touched their heads to the ground. They spread their arms wide and then, still on their knees, one leg out and one leg back, they began rocking on the rear foot. It was somewhere between a prayer and a warm-up, a stretch and a meditation.

'The *wai kru*,' Jesse said.

'Remember and respect,' Pirin nodded. 'Your ancestor. Your teacher. Your country. Your god. Your king.'

The fighters were in the centre of the ring, smiling – unbelievably smiling – gently touching gloves, gently touching foreheads, gently patting each other on the shoulder, offering an almost fraternal support to their opponent. No, there was no 'almost' in it. For even their smiles were gentle. They did not look as though they were about to fight. They looked like they shared a mother.

'Ah,' said Pirin. 'Showing more respect.'

But it did not look like respect. It looked like something deeper than that. It looked like something stronger than that. And I felt that for all the similarities that Farren saw between the British and the Thais, they had things that we did not. They were better at showing love to each other.

The fight began. With the fights that involved Westerners – and it wasn't just Jesse, there were a few *farang* on the bill – the fights all began at the same unforgiving pace. But when two Thais fought, they seemed to share a dance before the fighting began – rolling their heads, and practising a few shy kicks and bashful strikes, as though they might call the whole thing off and have a cup of tea and cuddle instead. But then it suddenly escalated and they tore into each other without mercy, and when you saw two Thais fight full out, the ferocity of it trapped the breath in your chest.

'Look at that,' Jesse said, perking up. 'It's like ballet with blood and broken bones and no protection. Can you believe it, Tom? No protection. No headguard. Not even a bloody vest. Just a genital cup and a magic tattoo.'

'A magic tattoo?' I smiled.

Jesse nodded at Pirin. 'Show him,' he said.

Pirin lifted up a T-shirt that said Stockholm Marathon 2002. There was a tattoo of a tiger covering his entire chest.

'Makes the wearer invincible,' Jesse said, and he chuckled, as the north of England staged a brief comeback in his traitor's soul. 'Until he gets hit by a *tuk-tuk*.'

Pirin was pulling down his T-shirt.

'Very good protection,' the Thai confirmed, as if discussing the contents clause of a reasonably priced home insurance policy.

Jesse began to weep and I put my arm around him and rocked him as I would one of my children as he hid his face against me.

'Maybe it's not for me,' he said into my chest. 'Maybe I was wrong. Maybe I am wasting my time. Maybe I have been kidding myself.'

Pirin tucked in his Stockholm Marathon 2002 T-shirt, and he stared at the broken boy in my arms thoughtfully, and then he told us about the man who would know of these things, as the band played faster still.

The fortune teller's office was a stone table cemented to the ground of an alley on the dimly lit edge of Phuket town.

The *mor duu*, Pirin called him – the fortune teller – was a plump old man with a fine head of white hair, and by his side was a battered briefcase that spilled out ancient books and pictures of holy men all sitting in the same position – legs crossed, hands resting lightly in the lap of their saffron robes, and nobody saying cheese for the camera.

There was a sign on the table, a drawing of the palms of a pair of hands, divided into sections. Pirin was ushered forward. Stuck to the wall behind the *mor duu* was a banner the size of a bed sheet, covered with drawings of elephants and warriors and peasants and gods and kings and assorted unidentified beasts. To me it looked more Hindu than Buddhist, more Indian than Thai. But what did I know? I assumed that the chequered board that was painted on the table was part of the routine. But as Pirin took his place opposite the *mor duu*, I saw that that was where the old men of the alley – they called it a *soi*, which could mean anything from a side road to a narrow little backstreet – played their games of chess. The *mor duu* took Pirin's hands and stared at them as my friend gave him all his latest news and worries.

The *mor duu* – and maybe the all-seeing doctor is closer

than fortune teller because Pirin was treating his session more like practical advice than an old girl with a crystal ball and big earrings looking into the future – read Pirin's palms, and then flicked through one of the ancient books, now and then pointing to numbers with the tip of his heavily chewed biro. I couldn't understand their conversation, but it sounded exactly like the meeting I had had with my accountant when he told me that my building business was finished and that I was bankrupt.

Pirin *wai*-ed and paid the *mor duu*, nodding at me as he stood up.

'Now you,' he said.

I laughed and shook my head, and pointed at Jesse, and said that this is the one who needs to know what the future holds, and if he is on the right path, and all that stuff, but the old seeing doctor was indicating the chair opposite him and Pirin was smiling encouragement, and Jesse was shoving me forward, and saying I should go first, as if he was scared of what he might be told, and in the end it would have seemed rude of me to refuse.

The *mor duu* took my right hand. I held out the left, trying to be helpful, but he shook his head and I pulled it away.

I grinned self-consciously at Jesse and Pirin as the old man rubbed the fleshy bit of my hand, where the thumb meets the palm, but they were both watching the face of the *mor duu*.

The tips of his fingers ran over my skin, and he poked and stroked the lines of my hand, as if they were the years of my life that remained.

I realized that I had stopped smiling.

He spoke to me in English.

'An inch ahead is darkness,' he told me.

I snatched my hand away and stood up and walked off, as Pirin and the old man barked at each other in Thai, something about money. Jesse came after me, but he was limping from the fight and I broke into a run and I did not stop until I found the *soi* by the stadium where I had left the bike. I shot past Jesse on the Royal Enfield, and he called out something but it was lost in the noise of my leaving.

I never rode faster in Phuket than I did that night. The roads, and the number of crashes, always frightened me, even during the dry weather, and I more or less attempted to stay within the speed limit at all times, and more or less on the correct side of the road.

But that night my heart was pounding with dread, and I flew home as fast as I could, up the long road out of Phuket City and past the wobbling flocks of drunken tourists who rule the beaches of the west, and then still further north, the fat *farang* and their burned faces and skinny girls way behind me now, up into the lush green far north of rubber plantations that were blacker than the night, even the green hills black, and passing through the villages that appear out of nowhere and are suddenly gone, as if you might have imagined them, and temples so big and golden and deserted that they can only be real but could be the ruins of some lost civilization, always on the lookout for dreamy locals taking a stroll and little children who stayed up very late and the odd water buffalo who had decided to sit down and take a nap in the middle of one of those dark dark roads, pushing the old Royal Enfield as hard as I could, the diesel roar mixing with the boom-boom-boom in my head, because I had to get home to my family.

The lights were all blazing. I left the bike out front and went inside, pulling off my helmet, my hair plastered down and wet, my entire body slick with sweat, and it took me a few long moments to realize that there was a row.

'She's being difficult,' Tess said, standing above Keeva at

the dining table. Our girl hung her head, a book open in front of her. In the corner Rory lounged in a chair, reading a handbook with some kind of rodent on the cover. He was keeping out of it.

'She wouldn't work today,' Tess told me, and Keeva did not move a muscle. 'She wouldn't eat her dinner. So I have asked her to read and now she can't even do that.'

'It's *hot*,' Keeva said, looking up with narrowed, resentful eyes. 'It's *hot all the time*.'

'Oh, do you want to lounge by the pool all day?' Tess said. 'Shall we rent a banana boat instead of working? Shall I get room service to send up a Knickerbocker Glory?'

Tess looked at me as if I might have something to say, or order from room service, but I shook my head.

'I didn't *say* I wanted ice cream!' Keeva said. 'I just said it was *hot*. And it *is* hot.' Then the clincher. 'I don't like it here, okay? Is that allowed?'

'I like it,' Rory piped up, although nobody had asked him. 'I like Mr and Mrs Botan. I like Mummy teaching us. And I like the island.' He settled comfortably into his chair, turning back to his book with the rodent on the cover. 'There's more animals than England,' he said.

Keeva erupted.

'You like it because you didn't have any friends,' she shouted at him. 'Only a hamster and me! Your sister and a pathetic hamster!'

'I had friends,' Rory said defensively. 'Just not special ones. I was friends with everyone.'

Keeva's face was cloudy with tears.

'But I had Amber,' she said, and her face crumpled at the thought of the lost friend back in London. 'I had her. Oh, Amber, Amber, Amber!'

I was by Keeva's side now and I touched her shoulder as lightly as I could.

'Angel,' I said. 'It's a big change and it takes some getting used to.'

She looked up at me as if I didn't get it. 'But I don't *want* to get used to it!' she said. 'I miss my school. I miss London. I miss Amber.'

'There's Skype,' I said, knowing how feeble I must sound to my daughter. 'There's email.'

'That's not being friends!' Keeva said. 'Don't talk rubbish!'

'Hey,' Tess said. 'Don't you dare talk to your father like that.'

'It's okay, it's okay,' I said, holding up my hands.

'No, it's not okay,' Tess said. She pulled out a chair and sat next to Keeva, who ignored her. 'Look at me,' Tess said, and Keeva looked at her. 'Listen to me,' Tess said, and Keeva raised her chin, her mouth set in a tight, unhappy line. Tess put her face close. 'We are here for your father's job,' she said. 'I didn't have a daddy or a mummy, okay?'

'Tess,' I said. 'Come on.'

'No, she needs to hear this.'

'But I know about all this!' Keeva said quickly, anxious to head her mother off. 'You don't need to tell me.'

She swallowed hard and there was a silent pause where we all took a breath. We rarely talked about this stuff and, when we did, somehow it was always more in anger than sadness. All families have places they never go. With us it was the childhood that Tess had spent in care. There was no reason to revisit all of that. We wanted it behind us. We wanted it in the past. But it was never really behind us and it was never really past.

Tess began to speak.

'The earliest thing I can remember is living in a home that wasn't a home,' she said. 'With lots of other children whose parents didn't want them, or couldn't take care of them, or who had to give them up. And then I was farmed to other people's homes – fostering, they called it – and some of them were all right and some of them were not so good. Because there were bigger children who didn't want me there, or because they enjoyed being mean, or because of the adults who were around.'

'Tess, this is enough now, okay?' Trying to catch her eye, trying to get her to stop. 'She's too young,' I said.

Tess ignored me.

'None of them were real homes,' she said. 'So you – you, Keeva – you're lucky.'

Keeva had begun to cry.

'I know, I know, I know.'

'You have a home,' Tess said, and the anger was leaving her now, but still she went on. 'And in that home is your father and your mother and your brother. And that home is wherever they are, do you understand me?'

'Yes. Yes. Yes.'

Keeva's tears fell on the pages of the ignored book before her.

'Good,' Tess smiled. 'Now come here and give me a hug.'

Then they were in each other's arms and apologizing to each other and telling each other how much they were loved. And I thought – She is a fantastic mother. Although when the time came she could be far harder on them than I ever could, I knew that Tess found their tears unbearable.

As the girls embraced, Rory looked at me and raised his eyebrows, as if confirming that we did the right thing by letting them sort it out between themselves. I began to breathe again.

'England is still there,' Tess said, rocking Keeva in her arms, wiping her eyes with her fingers. 'And when we go back to visit, Amber will still be your friend. But we are building a life here. Isn't that right?'

Tess looked at me. Outside I could hear all the noises of the night, the diesel engine of a distant longtail, the insect drone of the bikes, and the wind in the casuarina trees, making them sound as if they were breathing. I realized that Tess was waiting for a reply.

'That's right,' I said.

The fortune teller was wrong. The darkness wasn't an inch away.

But it was coming.

7

When the wind was strong enough to move the tops of the trees, the red satellite dish on the roof of the home of Mr and Mrs Botan flapped like a broken door. Tess and I stood at the window of our bedroom, watching it through the insect net over the glass.

'They're old,' Tess said. 'Can't you fix it for them?'

The red dish swung back and forth.

'You know I can,' I said, thinking of the tools I had seen at the back of the shed. There wasn't much, but then I would not need very much.

'It's not just dangerous for them,' Tess said. 'It's dangerous for us, too. It's dangerous for the kids.'

The shed was still full of bottled water. I could not imagine that we would get through it in a lifetime. But at the back, on a paint-splattered little workbench, I found what I was looking for. A drill. A ratchet. Some silicon sealant. A few odd plugs. The drill was dusted with rust but when I plugged it in and turned it on it worked. Tess watched me from the door of the shed. Keeva and Rory came and stood either side of her. They were both holding a book called the *Oxford Junior Atlas*.

'No ladder,' I said.

'I've seen a step ladder round the side of their place,' Tess said. 'Is that tall enough?'

'That'll do,' I said.

From the top of the ladder I could see water damage in the bracket that held the arm of the dish. But the real problem was that whoever put the thing up in the first place had over-tightened the wall mount so that there was no give when the high winds came. Mr and Mrs Botan had joined Tess and the kids at the foot of the ladder. I looked down at the little crowd.

'What cowboy put this up?' I said, and Tess was the only one who smiled.

Even with my broken old tools it was a simple job. I removed the whole thing, then drilled four new holes for the wall mount, secured the bracket and fitted the arm that held the red satellite dish. I called down and told them to try their television. They all piled inside, my family and the Botans, but only the grown-ups came out. I could imagine my TV-starved children channel-surfing, the *Oxford Junior Atlas* forgotten on their laps. Tess gave me the thumbs up.

'Looking good,' she said.

Mr and Mrs Botan were talking quietly to each other when I came down the ladder and I guessed that they were wondering if they should try to pay me. The old man looked at me and I looked at him and he did not attempt to give me money. I was happy about that.

'You know many things,' he said.

'I wasn't always a driver,' I said.

Despite the red satellite dish that now stood straight and tall on their roof, the Botans' place felt like a classic Thai home to me, because every part of it felt like it was bathed in a light of soft honey-tinted brown.

Buddha images stared from alcoves and the top of black lacquer cabinets. There was a photo of the King on the wall. Six chairs stood in perfect alignment around a long, wooden dining table, as if waiting to have their photograph taken. Everything immaculate, exquisite and very clean.

Although it had exactly the same layout as our place, it felt like another way of living. It had none of the jumble and mess that you get with children growing up in your midst, the endless books, the forgotten items of clothing and the discarded toys – not that we had brought many of those. Snacks were important to Rory and Keeva. The last snack. The next snack. The snack that they wanted and the snack that they were allowed. There was no evidence that any kind of snacking ever took place in the Botans' house.

But Mr and Mrs Botan were parents too.

Next to what looked like a small altar – more Buddhas, a few lit candles, and a solitary teacup – there was a silver-framed photograph of a large, prosperous-looking man in glasses standing next to his seated, tiny, very pretty wife with a solemn-looking little boy standing to attention between them.

'Our son,' Mr Botan said, the pride obvious. 'A lawyer in Bangkok.'

'What a lovely family,' Tess said. 'And do they visit you often?'

Mr Botan frowned with thought, and sort of slowly rolled his head, as though it was very hard to give a definitive answer. I could hear Keeva and Rory in the other room, laughing together as they changed channels.

'Not so often,' said Mrs Botan, bringing a tray of tea.

We all looked at the silver-framed photograph and, placed that close to the altar, I thought that the family in the picture looked as though they were being worshipped too.

*   *   *

We went back home after our tea but an hour later the Botans knocked on our door with two plastic bags, one for Keeva and one for Rory, both stuffed full of a jumble of banana leaves, candles and flowers ready to assemble. The Botans told us that tonight was the festival of Loy Krathong and although I had no idea what that might be, I saw that this was how they were thanking me.

When night fell and November's moon rose full and white, the children carried their hand-made baskets to the beach and walked with the Botans down to the water's edge. The baskets were lotus-shaped and decorated with banana leaves, flowers, coins and unlit birthday cake candles.

All along the bow-shaped beach of Hat Nai Yang, people were carrying baskets down to the sea where the candles were lit by parents before the baskets were gently set adrift. We arrived not long after sunset, but already there was fire on the water as a hundred pinpoints of flame floated out to sea, flickering in the moon-washed night.

Our first Loy Krathong. At the time I did not understand the importance of the festival to the Thai people. I had seen ready-made baskets being sold by the side of the road without understanding their significance. Without the Botans as our neighbours, we would have missed it completely.

Rory and Keeva were excited and happy about the whole concept. Putting down their *Oxford Junior Atlas*, spending all afternoon making baskets and then staying out late to send them out to sea – what was not to like?

Now, as we watched them prepare to push their baskets across the glassy black surface of the Andaman, the sea as unmoving as a skating rink, the Botans attempted to explain the significance of the night to us all.

'*Loy* means float,' said Mr Botan. '*Krathong* means . . .' He reached for the words. 'Leaf cup?' he said, looking at his wife.

Mrs Botan said, 'To honour the spirit of the water for providing life to the land.' She thought about it. 'To beg forgiveness for the sins of the humans who spoil the land.'

'Cool,' said Keeva.

Mr Botan took out a cigarette and hungrily eyed the unlit roll-up.

'For a better day,' he said simply, and as I watched the tiny lights shimmer in the darkness, I decided that is how I would define Loy Krathong to myself, and how I would understand it. A small prayer for a better day. But it was really much later before I really understood how important the ceremony was to Thai people. On that very first Loy Krathong all I saw was the beauty and magic of a night that seemed to be swarming with fireflies.

Mrs Botan shot her husband a look and the old fisherman slipped the cigarette into his pocket, deciding not to risk it. Keeva gave her basket a hefty shove and it spun away. Rory held his basket like a precious chalice, reluctant to release it. He turned his face imploringly to Mrs Botan, and the flames flickered on the pink and blue candles that he had pushed into the soft surface of the banana tree basket.

'Can I just keep it?' he said. 'Maybe I should do that.'

She laughed and shook her head. 'No,' she said. 'You have to let it go.'

Together they bent down and slipped the basket into the water with a soft splash. We watched their baskets disappear into the night, until the pinpricks of flame were lost among all the others.

The longtail boats bobbed in the darkness and we felt the soft white sands of Hat Nai Yang under our bare feet. I tried to work out where the sea ended and the sky began. Voices murmured all along Hat Nai Yang but I had never been in a place more still than that beach on Loy Krathong.

Tess took my hand and squeezed it and as I saw her smile

63

on the beach with her face lit by nothing but November's full moon, I knew that she saw it too. It was beautiful.

Suddenly the peace was shattered.

Voices were being raised. Fingers were pointed. There was an excited babble of Thai and I realized that there was a boat out on the sea. Not a longtail, with a diesel engine that split the night. But a wooden boat that slipped across the water with almost no sound and revealed itself as just the faintest silhouette – a blur of black against more black. Then, as your eyes focused on all that darkness, you could see why the boat was out there. Whoever was on it was scooping up the Loy Krathong baskets as if they were some exotic form of fish.

A cry of anguish came from further down Hat Nai Yang. The voices of men and women who were suddenly angry. A child began to cry and protest in Thai and I saw a basket with its tiny prick of flame lifted from the water and stashed inside the boat.

Out in the shadows a small body slipped over the side of the boat and into the sea. A small armada of Loy Krathong baskets were ushered to the side of the boat. Hands lifted them from the water and the birthday cake candles went out. There was no attempt to disguise the thieving now.

People were so angry that I expected someone to wade into the water and go after the thieves in a longtail. But nobody moved from the shore.

'Why would someone do something like that?' Tess said. 'Steal a child's basket?'

'They steal,' said Mr Botan. 'They steal and sell to tourists on the beaches of the south. The tourists who can't make their own Loy Krathong.'

'Good business,' said Mrs Botan, as if it was a racket that was worth getting into.

Then I heard his laughter, out on the water, seeming to

enjoy the angry cries of the people on the beach of Nai Yang. I heard his laughter and I saw his small hard body as he pulled himself back into the boat. And as the boat turned away, the moon caught the strange flash of light in his hair and it shone like gold.

My daughter looked up at me.

'Chatree,' she said, breathless with excitement.

My son did not take his eyes from the sea.

'That bad boy,' he said. 'He's so bad. He'll get punished for being so bad.'

'Maybe he's not really bad,' Tess said. 'Maybe he's just trying to feed his family.'

'They get it in the end,' said Rory.

8

I rode under the barrier and past the security guard and as I looked up at Farren's balcony I saw the grey uniform and sunglasses of a member of the Royal Thai Police.

I touched my brakes and sat on the Royal Enfield, the engine still running, staring up at him, and under the crash helmet my face was damp with bike sweat and dread. I glanced back at the security guard in his little hut as if his face might tell me what was happening, but he had gone. I wondered if something had happened to Farren, if there was an innocent explanation to have cops crawling all over his home.

The cop was up there staring at the infinity pool, his thumbs cocked inside his belt, and he seemed to be trying to work out how the trick was done, how this sheet of still water just seemed to stretch out into space and stop there. Then there was another cop, and then one more, all of them looking at the infinity pool and laughing. I swore under my breath, the sickness rising in my throat. I swallowed hard, forcing it back down, torn between running away and going up to the house. Neither of them felt like a good thing. Then I heard another bike.

The rider pulled up beside me and pulled off his helmet, and his face was pale and dark at the same time. The Russian from the night of Muay Thai. He looked briefly at the cops on the balcony and then jammed his helmet back on and rode off, swerving around the security barrier without waiting for the guard to lift it. I watched him go, and the petrol stink of the Royal Enfield mixed with the fear in my gut, making my head feel light and giddy.

'Tom!'

Jesse was jogging up the dirt-track road that led to the marina. He got on to the back of the bike.

'Just go,' he said, indicating the way he had come, and I rode back down the unmade road to the Wild Palm office, sitting among the trees like an air-raid shelter in a rainforest. Inside there was none of the usual babble of cajoling, pleading and promises. The Wild Palm staff talked in lowered voices. The phones were silent.

'We've got to get out of here,' Jesse said, and I watched him tearing things from his desk and throwing them into a rucksack. They seemed like important things. A passport. Keys. Phone. Thai baht and English pounds. 'We can take the bike to the end of the road and get out by the marina,' he said, hefting the rucksack on his back.

'But we're not doing anything wrong, are we?' I said, and he looked at me as if I knew it wasn't true.

'Let's go,' he said.

I took out my phone as we made for the door, the need to speak to Tess suddenly overwhelming. CALLING HOME, it said on the screen as the police came through the door, and I heard her say my name, once, and then again, with a question mark this time, before the connection was broken.

Without needing to raise their voices, the police were lining up the Wild Palm staff against one of the walls. Nobody was being touched, apart from Jesse. One of the cops was gently lifting his elbow, and at first I thought he was fascinated by the unearthly pallor of my friend's skin.

But what he was looking at were the three watches Jesse had on his arm, each of them set to a different time zone.

The cops all had a good laugh at that.

Through the barred windows of a police van I saw the name of Phuket Provincial Jail written in Thai script. They had not bothered to spell out the name in English, and looking at the mysterious letters I never felt more like a great big bungling *farang*. The sinking feeling came to rest in the pit of my stomach.

I was with Wild Palm staff I did not know. We sat opposite each other in the back of a small van with a teenage cop, so young that there was a smattering of acne on his smooth cheeks. None of us talking, all of us in handcuffs, all of us very scared. An Aussie guy. A couple of North Americans. A blonde Kiwi girl, quietly crying to herself.

The van passed through a set of gates, and then another and into a central courtyard. In the front pocket of my jeans, pressed hard against my thigh, I could feel my phone vibrate for a long time and then fall still. I could not reach it, and that made me feel a kind of shameful relief. Because I knew it was Tess calling me back, and I knew that I did not have the words to explain any of this. Tears stung my eyes and I blinked them away. The van came to a halt and they got us out.

There was a queue of women prisoners in the courtyard. All of them locals. Brown uniforms, barefoot, surprisingly cheerful. One of them smiled and laughed and gave me one of those looks that you saw in the bars. A professional look, full of longing and invitation, so well executed that the only way to tell it from the real thing was that you knew it could be switched off or directed elsewhere in a fraction of a moment. Some of them had their ankles shackled. Some of them were not women at all but men banged up between sex-change operations.

'Kathoeys,' said the Aussie. 'The second kind of woman.' Then he cursed when we saw that some of them were coughing. 'Jesus Christ,' said the Aussie. 'Tuberculosis! They're checking them for TB! There's TB in this fucking place!'

I swallowed hard and tried to control my breathing. Breathe in slowly through the nose, let the lungs fill, then exhale slowly through the mouth. Again and again and again. Trying to find control in a world where I had no control.

We were formed into rough rows. There was Farren, his face set into hard lines. Pirin, looking defiant, by his side. Jesse, his face whiter than ever, visibly struggling in the heat. The sun was hot now, and it blinded me after the darkness of the van. Voices called out to us in English. *Farang* prisoners, gesturing us to come closer, desperate to convince us of their innocence.

But the cops murmured to us in Thai and we were ushered inside the main building, like a tour group in handcuffs, our eyes adjusting to the light, my skin feeling burned after just a few minutes in the courtyard.

Then Farren stepped out of line.

'There's been a mistake,' he said, smiling coldly at one of the young policemen, and I thought it might have been the one with bad skin in our van, although a lot of them looked alike to me, very young, dangerously young; you had to be careful around cops that young. The cop looked at Farren without expression and held up his hand – *Halt*, his hand seemed to say. But his hand said far more than that, because the open palm struck Farren hard on the socket of his left

69

eye, and I watched him reel back, his hand on his face, the shock and the pain of the blow robbing him of breath.

He got back into line.

Because there had been no mistake.

We were kept in a giant cell where most of the prisoners wore nothing but shorts and a bandana around their mouths, like the villains in an old western. It was crowded with bodies, a great mass of stinking frightened flesh, and there were other foreign faces in here, it was not just the people from Wild Palm. The foreigners all had the same look, as if they had woken up and found that the nightmare they were having was real.

When the smell of the open toilets reached me, the bandanas made sense, and as I felt the heat in here, I could understand why men wore only shorts or pants. But I kept my shirt on, and kept my jeans on, no matter how hot it got, as if removing them was some kind of admission that I belonged here, and that I would stay here forever.

Jesse came and sat next to me. 'It's going to be fine,' he said.

'I know,' I said. 'It's going to be all right.'

Then he covered his face with his hands and I put my arm around his shoulders and I did not look at him.

Farren sat apart from the rest of us, saying nothing, as if he did not know us. He kept his hand over his wounded eye.

With my free hand I looked at my phone and when I saw that there was no signal I got up and moved through the bodies to where Farren was sitting.

'I should punch your lights out,' I said.

He looked up at me.

'You wanted a new life,' he said, his voice flat and cold. 'The good life. The soft life. I gave it to you. Stop whining.'

That wasn't true.

All I wanted was a better life.

I flew at him, wanting to rip his face off for whatever Tess would have to suffer now, but Pirin was on me at once, far stronger than me, and knowing exactly what he was doing, wrestling me away and down, the space opening up around us to make room for the violence, his thick arms tied in a complicated knot around my arms and neck, pushing my face into the ground, and I felt my nose and mouth and upper teeth being smashed hard into the concrete, slamming into it, banged into it again and again, trying to stop me struggling.

But my wife filled my heart and she choked it tight shut and no matter how much he hurt me, I would not stop struggling.

9

'Thomas Arthur Finn,' said the young cop, and I didn't get it at first, partly because my name sounded so strange in his mouth, and partly because of that middle name, hated and never used but there in my passport, and there on the computer printout the young policeman read from, the name of my father. About the only thing the bastard ever gave me, apart from eczema.

'Here,' I said.

Jesse's sleeping head was resting on my shoulder. I edged away without waking him and got up, every limb stiff and aching. I suppose I must have slept at some point because the day had drifted by, the sun shifting across the small high windows at the top of the communal cell, and it was fading fast now as the island prepared for another spectacular sunset.

I picked my way through the bodies, most of them stuck somewhere between sleeping and waking, and I thought of the last time I had seen my dad. I was eleven, and he was leaving us for his new life with a woman a few doors down. She was leaving her home too. *'You'll understand one day,'* my father had told me, but by now I couldn't even remember his face, and I still didn't understand, and I knew I never would, and I knew I would never want to.

I followed the cop down a corridor to a small, clean room with a desk and a policeman sitting behind it. The cop behind the desk was the one who I had first seen standing alone on the balcony, staring at the infinity pool. I had thought he was just some young kid, but now I saw there were the three stripes of a sergeant on the grey sleeve of his uniform. He ran his pen down the list of names in front of him and yawned. There were other papers on the desk, many of them with the Wild Palm logo.

He didn't look at me.

'I need to call my wife,' I told him.

'Your job at Wild Palm,' he said. 'Are you – an Account Opener? A Property Broker? Or an Investment Advisor?'

His English was good but careful, as if he was trying out these words for the very first time. There was a nametag in English script on his chest.

SOMTER, it said.

I shook my head. 'None of them,' I said. 'I'm a driver. My wife,' I said. 'Please, Sergeant Somter. I need to call her.'

He looked at me now, and sighed. 'You come to Thailand and do many bad things,' he said.

'Me?' I said. 'No.'

He pushed a sheet of paper across to me. 'This is your script,' he said. 'What to say to people to get money. What to say when the money is gone.' He shook his head. 'How to fool the people,' he said.

I shook my head. 'I don't have a script,' I said.

'You come to Thailand for cheap girl, cheap beer, cheap living,' he said. 'You come to Thailand for cheap life.'

I waited for a moment to make sure he had finished. There was a pounding in my head and everything hurt. I didn't know if he was talking about me or if he was talking about every foreigner that he had ever met. I genuinely could not tell, and not being able to tell scared the life out of me.

'I came to Thailand for a better life,' I said quietly.

He nodded, as if I had agreed with everything he had suggested.

'Many *farang* come to Thailand,' he said.

'Look, I want to help,' I said. 'Sergeant Somter. Please. I want to answer your questions. But I don't know anything about – what is it? – Property Openers and Investment Advisors? I don't know anything about that stuff. That wasn't me. I just drive.'

'Not just holiday,' said Sergeant Somter. 'To live. To stay. To suck what blood you can. Cheap life, cheap living.'

'That's not me,' I said.

'Men like your boss,' said Sergeant Somter. 'Farren. Is Farren your boss?'

'Yes,' I said.

I was every *farang* he had ever arrested. Every foreigner he had ever seen fighting in the bars, drunk in the street, shirtless in the temple.

'My wife will be worried,' I said. 'She doesn't know I am here. We have two children—'

'Your wife knows exactly where you are,' he said, cutting me off, and he nodded to the young cop who had remained standing at the door.

Sergeant Somter smiled at me, his teeth white and even.

'And you really believe that we are the barbarians,' he told me.

The young cop came back and Tess was with him, calm and controlled but her mouth set in a thin hard line, registering her shock at the state of my face with her eyes, only her eyes, and I grabbed her and told her how sorry I was and she told me not to be silly, all of our words less than a whisper. When she gently but firmly broke away from me I saw there was a man with her.

An Englishman in a baseball cap.

Tall and slim and untroubled by the heat inside Phuket Provincial. His jeans were neat and pressed and he wore a blue business shirt. Sergeant Somter rose from his chair and shook hands with the man. Then the man looked at me, but he didn't hold out his hand.

'James Miles,' he said. 'I help out at the British Office. At the Honorary UK Consulate. That's where Mrs Finn found me.'

There was a dragon in dark glasses on his baseball cap, and some words in Chinese. *Foreign Correspondents Club of Hong Kong*, it said.

'The British Office has a space on Patak Road,' he said, as if that explained everything.

'Karon Beach,' I said.

'That's it,' he laughed. 'More of a hole in the wall than an office. Above Klong Furniture.'

I stared at him, thrown by the small talk.

Tess took my arm and squeezed. I didn't understand what was happening. I looked at Sergeant Somter and his face revealed nothing. James Miles spoke to him in what sounded to me like fluent Thai. Sergeant Somter nodded and left the room, nodding to the cop at the door to come with him. When they had gone Tess threw her arms around me, her eyes shining, and I held her tight.

'I'm all right,' I told her.

'Phuket Provincial was built for seven hundred prisoners,' James Miles said. 'There must be twice that number inside. But there's worse than Phuket Provincial. A lot worse.'

'So you're from the embassy?' I said, my arm around my wife's waist. 'You're getting me out?'

James Miles laughed.

'I'm not that important,' he said. 'I write travel books. I'm a humble scribe. As I said, I just help out at the British office because they get so busy with no official consul or embassy on the island. But I'm going to try to get you out.'

That didn't sound too promising.

'The police think that Farren was running a boiler room,' he said.

'A boiler room?'

I had never heard of a boiler room. I felt stupid. Stupid and helpless. The relief that I had felt at seeing Tess was changing to something else. I did not want her to see me in this place. I hated it that she had to see me in this place.

'Boiler rooms offer investments in IPOs – Initial Pre-Offering Shares,' Miles said, and my face flushed at the extent of my ignorance. I looked at Tess and she nodded and smiled and squeezed my hands. James Miles was still talking. 'They're sold at a low base price to people in the know – usually directors. And when the company gets listed on the stock exchange, the price soars. And you make a fat profit.' He allowed himself a little laugh. 'If the company is real.'

I shook my head.

'But Wild Palm sold property,' I said.

'It comes down to the same thing,' Miles said, and he wasn't smiling now. 'Bogus investments. The glossy website is a front for a shack with a dozen telephone lines. Cold-calling the greedy and the gullible and separating them from their life savings. It may not have been a boiler room in the strict sense of the term. But our Sergeant Somter is right to smell a rat.'

I felt that something was slipping away from me.

'But,' I said, 'Wild Palm didn't do anything illegal.'

For the first time I saw a flash of irritation in his eyes.

'And how would you know that, Tom?' he said.

I said nothing. But I wondered whose side he was on. It didn't sound like mine.

'As far as I can see, the Thais are right to be concerned,' he said. 'Farren has been playing fast and loose with Thai property and land ownership rights. Wild Palm have been setting up Thai companies, but it's illegal to use nominees. These companies are meant to be genuinely controlled by locals. They have something called the Foreign Business Act of 1999 and they take it very seriously.'

I stared at him. 'Who are you?'

He laughed. 'I'm just a hack. I write travel books.' He glanced at Tess and seemed to soften. 'Look, I'm not here to make moral judgements,' he said. 'The Thais have been watching Farren for quite some time. Before you ever got here. I'm just here to help, Tom. But we have to help Sergeant Somter, too. What do you know about Farren?'

'He's a businessman,' I said. 'A property developer.'

He laughed. 'Farren will end up running a bar,' he said. 'They always do.'

'You don't know him,' I said, feeling suddenly angry at this man. 'And you don't know me.'

'Tom,' Tess said, but I didn't look at her.

'I know you're not like the rest of them,' James Miles said, and he was trying to be kind. I could see that. If not for my sake, then for the sake of Tess, and I wondered what terrors she was feeling when she found him at the British Office on Patak Road. 'I know you were just a driver,' he said. 'Isn't that right? You were just a driver at Wild Palm?'

I thought of the building business that I had once had in London before they took it away from me. I thought of the men who had worked for me and the things we had made with our hands.

'That's right, I'm just a driver,' I said, and I turned away.

I didn't give a damn what this man thought of me. But the thought of Tess looking at my broken face at that moment was unbearable.

10

They must have heard the bike bumping down the dirt-track road because they were all waiting for us when we got home.

Rory and Keeva, both holding copies of a book with a little girl and a pig on the cover. Mr and Mrs Botan, looking at me without meeting my eye. And, unaccountably, the boy with the gold streak in his hair, the boy from the beach, the *chao ley* kid who had tormented the turtle and thieved the baskets on Loy Krathong. He was also holding a book, but it was a different one from my children. He had to be a couple of years older than our kids, but the book he was holding was called *Stories for Six-Year-Olds*.

'I'm helping him with his English,' Tess said. 'He's had no formal education. His sister teaches him. Can you believe that?'

I nodded, because I could believe it very easily, and got off the bike, feeling dirty and tired, the kind of dirty and tired that would not come off in a shower.

Then Keeva was in my arms.

'We saw you! On TV! But we couldn't understand it! It was all in Thai!'

I guessed we must have made the local news. I looked

up at our neighbours. Mr Botan examined the unlit cigarette in his hand and Mrs Botan smiled sadly. It was my turn to look away.

Keeva was kissing my arm, but Rory hid behind Mrs Botan, studying the cover of his book.

'Rory,' Tess said. 'Welcome your father home.'

But the boy still held back, hiding behind the Botans, not looking at me. Tess said his name again – sharply, this time, with that classroom sting she could put into her voice when she needed to – and he slowly began moving towards me. I shook my head.

'It's all right,' I said. 'Rory doesn't have to welcome me home.'

I went inside the house, Keeva still holding my arm, rattling away about what they had seen on TV, and Tess thanking the Botans for looking after the children, and scolding our boy. I could hear all their voices but the words were not registering.

All I could think was – None of this is mine.

None of it.

The bike. The house. The furniture. It all belongs to someone else. What is mine?

'Mrs Botan turned it off quick, but we saw you and your friends,' Keeva said, her breath on my arm.

'They're not my friends,' I said. 'Jesse is my friend. The man with the gibbon. Not the rest of them. They're not my friends.' I thought of Farren. 'They've done nothing for me,' I said.

'Okay,' Keeva said, her eyes wide. 'Okay, Daddy.'

I smiled at her and touched her face.

'I'm sorry,' I said. 'About everything.'

'I don't mind,' she said quickly. 'It was Rory. He was crying. He didn't like it.'

'Well,' I said. 'I didn't like it much myself.' I got down

on my knees to look my daughter in the eye. 'But I haven't done anything wrong,' I said.

She smiled at me, her eyes shining with a love that I knew I did not deserve.

'I know,' she said.

Rory came into the house, and went into his room without meeting my eye. Keeva gave me one last fierce kiss on the arm and followed him.

I walked into the living room where the chair was not mine, and the table was not mine, and the air that I breathed was not mine. I sat in a chair that wasn't mine and my eyes closed without being told to. I was beyond exhausted. Then I felt someone standing in front of me and when I looked up Tess was standing there, as I knew she would be.

The Thai boy was at her side, still holding his babyish book. I felt a wave of frustration. My family were taking in waifs and strays when we were living under a borrowed roof.

'You still here?' I asked the kid.

He briskly nodded. 'Pleased to meet you,' he said, and his voice was thin and musical, and it seemed all wrong coming out of his body. 'How are you today? I am well.' He turned to Tess. 'Excuse me, I must be going.'

And he left.

'It's not his fault,' she said, and I felt a surge of shame.

'I'm sorry, Tess,' I said, and I meant – for all of it.

'Come here,' she said, and I got up and wrapped her in my arms, and I put my face in her hair as she told me what I was going to do now.

'You're going to eat something,' Tess said, and she had brought food from next door, and it was waiting on the table for me. Mrs Botan's Pahd Thai, the steaming noodles wrapped in a wafer-thin omelette. 'Then you are going to clean up,' she said. 'Then you are going to sleep.' She placed a kiss on my forehead and I felt myself slump into her arms. She gently straightened me up. 'And in the morning you're going to have to look for work,' she said. 'Okay?'

'Okay.'

But the big question hung between us, unspoken yet everywhere. Tess smiled at me, and waited for me to say it.

'And what about home?' I said. 'What about going home?'

She held my shoulders and gave them one gentle shake.

'We are home,' she said quietly.

The next morning I awoke at first light while my family was still sleeping and I wheeled the old Royal Enfield out of the shed.

It was so early that I could hear the *adhan*, the Islamic call to prayers. Foreigners think that all Thais are Buddhist, but our part of the island, that old Phuket, the far northern tip, was almost as Muslim as it was Buddhist, and by the time you reached the far end of Phuket, just before the bridge to Phang Nga, there were more mosques than temples.

I stood in the cool shadows of the dawn, listening to the calm certainty of the *adhan*, letting it still my heart. But again I was stabbed with the knowledge that none of this was mine. Not the bike, not the home, and not even the sense of calm that belonged to somebody else's religion. It was all borrowed and it would all have to be given back.

Mr Botan came round the side of his house, his arms full of ancient lobster pots.

'Don't worry about the house,' he said, his voice soft because everyone else was sleeping. 'It is paid for six months.'

I knew he was trying to be kind, but I felt myself tense.

'I'm not worried,' I said.

He placed the lobster pots on the ground and looked at his hands, as if noticing something about them for the first time.

'My hands are getting old,' he said. 'You could help me fish.'

I laughed bitterly. 'I'm not a fisherman,' I said.

'But you know many things,' he said, and I followed his eyes to the red satellite dish.

'Not fishing,' I said, my voice was flat and hard. 'I was a builder. I built things with my hands. All different sorts of things. And when that was taken away, I was a driver. Vans. Cars.' I touched the Royal Enfield. 'A motorbike. Now that's gone too.' I shrugged. 'But I don't need charity.'

I watched the anger flare in his face.

'It's not charity,' he said. '*It's a job.*' He shook his head, heading back round the side of his house. 'Just like my son – the big shot! – too good for fishing!'

I watched him storming off.

'I'm not too good for anything,' I said, but he had gone by then.

I wheeled the bike to the end of the dirt road so as not to wake my family or Mrs Botan, and then I rode south to the Bangla Road in Patong, where every night the music plays and the beer flows and the money pours in.

A river of money. I wasn't looking for much of it. We didn't need that much.

The rain came and I bought an umbrella made of transparent plastic from a street vendor on Bangla Road. Then I was suddenly hungry and I bought a coconut from another street trader, and I cruised slowly through Patong, one hand on the umbrella and the other hand on the coconut, sipping milk through a plastic straw, no hands on the bike, the Royal Enfield steering itself between my thighs, and the rain coming down.

I lowered my new umbrella and lifted my face to the heavens and the raindrops were so warm and fat that I had to smile. I felt the rain on my face and I tasted the thin sweet milk of a coconut and I realized that the island always made me feel this way. As if something would turn up.

But a few hours later I sat on the bike outside the Hotel Sala, and I looked at the long line of idle taxi drivers standing by the open doors of their cars, smoking and talking and waiting – mostly just waiting.

I looked at their blank, impatient faces and they looked back at me, staring straight through me, as if I was already gone.

As I put the bike away Keeva appeared in the doorway of the shed, a look of rapture on her face. There was a small dog in her arms. A mangy little mutt, ratty and brown, hardly more than a pup, although it looked as though it had been living rough for years.

I was immediately furious with her.

'What's the rule about dogs?' I said, my voice trembling.

It wasn't just the dog. It was everything.

Keeva's smile faded. 'We don't touch them,' she said, and she immediately put the mutt on the ground. 'We never touch the dogs.' The ratty little pup looked up at her and then shuffled over to me, sniffing at my boots, its grubby tail wagging away as though we were old friends.

'It's probably got rabies, Keeva,' I said, my voice softer now, and I pointed at the shed door as I fixed the mutt with a look. It cocked its head to one side, as if it didn't quite get my drift.

'Beat it,' I said, but the dog did not move.

There were stray dogs everywhere in Thailand. Mrs Botan had told me that it was because Thais respected all living things. Mr Botan had suggested it was because His Majesty the King had once adopted a street dog called Thong Daeng, so all dogs were favoured. But it always seemed to me that

the dogs were everywhere because Thais were totally unsentimental about animals, and yet they had no appetite for
dog meat. In their attitude to wild dogs, you could see
both that famous Thai tolerance, and that less famous Thai
indifference. And sometimes you couldn't tell them apart.

Seeing the mutt refusing to move, Keeva looked all
hopeful.

'Can we keep him just for a little while?' she said.

I could see Rory lurking outside the shed, still furious at
me with a rage that he could neither express nor explain,
but drawn by the dog.

'No,' I told her, as the mutt followed me out of the shed.
'Come on,' I said. 'Beat it, mister.'

The pea-brained creature capered happily by my side and
my daughter's eyes were wide. Keeva looked at her brother
and then back at me.

'Is that her name?' she said. 'Mister? How do you know
her name, Dad? Is she called Mister?'

'Here, Mister,' said Rory. 'Mister, Mister, Mister.' And the
filthy little hound was cunning enough to respond: *Yes, that's
my name – how did you guess? We were clearly born for each other*.

Rory picked the dog up, his love of animals greater than
his fear of me, and I shook my head and sighed as he aimed
the dog's tail at his sister.

'And Mister's a boy, see?' he said.

Mr Botan came out of his house and looked at the children
with the dog.

'What time do you go to work in the morning?' I asked
him.

But he ignored me and went back into his house.

Rory looked at me, and I felt that it was the first time he
had looked me in the eye since everything had fallen apart.

'Mister is hungry,' he said. 'Can we feed him before we
let him go?'

I nodded, and Rory and Keeva took the mutt into the house before I changed my mind. I could hear the voice of Tess, and their excited response. Mister began to yap as if this was its lucky day.

Mr Botan came out of his house carrying some kind of clothing. Clean, green and carefully folded. He gave it to me and I saw it was a pair of the lightweight trousers that he always wore. He nodded at my jeans, and I suddenly saw how unsuited they were to the island, how they were from another life at the other end of the world.

'I go when it is light,' he said, and when I nodded he went back inside his house.

I went inside my own house where Keeva and Rory were feeding the dog.

'I want it out of the house when it's been fed,' I said, and neither of them gave any indication they had heard. 'I mean it,' I said.

Then I touched my son's shoulder and he looked up at me.

'Are you still mad at me?' I said.

'I wasn't mad,' he said, turning back to the ravenous dog. 'Just worried.'

That night on the Bangla Road I saw the young sergeant.

He was on the other side of the street, standing by his car watching two Australians argue outside the No Name Bar, wearing his *Top Gun* shades even though night was falling fast. He had been waiting to see if the Australians were drunk enough to need attention, but when he saw me on my bike he strolled over to me.

'We got your file,' said Sergeant Somter. 'After you left.' He laughed and shook his head as if he could not quite believe my luck. 'All the files came on all the men. But after you had gone.'

The raindrops had started to fall, fat and soft and warm. I had my plastic umbrella with me but I did not raise it.

'I know what you did,' he continued. 'In your own country. I know about the trouble you were in.'

'I did nothing wrong,' I said. 'I protected my family. That's all.'

'We both know what you did,' he said.

The Australians had begun to swap wild, swinging punches. They grappled with each other for a bit and then tumbled into the gutter. A tiny woman in a tiny skirt began to scream, swaying precariously on her impossible heels. A few tourists stopped to watch the action, leering with delight.

'I don't want to see your face any more,' Sergeant Somter said, and pulled back his shoulders, preparing to deal with the Australians. 'So you go home now,' he said. 'Just go home.'

He wasn't talking about Hat Nai Yang.

It was after midnight when I came bumping down the dirt-track road. The house next door was in darkness, but on our porch Tess had left a light on for me. In the faint yellow glow I could see the dog looking up at me, as if waiting to see if I had a heart. He was patiently waiting in the same place after I put the bike in the shed.

'Come on, Mister,' I said, and I picked him up and carried him into our home.

PART TWO

Beach Dog

11

London.

The night it finally all fell apart.

I had been stuck out at the airport for hours, waiting for a delayed flight, and by the time I had dropped the client off at his hotel and got myself home it was the far end of the night, that brief moment when the entire city seemed to sleep.

As soon as I came through the door my last breath caught in my throat as I sensed the cold air coming in from somewhere. I looked into the blackness of the living room, and knew with a sickening certainty that there was something wrong with my home.

I was wearing a chauffeur's uniform that always carried the traces of some unknown driver's cigarettes, no matter how many times it was dry-cleaned, and a peaked cap that I usually tore off as soon as I was through my front door. But that night I did not take it off. I just stood there listening to the silence, the car keys still in my hand, the firm's limo still clicking and cooling on the driveway, and feeling the cold air on my face.

My family were sleeping. They were definitely sleeping.

So I let out the trapped breath, thinking it was just me, my nerves all jangled from too much caffeine and a long day behind the wheel. I went to turn on the lights. Then my foot touched the photograph.

I picked it up and saw there was a jagged crack of broken glass across the front, like a flash of lightning. It was a photo of the children, just two years ago but shockingly so much younger, feeding a banana to an elephant. Keeva laughing as she held out the fruit, and Rory standing behind his sister, looking at the elephant with dumbstruck love as it unfurled its trunk for the banana. Something stirred at my feet and I scooped up a twitching bag of fur and bones. The hamster's beady eyes shone with guilt when I showed him the broken photograph.

'Smashing the place up again, Hammy?' I said.

As I put him down the security light came on in the back garden. A fox stood perfectly still, staring through the glass doors that led to the little garden.

I saw that they were open.

The back doors were open.

That was where the cold air was coming from, and I felt it chill the sudden sweat on my face.

The fox was young, scrawny, but standing there like he owned the place. Eyes like yellow flares in the night, totally unafraid. The light went off and the shadow of the fox slid over the garden fence and into the night. For a moment I just stood there, not understanding what was happening, and not knowing what to do.

Then I was running upstairs, calling her name.

'Tess!'

The door to the children's bedroom was open and Tess was standing there in her dressing gown. She had a knife in her hand, a really elaborate knife that I recognized from our brief scuba-diving days, a couple of holidays before the children were born. Coral reefs and looking at the fishes and Tess in a wet suit. That's what I remembered. I didn't even know we still had that knife.

We heard a distant siren. Then it faded away. Tess shook her head as I looked from the knife to her face.

'It's not for us,' she said quietly. 'I only just called them. The police.'

We looked at each other for a moment.

'Maybe it's just the fox,' I said.

'It's not the fox, Tom.'

From beneath the folds of her dressing gown the twins appeared, as if by magic, their eyes sticky with sleep, one either side of her, clinging to their mother's legs. Different in ways that went beyond the boy's Harry Potter glasses and the girl's long hair. Rory was trying not to cry.

'Maybe they left,' Tess said.

'Who?' Keeva said. 'Who left? Mama?'

'Maybe,' I said, starting back downstairs, and stopped at the top of the stairs when I heard the gulping, snotty sound of someone trying not to cry. I knew it was Rory and I looked back at him, wanting to say something but not having the words.

'I'm going with Daddy,' said Keeva, and her mother silenced her with a yank on her arm.

'Just stay here,' I said. 'Everything's going to be all right.'

'Is Hammy all right?' said Rory, and he wiped his nose on the sleeve of his World Wildlife pyjamas.

'Hammy's fine,' I said, and I went downstairs.

This is what will happen, I told myself. You will check the back doors where they kicked them in and then you will check every room downstairs, but they will all be empty. Some stuff will be gone, but that will be okay. It's just stuff. Let them have it.

I did not want to fight.

And then the security light came on again and I could see the glow of the hard white light through the window on the stairs, knowing it wasn't our fox this time, and feeling the fear clogging my heart, my legs, my mouth.

Just go, I thought. Take what you want and go.

But when I got to the foot of the stairs and looked out at the back garden, all lit up in the dead of the night, I could see that he had not gone.

The shed door was open and this young man, this overgrown boy, this giant kid was coming out backwards, carrying my daughter's bike. The security light didn't seem to bother him and now I saw there was a dark pile in the middle of the garden and it took me a second to realize that it was our TV set, our DVD player, all that stuff that should be sitting in the corner of our living room.

Before the security light went off he looked at me with foggy eyes. Neither of us moved but he was still out there in the darkness, a black shape on more blackness, and he was not revealed by the moon or the light that never goes out in the city. Then somebody pulled the flush in the downstairs toilet.

And I thought to myself – *You're kidding me.*

I stared at the door of the toilet and another one came out, frowning as he buttoned up his jeans. He was wearing my old leather jacket. It was a bit small for him.

He stopped, looked up at me, and even then I hoped that it would all just go away. Even then I thought that they might make a run for it, carrying what they could, and I would give half-hearted chase until I heard the sound of the police siren.

But none of that happened. This is what happened instead.

The one in the garden carefully laid the bike on its side, as if he was afraid of damaging it, and he came into the house through the smashed back doors and the one who had just used our downstairs toilet waited for him before he started coming towards me and then somebody was howling with fear and rage and after a numb second, I realized that it was me.

But it was all right.

Because they were only fighting for all that stuff they had piled up in the back garden, while I was fighting for the woman and the two children upstairs.

In one corner of the police station there was a tangled mess of brightly coloured metal, this sad jumble of flaking yellows and reds and blues and greens, some of it deliberately curly-whirly and some of it deliberately bent out of shape. There was a sign above it: *Please be advised that this play area is unsupervised*, it said. As I stood there, waiting for my turn, I kept reading the sign, trying to make sense of it. I rubbed my eyes. I was very tired now.

Four in the morning, but the cop shop was still busy. All of us victims of the night. We queued with our complaints and our stories and an overweight policeman slowly wrote them down, speaking to everyone as though they had just had their brain removed or he was at the end of his tether or both. When my turn finally came, he really did not like it when I said that I needed him to come outside and take a look.

'I need to show you,' I said. 'In the car.'

'Sir,' he said, making *sir* sound like another way of saying *time-wasting moron*. 'I am not permitted to leave my station, sir.' He peered at me. 'What happened to your shirt?'

I had not noticed my shirt. It had lost all the buttons at the front. I tugged at it self-consciously and told him that the car was parked right outside. He looked up at my chauffeur's cap. Somehow I was still wearing my chauffeur's cap. His eyes narrowed as they drifted down to my face.

93

'Is that blood on your lips?' he said.

'Please,' I said, my fingers flying to my mouth.

In the end he came, lifting his massive bulk from his long-suffering chair, sighing with professional impatience, huffing and puffing as he waddled behind me out to the street.

I shivered in the night air, pressing the car key. The orange lights on the big black 7-series BMW flashed twice. The fat policeman stood by my side as I opened the boot. And there they were, their hands and feet tied up with jump leads. It was a bit of a squeeze.

One of them began to swear at me, telling me that his brother was going to kill me. The other one was sucking for air. I had seen that over the years with a few passengers. That desperation for some air. I knew it was an asthma attack.

The cursing did not stop. If anything, it was getting worse.

'You want me to shut this boot?' I said, and that was when I felt the hand of the fat policeman on my arm.

At work I sat on the fire escape overlooking the neat lines of cars, all black and shiny with money and love.

Men in dark suits, white shirts and dark ties moved between the BMWs and Mercs like parents in a maternity ward, gently removing smears on the paintwork, frowning at the spotless windscreens.

My body was stiff and aching from the hours in the police cell, the stink of the toilet in the corner making sleep impossible, and the sunshine on my face told my mind that it was a good thing to shut down for a while.

I loosened my tie and closed my eyes. All I could hear were the jets of a power wash smothering the sound of the city. I slept right there, sitting on the fire escape, my head nodding forward, dreaming of water. A voice broke the dream.

'Got a job for you, killer,' he said, and I opened my eyes.

Andrzej. A big, tough-looking Pole with a nose that had been broken so many times it looked like a ski jump. The only man at VIP Motors who was allowed to wear a T-shirt and jeans. He was holding out a piece of paper. I rubbed my eyes and yawned.

'What are the charges?' he said.

I took the piece of paper and stared at the name and address, scratching my head. The sun slipped behind some clouds, and I shivered in the sudden chill. 'Actual Bodily Harm,' I said. 'ABH and False Imprisonment.'

Andrzej pulled a face. 'Need a hug?'

'Maybe later.'

He shook his head. 'What a country,' he said. 'You need anything?'

'Like what?'

'To defend yourself,' he said, lowering his voice although nobody could hear him. 'Something to defend yourself with.'

'Why would I need that?' I said.

'In case they come back,' he said, genuinely surprised. 'Those guys you messed up.'

I shook my head. 'I don't want any trouble,' I said.

Andrzej looked at me with pity.

'Oh, you already got plenty of that,' he said.

Nick Kazan was young, a good-looking boy at the far end of his twenties, and that's all I noticed about him when I picked him up from the flat in Notting Hill. Most of our clients were older. Nobody used VIP Motors unless they were some kind of big shot with company money to burn. This kid – crumpled suit, no tie, a floppy head of Hugh Grant hair – looked like a struggling young professional. The Heathrow Express was more his price range.

We were turning on to the road to the airport when he spoke to me.

'For a driver,' he said, 'you don't say very much, do you?'

There was still a little bit of Liverpool in his accent that he had not managed to lose at university. I could feel he was watching me in the mirror, but I kept my eyes on the road, the traffic heavy yet moving along nicely, the first of the planes starting to appear as we headed west.

'The mouthy driver,' I said. 'That's a stereotype.'

He laughed, and looked out of the window. There is something hypnotic about the planes along that road. You look at them and you realize you can go anywhere.

'Do you think you're going to prison?' he said.

Now I looked at him.

'What terminal do you want?' I said, making my voice hard.

'Surprise me,' he said, leaning forward to place a business card on the armrest next to me. There was his name and the logo of his paper on the card. I did not pick it up. He placed a tiny voice recorder next to his business card, and it was as small as a mobile phone. There was a little red light on it to show you it was working. He also had a notebook in his hands. It was a bit belt and braces, especially as I wasn't planning to say another word. But he was good at his job. He knew how to make you open up.

'So what are you, Tom?' he said.

Tom. I loved that.

'The police think you're some kind of crazed vigilante,' he said. 'Those are serious charges. My editor thinks you're a noble have-a-go hero. Which one are you?'

A 747 flew right over our heads. I ducked down to watch it go. A light rain began to fall, and I flicked on the wiper.

'Why didn't you just knock on my door?' I said. A few reporters already had, and it was horrible. Shouting these questions at me, and at Tess, and taking our picture without

96

asking. I wanted to get one of their cameras and smash it, to make them go and to leave us alone, but Tess stopped me. She said it would make things worse.

Nick Kazan was smiling. 'If I had door-stepped you, would you have talked to me?' he said.

I looked back at him in the rear-view mirror.

'You think we're talking now?' I said.

I had pulled into the fast lane and put my foot down and we were nearly at the airport. The ride had been on account. One way. I was slinging him out at Heathrow whether he liked it or not.

'Not the first time you've had some trouble, is it, Tom?' he said. 'You had a business, right? A building business. You were good with your hands. Always have been, I bet. No real education, but clever.'

'Story of my life,' I said, and cursed myself. Why was I talking to him? I was meant to be saying nothing.

'And it collapsed,' he said, and I wondered how he knew all this stuff. 'Your business folded. You went bankrupt.' He was writing in his little notebook and the red light was shining on the voice recorder. 'You can find out about people so easy these days,' he said.

I laughed bitterly. 'You think you can just go online and get the story of someone's life?' I said.

'Tell me what I'm missing,' he said.

'It's all the paperwork,' I said. 'They kill you with the paperwork. The small businessman. They bury you. All these pen pushers who never employed anyone, who never ran a company, who never built anything in their soft little lives.'

He nodded, watching the planes.

'Couldn't pay your bills,' he said. 'Started driving cabs. Sorry – limos. Shipping shagged-out old businessmen to Heathrow and back. A bit of a comedown after having your own business.'

'Better than benefits,' I said, feeling the blood getting hot. 'Better than asking the state to take care of me.'

He was writing it all down as if this was all some story that we were telling together.

'Then one night you come home after a hard day's collar and there are two burglars in your house,' he said. 'Out of their minds on God knows what. Your family are asleep upstairs. You don't know if they've got weapons. But you overpower the bastards. Take them down the station, where you're the one who gets treated like the criminal. Your wife's name is Tess, right?'

'I don't want her in any story,' I said, and a lorry with Polish plates sounded its horn as I drifted into its lane. 'You leave her out of it.'

'This must be horrible for her,' he said. 'For Tess. It must be a nightmare. Trying to bring up your children – Rory and . . . Keeva? Is that Irish? – and you've got these scumbags breaking into your home. Your husband does what any man would do. And then he gets sent to jail.'

'I'm going to get out,' I said, seeing the signs for the airport, and realizing it only when I said it. 'This country is no good any more.'

'Get out?' he said.

'This was a great country,' I said. 'Look at it now. The crime, the grime. The lack of respect. The lack of fear. The wicked walk free and the innocent suffer. Defend your home, protect your family – the most natural things in the world – and they treat you like a villain.'

Nick Kazan was smiling at me. But I could see that he wasn't laughing at me.

We were silent. The rain came down harder. The Merc's solitary big windscreen wiper slapped back and forth.

'I love the rain,' I said, talking to myself more than him. 'It washes the streets clean. All the gangs, all the little hard nuts, all the scum – the rain washes it all away for a bit.'

Now Nick Kazan was staring at me with an open mouth. He began to write furiously in his notebook. He looked up and shook his head.

'You're Travis Bickle, aren't you?' he said. 'You're the Travis Bickle of Barnsbury!'

I must have looked blank.

'Travis Bickle. You never saw that film? You never saw *Taxi Driver*?'

He kept writing. I kept driving. There wasn't far to go now. I could see he was getting excited but I could not understand why.

'I'm getting out,' I said. 'One day soon, I'm getting out.'

'But a lot of people feel like that, Tom,' he said, and the rain-slick road to the airport hummed beneath us.

12

The screen of our television set was covered in white scratches where they had dragged it out to the garden, and it made Nick Kazan seem as though he was talking in a snowstorm.

'Tom Finn is the product of a state that can no longer protect its citizens,' he was saying. 'What else could he have done? He was damned if he did – and dead if he didn't.'

Tess took my hand, her eyes not leaving the screen, her face with the look that it had had for days, as though something in her was wound up tight, and would not leave her alone.

'He's getting better,' I said, and she shook her head, not really listening, and concentrating on the TV as though it was these journalists and presenters who were going to decide my fate. But it was true. He was nowhere near as nervy as he had been on the sofa of breakfast television this morning, just after his piece had appeared.

'My guess is that he is what the future looks like,' he said, and the man sitting on the other side of the presenter sneered at him.

'Then we don't have much of a future,' he said. He was thin with glasses and he talked a lot about human rights.

He had been brought in to disagree with everything Nick said. 'You are making this man into some fifteen-minute hero – and he is clearly just a thug.'

'You bastard,' muttered Tess, who never swore. 'You bloody bastard!'

The security light out front came on and a shadow seemed to fall across the window. I heard the soft clink of bottles in the recycling bin at the side of the house and both of us jumped up immediately.

'It's them,' Tess said, and she wrung her hands, and the gesture tore at my heart.

'It's not them,' I said.

When I looked through the slats in the blinds I expected to see the yellow eyes of our fox staring back at me. But there was only the glow of cigarettes in the darkness. The reporters were still out there.

'You're right,' Tess said. 'He's getting better at it. Talking more slowly.' She inhaled theatrically. The homework book she had been marking before Nick Kazan came on was still in her hands. 'He's taking a breath every now and then. It's calmed him down.'

She liked him. She thought he was on my side. I wasn't quite so sure.

I moved the stack of homework books Tess was marking and sat next to her. The presenter was talking now, sighing and rolling his eyes and acting as though everything was horribly obvious. I tried to connect the words to me but I couldn't. So I flicked open the top book. It was history.

The inhabitants of ancient Egypt are called Mummies. They lived in the harsh climate of Sarah Dessert.

I closed the book. There was a carefully drawn picture of a penis and two giant testicles on the front. I wanted to throw it away. I wanted to flush it down the toilet or stuff it in the rubbish bin, or leave it out with the recycled trash. But I knew that Tess wouldn't let me.

Nick Kazan was trying to speak, but the presenter was raising his voice, shutting him up. 'Surely the young men he assaulted have rights, too,' he said with a chilly smile. It wasn't a question. 'If I recall the film correctly, Travis Bickle was a psychopath.'

They flashed up two mugshots. A pair of mean boys with short hair. The bright cop lighting made their faces look very different from the two I had fought in the dark. I didn't recognize them.

But Tess did. She stared at me and back to the damaged screen.

'I taught them,' she said. 'Those two boys. Men, are they now? I suppose they're men now.'

I looked at her. The homework books were in two neat piles on the floor. Marked and unmarked. 'Not them,' I said. 'You mean lots of boys like them.'

'No,' she said. 'I taught them. Those two. I tried to. But you can't teach them. Not really. Because of what their homes are like and because it's hard and because it all takes years. And because, most of all, because they despise it.'

'A quick look at tomorrow's papers,' the presenter purred. 'The *Guardian*'s headline reads "Home Secretary Condemns Vigilante Cab Driver". The *Daily Mail* leads with "Now Bickle's Burglars Go Whining to Brussels" . . . The *Sun* has "Gotcha! Stick That in Your Swag Bag, says Travis Bickle of Barnsbury".'

Tess turned off the TV. Then she moved sideways and leaned against me, sliding into me. The kind of perfect fit that you only get after years together.

She was silent for a bit, thinking about it all.

'I just wish they had gone to someone else's house,' she said quietly. 'That's what I wish.'

I wrapped my arms around her, watching the firefly lights that rose and fell out on the street, and that was what I wished too. I wished the world would just leave us alone.

Tess shivered in my arms.

'You're shaking,' I said.

'Cold night,' she said, and I held her tighter.

But it was summer now, and the night was warm, and it wasn't cold at all.

We stepped out of the house and they were on us, shoving their questions and their cameras in our faces as we edged through the scrum, this mob of reporters and photographers who had washed up on our doorstep as soon as Nick Kazan's story had appeared. Tess was carrying a tray of fairy cakes, covered in tin foil, and she raised it high, struggling to protect it from the crowd. More than anything, it was embarrassing, because they all acted as if they knew me. They called me by my name as if I was an old mate met by chance, and as if they were truly worried about my family and me.

'Tom! Over here, Tom!'

'Tom! Are you a vigilante? Are you the Travis Bickle of Barnsbury? Tom?'

'Tess, Tess,' one of them went. 'Are you proud of him, Tess? Who are the cakes for?'

'The children,' Keeva said. 'It's the last day of term.'

'What if he goes to jail, Tess? Will you stand by him? What will it mean to the family if Tom gets put away?'

Over the tray of cakes, Tess shot me a look that was beyond worried. It was just a second, but it was enough. There was a world in that look. It said – What if the worst happens? And – What if they broke up our family? And – What is going to happen to us?

Then Keeva spun away, and was between their legs and into the garden next door where a smaller boy and girl were waiting with pens and notebooks, as if in imitation of the reporters. I had no idea what was happening. Then I saw Keeva sign a couple of autographs, and turn to flash a smile at the exploding cameras. The reporters scrambled towards her.

'Keeva, what do you think about your dad, Keeva?'

'Keeva, get over here,' I said, but it was Tess who claimed her, going next door and seizing her wrist and dragging her to the Mini where Rory already sat in the back, blinking nervously behind his glasses.

'I'll see you later,' I told Tess, and she nodded briskly and drove off without looking back, Rory with his head bowed and Keeva turning to wave to the cameras.

I pulled on my chauffeur's cap and the mob closed in around me. But I felt better now, with Tess and the children gone, because the reporters and the photographers could not touch me now, at least not in the same way, at least not in any way that really mattered.

Farren looked rich, even in faded jeans and a plain white shirt, and he looked fit, even in his forties, even after a twelve-hour flight from the other side of the world. But most of all he looked tanned. He had a face that had seen a lot of sunshine. The sunshine seemed to have seeped into his bones, and it made him look like he was having a good life.

'I'm Farren,' he said, in a London accent. 'We're going to have to get a move on.'

The flight had been late getting in from Bangkok. Most of our clients, if they came in this late, they would be ready for the hotel and something from room service and get down to business in the morning. But not him. Farren had a meeting that night, at a hotel not far from the airport, and his late arrival had made it tight.

I took his bags and he followed me to the car in silence. Some of the drivers try to be their friends. Asking about the flight, moaning about the weather, all of that stuff. I never bothered. I figured that if you have just flown halfway around the planet then you don't feel like small talk.

I held the door for him and got him settled in the back seat before loading his luggage and confirming the destination. His appointment was at one of those hotels near the airport where you stay if your flight is very early or very late. A lot of the trade at those airport hotels was conferences, seminars, somebody making speeches. Rooms full of people learning something or selling something. And that was what Farren would be doing tonight. He was selling the dream.

'This temperature all right for you, sir?' I said, and he nodded, not looking at me. He hadn't seen the news. That was fine by me, because when someone recognized my face they wanted to know all about it. But Farren wasn't interested. The big black car started out of Heathrow, and it was as if we were both alone.

They were waiting for him at the hotel. The room was full. A big air hangar of a conference room in darkness with a podium on the stage, lit by a single spotlight above, and looking like a pulpit with a small bottle of mineral water. All these people waiting for him. Older people, couples mostly, but some solitary men and women too, all of them with some money put aside, waiting to invest, but not so much money that they would never have to worry about it. They did not look rich the way that Farren looked rich. I watched from the back of the room as he walked on stage into the light.

Behind him the wall burst into colour.

It was an empty beach with the sunset on fire. Blue skies and green mountains rising above a swimming pool that

105

seemed to hang in the sky. The image changed, slowly fading into another view, this one of fields full of pineapple trees and coconut trees and palm trees, and after a while that faded too. It was a tropical island, an island in the kind of sunshine that Farren knew, and all of it seen from houses that seemed to be built from air and light and glass. Farren sold property.

But he sold far more than that. There were words on the screen behind him and although the images were constantly melting and changing, the words were always there.

ESCAPE TO PARADISE, it said.

'This country has let you down,' he said, and his voice was quiet, and tired, and totally convincing. 'This country has disappointed you. That's why you're here. You have done everything this country asked you to do. You have paid your taxes. You have educated your children. You have been good neighbours. And this country has broken its contract with you.'

I watched the wall behind him. The view from those homes full of clean air and bright space and sunlight without end.

There were no people in the pictures. And there were no prices. But to me it looked like heaven. That good, and that far away, and that impossible.

Just like heaven.

When we came through the big Victorian square, Farren was sleeping in the back seat, worn out from his performance, or maybe just overwhelmed by jet lag. I was trying to avoid the evening traffic on the main drag, to get him to his hotel this side of midnight, and that was when I saw the man with the woman.

The man was pushing the woman out of his car. A Renault or a Peugeot – some piece of French crap. The man was in

106

the driving seat and he had leaned across to open the passenger door and now he was trying to shove the woman out of the car.

The man had one hand on her and one hand on the wheel and he looked like his only hobby was lifting weights. He had a shaved head, and bad tattoos, and he was wearing the sleeveless T-shirt that his kind always wear just so you know that they have lifted a lot of heavy objects that they didn't really need to.

The woman was crying. She didn't want to get out of the car. The man was calling her names and before I had time to think I was doing something about it.

The knuckle dusters that Andrzej had loaned me were in the dashboard – a pair of them in this injected polymer, lighter than plastic and harder than brass, just four holes for the fingers and a grip that sat snug in the palm of your hand.

Just in case they decided to come back.

But now I was slipping them on, thinking that they weighed nothing at all, as I got out of the car and began crossing the square to where the man was pushing the woman from the car with the sole of his boot.

I was almost on them when I heard Farren call my name. *Tom, Tom, Tom.* It made the man in the car look up. I kept walking. Farren kept calling my name. I didn't even know that he knew my name.

The woman was completely out of the car now, tugging at the hem of her dress, struggling to stay on her feet as she had lost one of her shoes. She was crying. I held the knuckle dusters tighter, and I felt the grip dig into the palm of my hand, and the man was getting out of the car with this sneering smile because he knew he could take me, but then the smile was less certain because he saw the black dusters curling above my fingers and he wasn't sure what difference they would make.

Then all at once Farren was on me, his arms wrapped around me, surprisingly strong, and I could smell the money on him.

'It's not the smart move,' he said, his face almost touching mine, his mouth in my ear, the voice an urgent hiss. 'You don't know these people. They mean nothing to you. Think of your family, Tom.' I struggled against him but he held me tight. 'Listen to me,' he said. 'Your family needs you. Who are these people? Nobody. You can't worry about the rest of the world.'

It was true.

All of it.

I felt the fight go out of me, and let myself go loose in his arms, and I felt him slip the knuckle dusters from my hands. As we started back to the car, his arm around my shoulders as if I might change my mind, he quickly crouched and dropped them both down a drain. Then he patted my shoulder as my head fell forward.

'It's all right,' he said.

At the car I turned to look at the couple. The woman was wiping her nose with her fingers. She had found her missing shoe and put it on. The man had come around the car and the smile was more confident now.

'Change your mind, little man?' he said.

That's right. The little man had changed his mind. We got in the car. Farren leaned forward.

'You're a good man,' he told me. 'Let's just go.'

I nodded, not daring to speak, and as I drove Farren to his hotel the road ahead blurred through a veil of tears, and I felt him place a hand on my shoulder, as if checking that I was still there, and I felt my face burning with shame.

13

The next night I drove him across the river and we left it behind us, heading south, deep into the unvisited depths of the city, and all the while those sharp blue eyes in the dark tan face were watching me in the rear-view mirror.

Now he knew me.

Now he knew exactly what I had done, but he did not try to talk to me about it. It was as if we did not need to talk about it. Because he understood.

The further south you went, the faster the money ran out, and Farren turned his eyes to the bleak neighbourhoods of boarded-up shops, and groups of hooded figures on their mountain bikes, and the brutal flats rising on every side.

'The reason this was such a great country is because there was once a ladder,' Farren said. 'It reached into every corner of every town and every city. And then one day they kicked the ladder away.'

It was night now. We had spent the day wandering London and beyond. Most of the firm's clients covered a familiar patch, from Canary Wharf in the east and across the City and out as far as Chelsea in the west. That was where they did it all – making their deals, breaking their bread, resting their tired but wired executive heads.

But Farren was different.

I took him beyond the *A to Z* to a huge house with a gravel drive in Middlesex, and deep into the suburbs to a place with an Olympic-sized swimming pool out in Essex, and beyond the guards of a gated community in Surrey. While I was waiting for him at that one I found a glossy brochure on the back seat with a view of a still blue sea seen from the shade of a coconut tree on the cover. Wild Palm Properties, it said at the top, and in bigger letters below: PHUKET, THAILAND. ESCAPE TO PARADISE. I was putting it back when he came out of the house.

'Keep it,' he told me.

Now we went deeper into South London, the lady on the sat-nav gently urging me on, although I felt there had to be some mistake. There was no money here.

'You have arrived,' said the sat-nav lady, and the car idled near a patch of knackered grass on the edge of a dark forest of tower blocks. Faces watched us from the pavement, their eyes blank and shining. I looked at Farren in the rear-view mirror, waiting for instructions, and he met me with his blue eyes.

'Let's just sit for a while,' he said.

A pack of kids were nearby, lounging on the concrete steps that led up to the higher floors. They leered and spat on the ground, but it was all nothing. They wanted to do something to us but they did not know what. I felt a surge of admiration for Farren. He was not scared. He did not even notice them.

'What?' he said.

'I was just thinking,' I said. 'This doesn't look like your sort of place.'

He laughed. 'I think an Englishman is at home anywhere, don't you?' he said.

Then he stirred.

There was an old man with a plastic shopping bag, dragging himself home, heading towards the concrete steps of the nearest block of flats. The spitting and smoking kids made no effort to make way for him, so the old man edged around them, and between them, his eyes on the ground, his hair grey and thinning, moving slowly and carefully, as if they were wild animals he had no wish to alarm. Without saying anything, without even looking at them, the old man seemed to apologize for existing.

'Who do you think he is?' Farren asked me.

I shrugged.

'Some poor old bastard afraid of getting stabbed coming back from the shops with a can of cat food,' I said. 'Probably fought in their wars, and worked in their factories, just so he could have a bunch of acne-adverts on mountain bikes pissing on his doorstep. Lovely.'

Farren watched the old man climb the stone steps until he was out of sight. Up on the second floor, at the end of a windy walkway, a solitary light came on in one of the flats.

'I'll tell you about that old man,' Farren said. 'His wife left him. Years ago. I am talking about years and years ago. Half a lifetime ago. And he had a son. She left them both. The child – the child was four when she walked out the door and left them to get on with it. And the old man couldn't cope, so the boy was farmed out. Grandparents – that was all right. Your grandparents love you, don't they? But they were old and they got sick and died. First one, and then the other one. The man first. It's usually the man first. So then it was other relations. Then foster parents.' He was silent for a bit, thinking about it. 'The levels of indifference and negligence and cruelty always rising,' he said.

I thought of Tess, and the unknown terrors of a child growing up in care, and parents who brought children into the world but did not stick around long enough to bring them up, but I said nothing.

Farren was leaning forward, making sure that I got it. I turned to look at him. Somehow the mirror did not seem like it was enough.

'All because a man could not cope with one hard knock,' he said. 'What do you think about that, Tom? Someone who doesn't raise their own child?'

'I don't think much of it,' I said.

Farren gave me the nod, satisfied. I started the engine, and the faces in the darkness turned to watch us leave. The blue eyes were on me in the mirror.

'You know who that old man is?' he asked me. 'That disappointed old man?'

I could guess. There had been too many years apart to ever make it good between them. Maybe they had tried, later, but there had been a falling out. Strong words, harshly spoken, all the old resentment and bitterness coming out. My parents had been gone for a long time, but I could see how it was the kind of thing that could happen between fathers and sons, between parents and children. How you could lose each other and then never find each other ever again.

Farren was waiting for my answer.

'Is he your father?' I said.

Farren smiled. 'No,' he said. 'That's you, Tom. That's you if you don't get out of this country. That's you in thirty years. That's you if you stay in this place with no ladder. And you deserve better,' Farren told me. 'You and your family. A better life than that. You know you do.'

Then he slept. Farren never really got over the jet lag on that trip. I don't think he wanted to. I think that getting on local time would have brought too much back. The little flat. The mother that left. The father who could not cope. So Farren stayed on Thai time and he slept when he could.

It felt like he was already in that space between time zones, neither really here nor over there, pulled in two opposite directions.

And I sort of felt the same way. Trapped by my life in this city, knowing that if I got any kind of criminal conviction I would lose my job, and trapped by the mad dream that, if we want it bad enough, then there is still time left to break free.

'It's time,' Rory said.

Tess and I stepped through the broken glass doors that led to the garden. The children were waiting for us. Keeva with a shoebox, Rory holding a lifeless bag of brown fur.

Keeva solemnly handed me the shoebox and I held it open for Rory as he gently placed the dead creature inside. A tiny collection of fur and bones that seemed to curl up on itself now that the spark of life had gone.

'The fox did it, didn't he?' said Rory, nodding bitterly. 'Just scared him to death. Just frightened him so much he . . .'

I kept the lid open, giving him a long last look, and we both stared at the dead animal.

'They don't live long,' I said softly. Hammy wasn't the first pet we had buried. Our back garden was a mass grave of goldfish, budgies and hamsters. 'You know they don't live long, Rory.'

I slowly closed the lid. Rory's chin trembled with emotion. On the front of the shoebox he had carefully printed an epitaph:

Hammy Finn – born 2004 – died 2004 – A Gud Pet

'Longer than *that*,' Rory said bitterly. 'They're meant to live longer than *that*.'

Our little funeral procession made its way to the end of

the garden, the graveyard for the Finn family's dead pets. Keeva was in her own little world, muttering to herself and taking long careful steps in some secret game. She could be lavishly sentimental about our animals, but she never really loved them the way that her brother did. As we passed the Wendy House she slipped inside and looked at her bike.

'The front wheel's gone all wonky,' Keeva called. 'From where they laid it down and trod on it or something. The bad men.'

There was a small flowerbed by our back fence. We knelt down on the grass and I began digging a shallow grave with a toy spade. We all knew the ritual by now. Keeva had joined us again and bowed her head until the shoebox was placed in the grave and covered up with soil.

'Can I have a new bike?' she said hopefully.

'Yes, and I'll be needing a new hamster,' Rory said, wiping his nose on the back of his hand.

Tess exploded.

'There's no money, okay?' she said. 'Jesus Christ! Don't you two get it?'

The four of us were silent.

'I'll get the money,' I said.

I came out of court and they were waiting for me, sticking their cameras and their microphones and their questions in my face, asking me how I felt. But there were not so many of them now. Other stories had come along to replace me – the man who shot two intruders with his crossbow, the woman who stabbed a burglar in the neck with an oyster knife. They were bigger news, fresher news. The Travis Bickle of Barnsbury was already yesterday's man.

I would never be much of a story now. Because I wasn't going to prison after all.

Over their heads, I saw Tess waiting for me at the bottom of the steps, and when I started towards her, it wasn't like before. They let me go to her.

She wrapped me in her arms. 'It will be all right,' she said.

On the advice of my lawyer, I had pleaded guilty to the lesser charge of causing an affray. Six months sentence, suspended, and a £1,000 fine. So that was both a slap on the wrist and kick in the head. Because I was a free man but it was still a conviction. So I wasn't really free at all.

Tess took my arm and pulled me close, and as we walked away from the courtroom Nick Kazan was waiting for us, away from the rest of them, as though he was different. And he was, because I believe that he just wanted to see me. He held out his hand and smiled, as if we had come through something together.

'Congratulations,' he said. 'I'm so glad it's over.'

I shook his hand, nodded and said nothing. It was no good trying to explain. Nick was a good kid, and I liked him, but he would never get it. For a man like me, it can never be over once they have you on one of their lists.

'Coming home?' Tess said. She understood what today meant. But I shook my head because I had to go to work to give it all back to Andrzej. The car keys. My laminated ID card. All the stuff that I wouldn't be needing any more. Andrzej would be sorry to see me go. But the firm could not employ a driver with a criminal record. It was nothing personal. It was just the rules. I would lose my job the moment I stuck my head in the door.

So first I was going to make one last run to the airport.

I caught up with Farren just before he was about to go through security.

I later learned that the journey he was about to make – that long overnight flight from Europe to Asia – can propel you from the old life and into the imagined future, where the time is always racing ahead of the old place, and you can become the person you always dreamed of being.

The Thai Airways flight to Bangkok left Heathrow just after noon and with the time difference it would get him into Bangkok at around six tomorrow morning. He had already told me that he would not stay in Bangkok but would get another plane to Phuket – a short hop, he had called it – and as I watched him at the edge of security I thought of how he would be arriving on a day that had yet to dawn for me.

He looked at me with more kindness than surprise, as though he had been half-expecting me. Businessmen went rushing past him to their fast track. He was the only one who wasn't wearing a suit.

'I need a job,' I said.

We stared at each other.

'That's it,' I said. 'I have a family to support and I need a job.'

'I can give you a job,' he said. 'Phuket is a great place for families. Cheap. Child friendly. You don't have to be afraid when they walk down the street.'

'What would I do out there?' I said, and the words came tumbling out, and they seemed to measure all of my limitations. 'I don't have any education. I was a builder – had my own business – but that didn't work out. That's all I know. That and driving. If I left – what would I do? Would I drive? Would I be a driver out there?'

His blue eyes studied me. 'Well,' he said, 'the driving would be a start. But you have to start thinking bigger than that. A foreigner doesn't come to Thailand to pick rubber.' He watched a giant 777 roar into the sky. Then he looked back at me and smiled. 'He comes to run the plantation,' he said.

'I can do that,' I said.

Five on a summer morning.

The sky was still dark but it was not late any more. It was early.

I unlocked the back door and went out into the little garden. The glass had been replaced but parts of the wooden frame had been ripped off and looked like fresh wounds in the half-light. I sat on the step with the Wild Palm brochure in my hand, leafing through it in the dawn chill, although I knew its glossy pages by heart.

Escape to paradise, it said, and I understood now why there were no prices, and why there were no people in any of the pictures. You were meant to put yourself in there.

I heard a rustling noise at the end of the garden and the fox appeared on our neighbour's fence, hung there for a long moment, seemed uncertain, then dropped, tripping the security light. It came forward, not looking at me, and I saw there was something wrong with one of its legs. The front left leg. The fox was hobbling, unable to bear weight on it. Then it stood still, head sunk with exhaustion, and the light went off.

'Can't we help it?' Rory said, suddenly by my side, rubbing his eyes, barefoot in his WWF pyjamas. I pulled him to my lap. He was still young and small enough for me to do that, but I guessed that he wouldn't be for much longer.

'I don't think we can,' I said.

Then Tess was there with Keeva, my wife fully awake but my daughter swaying with exhaustion. The girls sat down with us and we all watched the fox carefully cross the garden.

'Call the RSPCA,' Keeva said.

Rory dismissed the idea.

117

'They can't catch him,' he said.

Every movement the fox made came with a jerky dip as it kept the weight from the bad leg, and after every careful step it seemed to lurch forward and then immediately lift its head and right itself, like a drunk trying to seem sober. The effort was taking its toll, but apart from the injury, the fox still looked young and strong and proud.

The sun came up over the rooftops and with the warmth on my face I began to feel better about everything and to believe that the sun would never fail us, and that as long as my family were in its light and heat, then we could never truly come to harm. I still had the Wild Palm brochure in my hand. I looked up at Tess to speak, to try to explain, to tell her that it wasn't over yet, that I had one more chance to get it right, and there would be better times to come if she could believe in me for a little longer.

But she was already smiling at me.

She reached out and took my hand and I knew that something had already been decided.

'Look,' Keeva said.

With great effort, the fox hauled itself on to the fence on the far side of the garden. I hoped that perhaps it was not something as serious as a broken leg, that perhaps it had only damaged its paw and the wound would heal.

The fox looked back at us from the top of the fence.

'He's just trying to survive, isn't he?' Rory said.

As the words left my son's mouth, the fox dropped to the other side, and he was gone.

14

'I need you to do something for me,' Jesse said. 'A favour.'

'Name it,' I said.

I was shocked at the state of him. He was in the special uniform of T-shirt and shorts that prisoners wore for visitors, and with the weight that he had lost they were hanging off him. His face was covered with pale stubble and beneath it his skin was sallow, sick-looking. His fingers picked nervously at a plaster on the top of his arm. He caught me staring.

'They gave us a shot of Twinrix,' he said. 'Wonderful stuff. Wards off Hepatitis A, Hepatitis B and tuberculosis.' He smiled faintly. 'We've got all the mod cons.'

I touched his other arm. 'Are you all right?' I said.

'I'll be out soon,' he said. 'Packed off home. Everybody else has already been deported. You were lucky to get out.'

'Farren?' I said, unable to imagine the island without him.

'He was the first,' Jesse said. 'Must be back in London by now and freezing his butt off.'

I thought of December in London and saw Farren's tanned face in those cold streets.

'So no court case then?' I said, suddenly relieved. 'No trial? No Bangkok Hilton?'

'Easier for them to just kick us out,' Jesse said. 'As soon as the money comes through from my mum I'm off to the airport and then they'll be tucking me in at 35,000 feet and handing round the nuts. The deportation isn't so bad. The painful bit is if they deport and blacklist you. That means you can never come back to Thailand. Well, not for ninety-nine years, anyway.'

'So after ninety-nine years, you can come and go as you like?' I said, and we smiled at each other. But I was shocked. 'They can't really do that, can they?' I said.

Jesse chuckled.

'They can do what they like,' he said. 'It's their country, mate.'

It felt like something we had only just started to learn.

I watched him remove the chain that he always wore around his neck.

'I want you to have this,' he said.

He laid it before me. A chain with maybe a dozen amulets. I could see a tooth, an image of the Buddha, an inscription of a language I didn't recognize that I later learned was Khmer. There were pieces of bronze, and wood, and tin, and a tiny sliver of clay that seemed to have some kind of sparkling dust buried in it. They were shaped like bells, or round like coins, or oval with images of monks who had died a long time ago.

'Charms?' I said. 'You should keep your lucky charms. Your plane home might crash.'

He wasn't smiling now. 'You shouldn't mock amulets, Tom,' he said. 'These are not lucky charms. These are real. And I want you to have them so that you can do me this favour.'

I thought he might tell me about the favour. But instead he wanted to tell me about the amulets. He leaned forward.

'There are four hundred and forty-three Thai troops in Iraq,' he said. 'And they are guarded by six thousand amulets.'

'That's good,' I said. 'For a minute there I was worried about them.'

'I mean it,' he said. 'You shouldn't laugh about this stuff.'

'I'm not laughing,' I said, laughing at him.

He began pointing his index finger at the individual amulets. The nail was filthy.

'This one will guard your pineapple crop against insects,' he said. 'This one will protect your water buffalo from sickness. This one will ensure good relations with your mother-in-law.'

'Thanks,' I said. 'It's really going to come in handy.'

'This one will make sure your fishing nets are never empty,' he said, ignoring me. His eyes lit up with excitement. 'Oh, this is a good one – it ensures you pass your driving test at the first attempt. This one—'

'Jesse?' I said.

He looked up at me, the chain of sacred amulets between us. 'What?' he said.

'Are you honestly telling me that these things work?' I said.

'Satisfaction guaranteed,' he said. 'Or you get your money back.'

Then he told me about the favour and I decided it could do no harm to take his lucky charms.

I held my hand under the cold-water tap and let it run until the wound between my thumb and index finger began to feel numb. The pain eased off slightly but the blood did not stop. I tore off a strip of kitchen towel and pressed it hard against the cut.

Tess was watching me.

'How did you do that?' she said.

'When I was out with Mr Botan,' I said. 'Caught it on a fishing hook.'

I did not look at her face. Because she was my wife and

she knew everything about me and she could tell when I was lying with just one look.

Keeva was sitting at the kitchen table with Chatree's big sister, whose name was Kai. She had started coming round for English lessons with her brother, but she wasn't studying now. My daughter had tied the older girl's hair back and was holding up a hand mirror.

'See?' Keeva said. 'You're so pretty, and you don't even know it.'

Kai smiled politely.

Tess was still watching me.

'I'm fine,' I said, heading out of the kitchen.

Rory was on the living-room floor with Chatree, staring at an atlas.

'See?' my son was saying. 'Thailand looks just like the head of an animal.' The tip of his finger moved slowly north, along the borders of Cambodia and Laos. 'See that?' Rory said. 'That's the ear. A great big flapping ear.'

Chatree laughed. 'Great big flapping ear,' he said, liking the sound of it.

Mister moved between them, wild for attention, his tail wagging furiously. Rory picked up the dog and let it slobber all over his face.

'And up there,' Rory said, his finger drifting south-west, along the border with Burma. 'That's the head.'

Rory's finger made the long journey south. 'And down here – Peninsula Thailand, where we live – that's the trunk. See?' Rory closed the book – *The Traveller's Wildlife Guide to Thailand* – and smiled at his friend. 'Our country is shaped like the head of an elephant,' he said.

Tess was in the doorway of the kitchen. She looked at me and smiled. We were both thinking the same thing.

Our country. It did not sound as strange as it would have a few months ago.

'I'm just going to the garage,' I said, keeping my voice light. 'Do some work on the bike.'

'Okay,' Tess said, not suspecting a thing. I went out to the shed and stood outside the closed door, listening. A light went off in our neighbours' house. The Botans turned in as soon as the Almost World Famous Seafood Grill had closed its doors and fed its staff. Everyone went to bed early in Nai Yang, and I was happy about that tonight.

I opened the door of the shed and went inside.

There was a pile of towels and blankets that I had gathered from Jesse's apartment and at the sound of the door the gibbon's head emerged from inside them, baring his teeth at me.

At first I had thought he was trying to give me a smile, but now I knew it was a sign of aggression. He had given me one of those toothy smiles right before he took a chunk out of my hand on the ride back to Nai Yang from Jesse's apartment. But it was a half-hearted gesture, and I somehow knew that Travis – and I thought of him as Travis, rather than just another gibbon – was not going to hurt me. It was as if he knew I was his last hope, God help him.

He only came halfway out of his bedding, and a towel with *Amanpuri* on it drooped over his head like a shawl. He looked like ET's stunt double. I slowly and gently lifted the shawl back to take a look at him, and he gave my bloody hand a quick sniff.

'Yeah, I wonder who did that?' I said.

He glanced away and then back at me. The black skin of his face looked as tough as leather, but the eyes were huge and perfectly round. They seemed to have no bottom to them, no depth, they just went on forever. I had never seen a face so expressive, or so full of sadness.

It was all there, I felt. Whatever someone had done to catch him. Whatever they had done to keep him up late and pulling in the happy punters on the Bangla Road. All right there. It was a look that said – *Sorry, so sorry, but there is nothing that can be done.*

But I didn't believe it.

I was going to set Travis free.

Put him back into the wild, where he belonged. I reached out my hands and he came to me in one nimble movement, perching, those endless limbs wrapped lightly around me, taking his own weight. I had no doubt that he was completely wild and yet there was something delicate about him, something that had not yet been touched and spoiled and hardened. He was only going to hurt me if he meant to hurt me.

'Come on, Travis,' I said, and carried him out of the garage, the towel from the Amanpuri resort again wrapped around his face, and we headed down the dirt-track road. I glanced back once at the house and then stepped off the road and into the trees.

Few foreigners who came to Phuket had any idea of the lushness of our island, how green it was, and how dense. Avoiding the lights that glittered and showed signs of life below, I carried Travis towards the darkness of the thick forest. Soon we could go no further.

It was not as far from the lights of civilization as I would have liked, but the forest was too dense to go on without a machete. The forest was that thick. I lifted the Amanpuri towel and we looked at each other.

'Time to go,' I said, and carefully lifted him on to a thick branch that blocked our way. The towel was in my hands. The gibbon stared at me. 'Scoot,' I said. Then I heard the boy's voice.

'What are you *doing*?' Rory cried, coming down the hill, and I had never heard him so upset. 'You're going to *kill* him!'

Rory came crashing through the undergrowth. Chatree was behind him. My son pitched forward flat on his face, picked himself up and staggered on, straightening his glasses. Travis considered him with interest, as if he recognized the boy from somewhere but couldn't quite place him.

'Calm down, Rory,' I said.

'You bloody bastard,' my son said. 'Oh, you bloody, bloody bastard.'

'Hey,' I said. 'Watch your mouth. What do you think is happening here?'

He pointed at the gibbon, who had hopped away from us and now clung to the thick leaves of a pineapple tree.

'You're killing him!' Rory said.

Now I was angry too. 'You think I'm going to kill an animal, do you? You think I'm taking him out here to kill him, Rory? I'm putting him back in the wild. I'm setting him free.'

My son shook his head, swallowed hard. Chatree stared at us looking worried, but closely following the action.

'You don't understand, Dad,' Rory said. 'If you just put him back in the wild, *then he is going to die.*'

I stared at him. For a moment all I could hear was the distant buzz of the bikes on the road, and the wind that moved through the thick canopy of trees above us. I shook my head.

'I don't understand,' I said.

'That's right,' my son said, and his face crumpled into a teary sort of smile. 'You really don't understand, do you?' He nodded at Travis, who seemed to be listening carefully to the conversation. 'Gibbons only survive in the wild if they are part of a family unit,' Rory said, speaking very slowly, so that the lesson would sink into my thick head once and for all. 'Okay, Dad?' he said. 'Without a family – they don't survive. It's that simple.'

I sat down on the nearest branch. Rory sat beside me. 'We can't keep him,' I said. 'You saw what happened at Jesse's place.'

'I know,' the boy said. 'I know that we can't keep him. I know that he will never be a pet. I know that, Dad.'

'So I have to let him go,' I said, feeling helpless, and suddenly believing that my son was right – leaving him in the forest would be as bad as dumping him by the side of the road. 'I have to let him go and he just has to take his chances. What else can I do?'

Behind the glasses his weak eyes drifted from my face to the chain of amulets that I wore around my neck.

'I know a place,' he said.

The next day I borrowed Mr Botan's pick-up truck and Rory and I started out towards the Bang Pae waterfall with Travis sitting calmly between us, the shawl from the Amanpuri over his head. At a red light a scooter carrying a family of five gawped at the gibbon and Travis stared right back. *Yeah – I'm a gibbon. Get over it.*

The three of us drove towards the last of the island's rainforest.

'There were tigers and sun bears in there once,' Rory said. 'Even now, there are wild boar and flying foxes and cobras.' Then he smiled. 'And gibbons, of course,' he said.

The Bang Pae waterfall is just inside the Khao Phra Thaew National Park. We left the pick-up truck outside a small café and bought some bottled water from the woman who owned it. She did not seem remotely surprised to see Travis in my arms.

'He looks like my side of the family,' I said, and she nodded in agreement.

We walked towards the waterfall and that was when we heard the singing. It was a kind of smooth, melodic hooting

126

– high and musical and hypnotic, and unlike any sound that I had ever heard.

'Can you hear them?' Rory said. 'The gibbons are singing.'

'Why do they sing?' I asked the boy.

'They sing to find a mate,' he said. 'But even after they have found a mate, they keep singing.'

We stood there listening to them but it was only much later that I felt I began to understand the songs of the gibbons. Rory was right – they sang to find a mate. But then they sang because they were gibbons, and they sang because they were alive.

We climbed the hill to a small hut. In the distance, towards the Bang Pae waterfall, there were giant cages that were more than cages – part of the rainforest itself, built around it, but protected and watched over. Inside one of the massive enclosures I could see a black gibbon hanging from a large wooden triangle. But we heard them more than saw them, heard their songs stretching all the way to the top of the Bang Pae waterfall and beyond.

We were at the Phuket Gibbon Rehabilitation Centre. A young American stepped out of the hut to meet us. We had not phoned ahead, or given anyone any indication that we were coming, but somehow it was as if they were waiting for us.

'Who have we got here?' the young American said.

'Travis,' Rory said. 'We have Travis here.'

The young American took Travis from us and handed him over to an even younger Thai woman, who took him away before we could say goodbye. Rory and I stared at each other, dumbfounded. The young American smiled.

'Don't worry,' he said. 'We'll get Travis checked out. Test him for Hepatitis A and HIV.' I must have registered shock, because the young American held up his hand. 'Don't worry, we'll take him in, whatever the results are,' he said. 'But he can't be released into the wild if he's HIV positive or if he's disabled.'

'Because he wouldn't survive,' Rory said.

Somehow the fact that Travis had been brought to this place of care and love made his past seem all the more terrible. I felt I should apologize, or at least try to explain.

'A friend of mine found him in some bar,' I said, looking up at the giant cages. I could see a dark brown shape move swiftly through the trees. 'I don't know what they've been giving him to keep him awake.'

I was trying to say something about the horror in this animal's past that had been inflicted by men and how we wanted to put it right. But the young American was way ahead of me.

'It's illegal to keep a gibbon as a pet in Thailand,' he said. 'But people do and they don't treat them well. They don't treat them like they're living creatures who share most of their DNA with us.'

'He's forgotten what he is,' Rory said. 'He doesn't know how to feed himself. He doesn't know anything.'

The young American nodded. 'This is where he'll remember,' he said. 'If he checks out okay, we gradually reduce the amount of food and human contact he gets. Encourage Travis to forage on his own and hope that he finds a mate. Move him up the hill to bigger cages. Soft release, we call it.'

'Soft release,' Rory said, making a mental note.

Then the young American smiled.

'Happy holidays,' he said, and I remembered that it was Christmas Day.

We kicked off our shoes at our front door, and just as I felt the cool hardwood floorboards worn smooth by generations of bare feet, I smelled the roast turkey in the oven.

128

Keeva was there, Mister in her arms, going wild.

'Somebody wants the leftovers,' my daughter laughed. Her brother stroked the dog and looked at it thoughtfully.

'It might be something else,' he said.

Tess came out of the kitchen and threw her arms around me. 'Merry Christmas!' she said, planting a kiss on my mouth.

'Merry Christmas,' I said, kissing her back. I hugged her and turned to our girl. 'Keeva, that dog doesn't want to be held,' I said.

She put Mister down and with his paws skidding on the smooth wooden floorboards, he dashed straight out of the front door.

Rory and Keeva went after the runaway dog and thirty minutes later, after Tess had called them from the front door, they came back without the dog, both of them silent with worry. I had laid the table and as Tess was getting the turkey out of the oven she gave me a look. I went to the door and called the dog's name.

But all I could see was our island.

Inland there was the thick forest with its fifty shades of green. Towards the shore there was the endless line of casuarina trees along Hat Nai Yang and Hat Mai Khao, and the still blue of the looking-glass sea beyond. The dog could have been anywhere. I went back inside.

'He'll be back,' Tess said.

'And if he's not, I'll look for him in the morning,' I said.

The children had perked up.

'It's not even our bloody dog,' I grumbled.

But my family just laughed at me.

15

It was just after breakfast on Boxing Day. A Saturday morning. The sea was flat as a mirror, and it shimmered with gold as the sunshine came through the casuarina trees.

'Mister!' I called. 'Mister! You dumb dog . . .'

There was a gang of dogs on the beach. But as I came out of the trees and on to the sand, the small pack trotted off, one of them with a dead fish in his mouth, and none of them was our dog.

I walked down to the edge of the sea and turned north, towards where we had seen the turtle lay her eggs, my feet sinking in the wet sand. I felt good. I knew I would find him – he wasn't so dumb that he would run away from home – and it seemed like magic that I was feeling the wet sand and the warm sun on Boxing Day.

I passed an old massage lady sitting under a tree. I had seen her before at this far end of the beach. She seemed to do more knitting than massaging. There was some formless pink thing she was making on a long piece of wood that bristled with nails. She had been working on it since the first time I saw her, and she didn't seem to be in any hurry. The knitting seemed to be the thing. She

130

waved and smiled, her sun-dark face splitting in a wide grin.

'*Sa-wat-de!*' I said, lifting my hand.

'*Sa-wat-dee,*' she called. '*Ah-gaht dee na!*'

I nodded, and stopped for a moment to look at Hat Nai Yang stretching out before me. The scattering of longtail boats on the glassy sea, the bow-shaped perfection of the bay, and beyond the treeline, the endless shades of green that grew inland. I felt the early morning warmth of the sun on my face.

She was so right.

It was a beautiful day.

A bit further on there were some local men playing the special kind of volleyball you saw on the island – dazzling displays of acrobatics as they kept the ball in the air with head and feet and heel. Nobody ever kept score. It was just *sanuk*. It was just for fun.

They called out to me to join them and I laughed and shook my head, miming a bad back, and that made them laugh as I kept going. The beach was empty here. I walked the length of Hat Nai Yang and saw no more people and no more dogs.

I paused at the sharp tip of the bay and wondered if I should turn back. There was only one more beach on the island, Hat Mai Khao, the longest, least-developed beach on Phuket. After that there was just the bridge across to Phang Nga on the mainland, and the end of our island. After a moment I kept going, but now I had to turn inland, the sea a still blue world on my left as I called Mister's name and trudged through the thickening casuarina trees.

The tangled roots and the mud of a mangrove swamp rose ahead of me, barring my path, so I walked back to the sea and the great expanse of Hat Mai Khao lay before me.

It looked like the beach at the end of the world.

These were the widest, whitest sands on the island, banking steeply, because the developers had not been allowed to flatten the land the way they had on the tourist beaches further south. Hat Mai Khao was part of a national park and the nesting ground for sea turtles. Despite the crowds that flocked to this country, the Thais knew how to protect what they valued.

There was one hotel ahead of me. I could see a line of sunloungers, and the first sunbathers of the day, and further back, beyond a strip of grass, a small dining area where a couple of wild dogs moved panting and hungry among the breakfasters, trying to avoid the attention of the staff as they scavenged for scraps. None of them were Mister.

'Oh, you silly thing, Mister,' I said out loud. 'Maybe you are gone for good.'

The lazy commerce of a Thai beach was just getting started for the day. A local was leading a small horse, offering rides. The old lady that I had seen knitting under the trees was walking between the white bodies on the sunloungers, shyly offering foot massage. She must have come by the road, I thought, and have a motorbike or scooter, and I made a note to ask her about getting decent spare parts for the Royal Enfield. Maybe I would get a foot massage too. She waved to me, and smiled, and knelt before a woman in a big floppy hat. Out on the sea a few fishermen moved silently on their longtail boats, ancient nets in their hands, the diesel engines puttering in the calm of the early morning, and I wondered if the fishing was good up here.

As I passed the hotel I waded out to the sea. There was meant to be a strong current off of Hat Mai Khao, another reason why it was undeveloped, but the Andaman felt warm and still and calm, and under my feet there was nothing but the soft shift of perfect white sand.

There were a few people in the shallow water. Swimming

and snorkelling and paddling. Or simply standing there, feeling the sun and the soft golden glory of the day.

Voices travelled across the water. German, Swedish, English. Then I stopped, feeling a wave. Nothing more than a gentle movement of the sea. But unmistakable, and insistent.

I looked at the hotel.

There were swirling pools of water on the grass between the beach and the dining area. That was strange. I stared at them, not knowing what I was seeing, and I felt the wave move back out to sea.

And then the water just kept going, as if God had decided to pull the plug.

With the sea sucked out towards the horizon, a fish flapped and gasped on the sudden sand. A small boy laughed, chasing after it as the dying fish beat against the sand with its final breaths.

There was laughter on the beach and I looked up to see that a tourist had climbed on to the horse and it was bolting inland. The tourist shouted out with a mixture of strained humour and pure terror, trying to be a good sport even as he fought to control the animal. The Thai ran after them, grinning with embarrassment.

'But I *know* this,' said a child by my side, and I looked down to see a girl of about Keeva's age. The girl was the older sister of the boy who was chasing after the dying fish and she remained protectively close to him. She stared up at me as she went off to retrieve her brother.

'We did this with Miss Davies,' she said. 'Last year. In school. We have ten minutes.'

'What?' I said, understanding nothing.

I watched her take her little brother by the hand and run back to the dining area, calling out to her mother. I heard a dog bark and I looked up. But it was not our dog. It was not Mister. Then I heard the birds screeching high in the casuarina trees. They took off in a black scattering mass and I could feel the magic draining out of the day. I began to feel frightened. The water was still going out.

One of the longtails that had been sitting in shallow water was now aground, and the young fisherman stared down at the wet sand beneath him.

'Look at that,' someone said. 'It's beautiful.'

They were looking out to sea.

And far out to sea, all the way to the end of what could be seen with the naked eye, as if it was the very edge of the world, the sea was a foaming white crescent of wave.

It looked very clean.

It looked as though it was not moving.

The water was blue-black beneath it.

And when I looked at the blue-black water beneath the foaming white crescent, I could see that it was moving after all.

Although still very far away, it was getting closer. The sea began to come back in, and it was not like that first wave. This time it was strong and I felt my fear grow. I steadied myself against the movement of the water, digging my toes into the sand, and an old fisherman in the water next to me was knocked off his feet.

He nodded as I helped him up.

'Go now,' he said in English. 'Run now.'

I stared at him.

'*Run!*' he told me.

Under the trees I saw a group of old massage women, unmoving, ready for the working day. There were still people coming into the water, staring out to sea at that moving horizon, and so I just stood there.

'My camera,' a woman said sleepily. 'Don't let it get wet.'

Then I heard the dog barking. It sounded so much like Mister that I had to smile.

134

I walked off the beach, through the people all staring out to sea, and I crossed the deserted dining area and walked to the back of the kitchen, all the while calling his name. But it was some other dog. The dog was tied to a cold-water tap with a ragged piece of string. Its eyes bulged in its head as it fought to free itself. It was wild, maddened, and I was afraid that if it wasn't untied, it would hurt itself, so I crouched down beside it, releasing the knot that held it, and all the while the dog was snapping at my hand, catching me just as I untied it, making me curse, and then it was gone.

I touched my hand, relieved that its teeth had not broken my skin, and that was when I heard the sound, a roaring white noise, like some kind of terrible engine. I felt the air shudder. Then somebody screamed and I turned to look at the sea.

The wave was rushing to the shore now, and it was as if the sea was trying to fill the sky. There was a man standing on the beach, staring up at the wave, as still as a statue. There was a beach towel wrapped around his shoulders to prevent sunburn. Then he was gone, lost in the rushing water, and the wave was even closer.

The wave will break, I thought, even now, it must break. But it did not break. It just kept coming, up the steep incline of the sand, and across the dining area, and into the hotel, and the sound of that wind filled my head and choked my throat.

The water lifted me off my feet as if I weighed nothing and it carried me backwards, half-turning me around, and it was not clean, or at least it was not clean now, it was filthy, like boiling mud, swirling and stinking and brown.

Then my head slammed hard against a wall, my forehead and the bridge of my nose taking the full force of the blow. The water pinned me there, the rough surface of the bricks rubbing against the skin on my face, the water just nailed me there and would not let me move for some unknown length of time, minutes or maybe seconds, and I was dizzy and sick and there was something in my eyes and when I saw that it was blood my heart tried to burst open with the flying panic.

I cursed and begged and prayed, and when I managed to turn my numb and battered head, I recognized nothing. I was all at once in some other place and my skin crawled with blind dread.

Tess, I thought. *Keeva and Rory.*

The beach that I had been walking on a few minutes ago was gone.

I did not know or understand what I was looking at. None of it was familiar, none of it made any kind of sense, all of it was new. The world was suddenly insane, ripped apart, drowned in the avalanche of water.

A longtail torn from its moorings floated by. And then a car. And then a man. And then a beach house, intact and whole, but dipping forward at a rakish angle. People I could not see were screaming and calling for help and the people they loved in a babble of languages.

I thought perhaps the worst was over, but then I saw that the water was still rising and I whimpered like an animal as the water swiftly rose from my chest to my chin. The terror flew inside me as I took a mouthful of the filthy water and gagged and felt the blood pounding in my head, knowing that I was going to die today if I did not move right now. But I could not move. The water was the most powerful thing I had ever felt. I could not fight it.

Then from somewhere there were hands pulling at my T-shirt and I was dragged sideways and away from my wall and on to some concrete steps.

Then I was on my hands and knees for a bit, kneeling on stone steps as I brought up filthy water and shook with fear, and when I looked up I saw that I had been pulled on to some kind of staircase. Faces were peering down at me from a balcony. The man who had saved me helped me to my feet, and he spoke to me in a language I did not know.

'I don't understand,' I said. 'Sorry.'

Tess, I thought. *Keeva and Rory.*

The man who had saved me helped me up the stairs. It was a restaurant. The tables were set and there was a large breakfast buffet. It was all untouched by the water.

A child looked up at me and I saw that it was the small girl from the beach, the one who knew about the water from school, the one who had understood what was coming, the little one who had said we had ten minutes. She was holding the hand of her brother. But I still didn't understand any of it.

I went to the balcony with the others and it was as if we were on some strange ship in some murderous storm.

Below us the water was white now, and under the scum of debris and dirt on the surface, and beneath all of the beach loungers and smashed trees and splintered tables, and below all the chairs and sun umbrellas that it carried away, the water seemed to be full of small explosions. The water seemed to be alive, the water was this living thing that wanted to kill you, and it made me sick with helpless panic.

There were people in the water. The lights in the restaurant suddenly went out and I glanced up at them and when I looked back the people in the water were gone. Apart from one man, a local, probably one of the fishermen I had seen out on the longtails, dark skinned and lean limbed, and he had climbed halfway up a casuarina tree. Then the water tore the tree down and he was gone too.

The earth fell away.

We looked down from our balcony and we were above the uprooted trees. They floated by in a world that was water. Moving, filthy, murderous. There was a car, turning in circles like some fairground ride in hell, and I saw the pale, frightened faces at the window before it was taken away.

'It's not just our beach!' cried someone, but it seemed impossible to me that this force could go beyond what I could see in front of me.

'There's another one coming in!' someone else said, and I believed that, I believed it with all my heart, and we all looked out to the horizon, sick with fear, waiting for the water to come again and claim us.

The water was going out now, and people were staggering down the steps, and some of them were crying, and even more of them were calling out the names of the missing. The world had fallen apart and the same thoughts were everywhere.

Are you gone?

Have you been taken from me?

Shall we ever meet again?

I began to cry, these useless, ragged sobs that came from deep inside my chest and sounded like nothing human.

Tess, I thought. *Keeva and Rory.*

I saw my family lost in the water, I saw it clearer than anything I had ever seen in my life, and the sight was like a knife being shoved in my face, again and again and again.

16

I slowly crossed the shining field of mud that had replaced the landscaped gardens of the hotel.

My legs were gone, as if what had been bone was now jelly, and my feet stuck in the mud. I looked down and saw that my feet were bare. I had lost my sandals and I swore because I knew it meant it would make it harder to get home, or to whatever stood in the place of home.

There was a sharp pain in my forehead, where bare skin had banged against brick, and when I touched it my fingertips came away slick with fresh blood. There was a man standing with me in the field of shining mud and it took me a while to realize that he was the man who had pulled me from the water.

'But you must rest,' he said. He had followed me down the stairs and into the mud and now he touched my arm.

'No,' I said, pushing him away, harder than I meant to. 'I have to find them – my family.'

'Of course,' he said. 'Yes. Your family. Good luck.'

I staggered away, dizzy and sick, my bare feet sucked by the mud, and then I stopped and turned back, looking at him. 'Thank you,' I told him, as though he had opened a door for me rather than saved my life, and he nodded, just watching me. 'And what about you?' I said.

'My family were at breakfast,' he said, glancing back at the hotel. 'My wife and our baby. They were upstairs at breakfast. They're safe.'

I nodded, glad for him, of course, but also pushed down by the weight of what had happened, the weight of knowing that it took nothing at all to live or to die, how you carried on living if you went to breakfast instead of the beach, and how this was the day you died if you went to the beach instead of breakfast. Then a pretty woman with a new baby in her arms was calling to him and he turned away, and I walked towards the sea, and I wished that I had asked him his name.

The sand on the beach was unchanged, it was still that soft sand you find on the beaches in the north of Phuket, far closer in colour to snow than to gold. It looked untouched, apart from the dead fish that were now scattered across the sand. The dead fish were everywhere.

I looked at my bloody hand as I wobbled on, wiped it on the front of my T-shirt, and when I looked back one last time at the hotel I saw a nightmare in the sunshine. Everything that had been made by men had been smashed to pieces. The contents of the ground-floor hotel rooms had been sucked out and trashed by the water.

Hearing the voices calling to the missing, I lurched on, willing some strength into my legs. The vision of Tess and the children refused to leave me. It stung my eyes and churned my stomach and clawed my heart.

I did my best to avoid the dead fish. Sometimes I accidentally stepped on one of them and, when that happened, something inside me seemed to scream to be released.

I could not understand what I was looking at.

Sitting inland in the middle of the mangrove swamp,

among the exposed tangled roots of the trees and the slick black mud, was a boat. It was upright and untouched, and presenting itself in perfect profile, like the pictures of boats that Keeva and Rory had drawn when they were younger.

It was grey – a police boat, or an army or navy boat – with a number stencilled on the side: 813, it said, on its unscratched side, as though that might still mean something to someone. When I called out there was no reply, and I looked at my watch but it was gone, so I turned away, touching my bare wrist, and walked out of the mangrove trees and towards home.

Just outside the mangrove swamp a man was waiting for me. Tall, muscular, his hair fair and cropped. His T-shirt was ripped to pieces and hung on him like rags. He was a big man who had been crying.

'I saw you looking at the boat,' he said, and I felt the sand burning my feet and I stared down and wished I had my sandals. 'There's nobody on it,' he said, glancing back at the mangroves. 'I checked. It took me a long time to get to it.' He had the perfect English of the Scandinavian. 'The trees are so thick.'

I had not stopped walking.

I wasn't moving fast but I had kept going.

The man was behind me now. I was heading south, the direction of home, towards Hat Nai Yang, with the quiet sea on my right.

So still, the sea.

But I kept looking at it, not trusting it, not believing it.

The man was by my side, trying to keep up. He touched my arm and left his hand there. I stopped and looked at him and I felt my hands curl into fists.

I felt sorry for him. But I had to get home. That was the only thing in the world that mattered.

'I am searching for a boy,' he said. 'My son. I wish I had

a photo. But I have no photo.' He turned in the direction I had come from. 'We were on Khao Lak beach. It was hit hard.'

We both glanced north. The dead fish had gone now and it looked like a postcard that you would send to someone, trying to make them understand the beauty of this island.

'I haven't seen a boy,' I said. 'Sorry.'

'If you see my son . . .' he said. He touched his swimming trunks. 'I wish I had a picture. He is four years old,' said the man. 'A Norwegian boy called Ole. Like the famous footballer. *Ole*. A very special boy.' He smiled, lighting up his big face. He was smiling at a memory. 'At his nursery, Ole would hug all the children when he arrived. Every morning. Every child. He is a very special boy. He hugged every child. A happy, loving boy.'

His voice cracked and he hung his head and cried. I held him then and I let him cry in my arms. It didn't last long. A few seconds. We broke apart and he wiped his nose on the back of his hand, looking down. I put a hand on his shoulder.

'You will find your son,' I said – a ridiculous, absurd, foolish thing to promise, although I believed it. I needed to believe it.

'He is a loving, special boy,' the man said.

I nodded.

Then I saw the others.

Coming from the north, emerging out of the trees and on to that endless white beach, came the refugees from Khao Lak. Cut and bruised and wearing T-shirts and shorts and beachwear that had been shredded to tatters. A few of them sobbing, but most of them blank as the grave.

All of them were moving as if in a dream, as though they did not believe what had happened that day. For the first time I knew there were a lot of people who were missing.

The Norwegian man moved towards them, asking if they

had seen a boy, and I turned away, breaking into a tumbling sort of run, the tears suddenly streaming.

'Tess,' I said out loud, and my wife's name choked at the top of my throat and got stuck behind the back of my eyes, and then I said it again.

The sun was high and I felt it burning my face, my legs, and the top of my feet.

The mangroves of the far north of the island were behind me now, and the beach was lined with the familiar casuarina trees, tall and feathery and looking like the trees of home.

I stopped when I saw the place where the old massage lady had sat with her knitting. But she was no longer there.

I walked in the edge of the water, which helped soothe the burning skin on my feet, until I came to the first hotel. I wandered inside, desperate for water, desperate for the phone, steeling myself for what I would see. But there was only strange, inexplicable normality.

At the hotel desk a young couple had just arrived and the receptionist was giving them a welcome cocktail and a garland, a deep *wai* and a professional smile so slick that it appeared to glow with love. There were planes? But how could there still be planes? How could people be starting their holiday today? The world should have stopped turning.

But the world had not stopped turning, and I felt a rage unlike anything I had ever known.

An older couple were standing at the desk, and they had the deep tans of a month in the sun on their well-fed faces. There were suitcases at their sandaled feet. On their way home and unhappy. They were arguing about their bill.

'But we have not had full use of the spa,' said the man. 'Do you speak English? Fetch me your manager. We have not had full use of the spa!'

143

People were strolling into the restaurant, piling their plates high at the seafood buffet. A lone guitarist was playing 'Hotel California'.

A bellboy scuttled towards me and asked me if I needed help.

'I need to use a telephone,' I said. 'I need to call my wife. It is very urgent. Do you understand?'

'Sir,' he said, backing away from me, really looking at me for the first time, seeing the mess I was in, the sunburned skin streaked with blood and mud and tears. 'The telephones are all out,' he told me.

The little line of seafood restaurants that had stood on Hat Nai Yang were gone. The Almost World Famous Seafood Grill was gone. All of them were gone. Nothing remained. No debris, no sign, no people. As if none of it had ever existed.

My eyes scanned the bay, the perfect bow-shape bay of Hat Nai Yang, and the sea was as calm as ever. I must have walked all day, for the sun was going down fast now, bleeding extravagant red and orange streamers across the horizon, and all at once I felt all the parts of me that ached and were sore and had bled, and it was nothing next to the fear that something had happened to my family.

I craned my neck and stared up at the little green hill that rises high above the southern tip of Hat Nai Yang, and I headed up the hill towards my home, the dread growing inside me like a tumour.

The dog saw me first.

Mister barked once, twice, and came running down the dirt-track road, his wild eyes gleaming, mad with joy to see me, as if we had reached the end of some glorious game. Then Keeva and Rory were running behind him, trying to keep up, and when the dog reached me, sniffing and jumping and barking, they stood back for a moment, hovering uncertainly between smiles and tears, until I went to them, took the pair of them in my arms, kissing their heads, smelling their smell of sea and sunblock.

'Do you know how much I love you?' I said, looking at their upturned faces.

'We know,' Keeva said, and her face crumpled. 'We love you too. We thought that you were . . . gone.'

She buried her face against my chest.

'No,' I said. 'I'm all right.'

I saw Tess appear in the doorway of the little house and she looked at me for a moment and began running down the dirt-track road.

'Mister went to the top of the hill,' Rory said, dry-eyed and pale, holding the dog. 'That's where we found him.'

'We saw the big wave,' Keeva said, crying quite hard now. 'Is that what cut your face, Daddy?'

Then Tess was there, and she said my name once as she crashed against me and I gathered them all up in my arms, the three of them, the dog barking somewhere around our feet, and we stood there with no more words to say just yet, and the four of us held on to each other as if the world might end but we would never let go.

17

Mr Botan was staring out to sea, as if really looking at it for the first time, and when I said his name he turned to face me. He took my arms in his hands and squeezed them, as if making sure that I was really there.

'Good,' he said. 'You are safe. We are all safe. The two families who live on this road.'

'Yes,' I said. 'We're safe. Thank God.'

'Thank God,' he said, and he glanced at the sea, still holding my arms. 'We have lost everything,' he said. 'The restaurant. The boat. But thank God.'

I felt a choking sob rise in my throat, a sob with shock and grief and relief all mixed, and I forced it down, as if it was a gutful of filthy water. I leaned against Mr Botan for support and he smiled at me and held me up and my eyes burned with gratitude. He took my arm and led me to our homes. Mrs Botan was sitting on their front porch. Tess was by her side, holding on to the hem of Mrs Botan's apron. The children watched uncertainly, not sure how to act, not responding to Mister's invitation to come and play. Mrs Botan stood up as her husband and I came towards them. She had been rolling a cigarette and now she handed it to her husband.

146

'*Mai nam mai,*' Mrs Botan said, addressing me, as if I could speak Thai. And somehow I found that I could.

Mai nam mai. There is no water.

'No,' Tess said, suddenly standing up. 'We have water.'

It was not just the water that was out.

There was no electricity and the red satellite dish could not bring us the news we needed, the news that would tell us what had happened today. I thought of the hotel where they acted as if nothing had changed, and I found it hard to believe that the entire island had been hit. But then I remembered the Norwegian from Khao Lak, and the missing boy, his special boy, and I sensed the enormity of the day.

The children played in the yard with the dog, not going far, and as I brought the bottled water from the garage I watched them, feeling anxious when they were out of my sight.

I paced the area around the house, for I found that I could not sit still more than a short while. And when it became too much I would take myself to a quiet corner of the shed where I kept the bike, and there I would weep, silently and helplessly, crying as if I was broken, as if something inside me had been smashed to pieces by the day. I lost count of the times I went alone to the garage to empty myself of all those feelings that I could not even name, and it would have gone on, but in the end I looked up and Tess was standing there.

'Come inside now,' she said.

Night fell fast and with the electricity out it became very dark very quickly, but the moon rose silver-white and full. From the light of the full moon we could see the people coming up our hill, seeking the higher ground. There were rumours of another wave, constant rumours, and I believed every one of them, I had no trouble believing in them totally, and every rumour of another wave made my heart fly with raw panic. How could I not believe the rumours? There were people who had lost everything.

We had taken a few of the pallets of bottled water from the shed, the Botans and ourselves, and we had placed them in our front yard and opened them up, so that the water was ready to hand out as the people came up the hill or down our dirt road to our front door. They were all in need of water. They took the water with a *wai* and sat down nearby, talking quietly among themselves. They sat just beyond our fence, as if not wanting to impose.

Without the air con the house was hot and airless so we sat on the veranda, Tess with Rory in her arms on the steps, Keeva and I together on the old rattan chair, slapping at the mosquitoes that settled and fed on us, the insect spray never quite enough to deter them. I could sit still at last, but it was with exhaustion more than anything resembling calm, a mind-numbing exhaustion that left me sick and dizzy.

I looked out at the bay, watching the point where the sky touched the sea. I wasn't sure how I would ever sleep on this island again. My hands were shaking.

'It was the shape of our bay,' said Keeva, looking up at me, her head nodding with tiredness. 'That saved us from the wave. The special shape.'

I squeezed her. 'That's good,' I said, and the tears came unbidden at the sight of my daughter's beautiful face.

Keeva was right. The perfect semi-circle of Nai Yang bay broke the force of the wave, and stopped it from surging inland and taking everything with it, the way it had in Khao Lak on Phang Nga to the north, or on the Phuket beaches further south, where some of our visitors had come from.

The Botans were as numb and disbelieving as survivors of a car wreck or a war. They helped hand out water, and

148

they smiled at the children, and Mrs Botan cooked all that she could. But behind the bustle was a real and shredding grief.

There were people missing from the strip of restaurants on Hat Nai Yang, the neighbours of the Almost World Famous Seafood Grill who had gone into work early. Waiters, cleaners, cooks. Friends, neighbours, women and men they had watched grow up since they were babies. And nobody knew who was missing and who was gone forever.

'Look!' Keeva said, waking up, and I saw Chatree and Kai walking down the dirt-track road alone.

Tess went to greet them, the children and the dog bounding alongside her.

'And your father?' Tess said.

'He was fishing,' Chatree said, and he looked at his sister. 'He was out fishing.'

Kai shook her head. 'We can't find him,' she said.

'He'll turn up,' Tess said, and she put her arms around the pair of them, and they stood there, stock-still, letting her hold them.

'Can they stay with us?' Keeva said.

'Of course they must stay,' Tess said.

I gave them each a bottle of water, and the two young *chao ley* took it without expression as they stared at the ground, wondering what would happen now. Then we all turned to look at a flame of pure fire that had suddenly pierced the darkness.

Mr Botan had his blowtorch in his hand, and was heating up the garlic and bread that someone had carried with them up the green hill of Nai Yang. Mrs Botan began to light candles as the smell of toasted bread and garlic drifted across the yard and I felt my mouth flood with saliva. I had not eaten since breakfast and the bread and garlic smelled like the finest meal in the world.

Then there was other food. Thais came shyly to our porch and offered us cold rice wrapped in banana leaves, and pieces of mango and watermelon and pomelo. Tess kept handing out bottles of water, and soon we all realized how hungry we were.

And when the food was gone, Keeva and Rory took Kai and Chatree by the hand and led them to their bedroom. Then our kids brushed their teeth and staggered off to our big bed while Tess stood in the doorway of the children's bedroom, smiling to say that everything was all right. But Chatree seemed unsure if they should accept the offer of a bed.

'We should look for our father,' he said.

'You can look for him in the morning,' Tess said briskly.

'*Jah?*' said the boy. *Sister?*

'Thank you,' the girl said to Tess, deciding the matter, and then to the boy, '*Bang*,' with a small nod of encouragement. *Brother.*

But they made no motion to get into bed. Tess smiled at them and closed the door. We stood there for a moment, hearing their soft voices before we walked quickly away, as if we had accidentally overheard somebody praying.

With Mister in my arms, I kissed my family goodnight – Keeva and Rory either side of Tess, the bed completely full, all three of them more asleep than awake – and went out to sleep on the rattan chair.

There was work going on in the darkness, as the people who had come to our hill pulled palm leaves from trees and spread them on the ground for their beds. I left the dog settling down on the rattan chair and went out and helped them in their work, surprised that I needed all my strength to pull off the largest leaves, some of them as big as a man.

In the end we had more leaves than we needed. The

150

people who had come up the hill began to bed down for the night and I felt the surprising softness of the last palm leaf that I had torn from the tree. The feel of it made me weak with tiredness and I placed it on the ground and lay down. Immediately I felt myself ordered to sleep.

I smelled the garlic and the bread that Mr Botan had cooked with his blowtorch and my eyes started to shut, and I knew that soon the darkness would come, despite the fragile flames of the candles and the white blaze of the moon.

The first time I awoke in the night I cried out with fear, but Tess was by my side, her body curved into mine, knowing every twist and turn, and in her sleep she placed a light hand on my arm and it calmed me. I turned over to face her, but she turned over too, so I slept with my face in her hair until I woke again, the sky still black, the moon and the candles all gone, and this second time I found that I was alone, and Tess had gone back to the bed with our children, as if she knew that I would not cry out again.

18

The traffic started before dawn.

I got up, leaving the others still sleeping around me on the ground, and walked down to the main road.

A pick-up truck went by, the back loaded with young *farang* and their luggage, and then another. The road was full of them, and scooters, and motorbikes, all kinds of motorbikes, everything from little hairdryers to giant Harleys. In the half-light you could see them coming, this ragged convoy of trucks, taxis and even the odd *tuk-tuk*, crammed with foreigners and their belongings, a river of traffic moving north to the airport.

I held up my hand and called out for someone to stop, but nobody even looked at me. On their faces there was nothing but that animal need to get away. And it was in me too. The animal need to be somewhere else. A single thought of pure terror.

I watched the traffic and when a pick-up passed by and there was nothing but a flock of scooters ahead for a bit, I stepped into the road, my hands held high. An elderly Vespa slid to a halt so close to me the front twisted hard against my leg.

'Please,' I said, my hands still held high.

'I'll kill you!' the driver screamed, one hand for the scooter and the other in a fist, waving it in my face. He was some kind of American. 'You speak English, you dumb bastard?'

'Please,' I said. 'What happened?'

He stared at me, and slowly unclenched his fist.

'What happened?' he repeated. 'You're asking me what happened?'

I nodded.

'I don't know what's happened,' I said.

And then he told me.

'It was an earthquake,' he said. 'Below the Indian Ocean. CNN said it was the biggest earthquake in – I don't know – the history of the world. You believe that? And the earthquake made the tsunami.'

I shook my head. 'Tsunami?' I said.

'The water, man! The fucking water! Jesus Christ! You see the water?'

'I saw the water,' I said.

'Okay,' he said, calming down, his eyes moving from me to the traffic and back again. He was wondering how long this was going to take. 'And the water hit all over,' he said. 'India, Sri Lanka, the Maldives, Indonesia, Malaysia, Thailand . . .'

I couldn't understand. The terrible reality of it was too big to fit inside me.

'So it's not just the island?' I said.

He laughed out loud.

'It's not just the island, man,' he said. 'It's not even just the country.' He looked at the fast-flowing traffic, ready to go. The Vespa came to life. 'It's more like the whole world,' he said.

I walked quickly down the dirt-track road. Through the trees the sea was smooth and flat and still, more like a lake than an ocean, more like turquoise stone than water, but I thought of the strong currents that kept the swimmers from Hat Mai Khao, and of the surfers who came for the big waves further south, and above all I remembered the white line that had stretched across the horizon.

How stupid I had been, how suicidally trusting that Nature would be kind. I stared at the sea for seconds and minutes, trembling with fear and anger, and then I began to run back to the house as fast as I could.

I went into our bedroom, Tess and the children still sleeping, and pulled out a suitcase from the wardrobe and began to stuff it with clothes. Her clothes, my clothes. I just wanted to fill the suitcase. I didn't care what we took and what we left behind. I just needed for us to be on our way.

'We have to go,' I said.

Tess stirred, sat up and then settled back down under the sheets, Keeva moaning in her sleep beside her. Rory was out for the count.

'I mean it, Tess,' I said. 'We've got to get out of here.'

Now she was sitting up in bed.

'I talked to someone on the road,' I told her. 'You can't imagine. It's not just the island. It's everywhere.'

She pulled back the sheet, eased herself over Rory and out of bed. She came to me and placed a hand on my arm.

'Tom,' she said. 'Stop.'

I stopped for a moment and looked at her.

'We have to stay,' she said.

I could hear the traffic on the road. The sky was getting light. I went back to my packing. It wasn't really packing. I was blindly shoving whatever I could into the suitcase. Already it was nearly full.

'No,' I said. 'We have to go, Tess.'

She wiped her forehead with her hand. With the air con out, the heat of the night was still in here, and it was difficult to breathe.

'We have to stay,' she said. 'These people have nothing now. Mr and Mrs Botan, they've lost everything. Those children sleeping in Rory and Keeva's bedroom. So many people have nothing now.'

'We have nothing!' I said, too loud, and Keeva sat up, rubbing her eyes.

'We have water,' Tess said.

I couldn't believe what I was hearing.

'What's wrong?' Keeva said.

'That's why we're staying?' I said to Tess. 'Because we have a few bottles of water? Because the man got the delivery wrong and we ended up with twenty pallets instead of twenty bottles?'

'If it's as bad as you say, then there's going to be disease,' she said.

'That's not a reason to stay,' I said. 'That's a reason to head for the airport.'

'Cholera,' she said. 'Bottled water will prevent cholera. And dysentery. And – I don't know what else.'

'Just give it to them and go!' I said. 'They can have the water!'

'Is it time to get up?' Keeva said.

'Go back to sleep, angel,' Tess said.

'No,' I said. 'Don't go back to bed. Go to your room and get your backpack and start filling it with your stuff.'

'Are Kai and Chatree already awake?' she said.

'Keeva,' I said, 'please, just do it.'

Our daughter looked at her mother for a moment, then yawned widely, and got out of bed.

'You're telling me two different things,' she muttered, and stumbled from the room.

The air con suddenly came on. I heard the rattling hum, felt the blast of cold air and I saw Tess smiling at me.

'Tom,' she said. 'It will be all right. Do you really think I would stay if I thought the children were in danger?'

'Everybody is leaving,' I said. 'All the foreigners. They're all getting out.'

'Let them go,' she said, her face darkening. 'But we're not leaving. We're not running away again.'

'What does that mean?' I said.

'In the end you have to decide if you're going to have a real home somewhere,' she said. 'Or if you are just going to spend your life bouncing from one place to the next.'

I could hear voices through the wall speaking softly in Thai. Kai and Chatree were awake. Keeva's voice came through the wall.

'Do you think their father is going to come walking up the hill any time soon?' Tess said quietly.

'No,' I said. 'And it's a tragedy. But what's it got to do with you?'

Rory groaned in his sleep and we both looked at him.

'I teach those children,' Tess said. 'That's what it's got to do with me, okay?'

'A few free language lessons,' I said. 'That doesn't make you their guardian.'

'It's more than that.'

'We're staying so you can play teacher with the locals?'

The first flash of anger.

'Teaching is not something I play at,' she said. 'It's who I am.'

'Tess,' I said. I was begging her now. 'Please. Let's go.'

But she held my arms, wanting me to understand. 'Look,' she said. 'You don't go to another country to be someone else. You go to be yourself. You go to be the person you couldn't be back home. The person you want to be.'

156

'I don't know what you're talking about,' I said.

'Yes, you do,' she said. 'And – more than anything – *that's* why I want to stay,' she said. 'We can be ourselves here in a way they wouldn't let us back home. You can be a good man, Tom. I know you can. The man you want to be.'

Rory was sitting up in bed, rubbing his eyes.

'Am I meant to be getting my backpack?' he said.

Before either of us could answer, Keeva burst into the room.

'Next door,' she said. 'Come and see. The TV's working.'

The Botans were watching a local station. They did not look up at us as we came into their home and stood behind them while on the screen a young Thai woman pinned a photo of a young Thai man to a board.

When the camera pulled back you could see that the messageboard seemed to go on forever, and there were already many photos pinned to it. The faces in the photos were from every nation on earth, but what you noticed about them was that they were all happy. They were faces captured on birthdays, weddings, holidays. Some of the foreign faces smiled with Christmas trees in the background, and you did not know if the picture had been taken in some other time on the other side of the world or here on the island, the day before yesterday. All ages, all races, all smiling.

I could feel the choking sob of grief, that sob like filthy water, rising to my mouth and my nose and my eyes, sickening me, and I could not imagine a day in my life when it would not be there, waiting for the chance to come again.

My daughter tugged my hand. Rory and Keeva both had empty rucksacks, as if trying to please both Tess and me at once by getting their bags but not packing. Then Chatree and Kai came shyly into the room, and sat on the polished wooden floor, eyes solemnly fixed on the TV screen, too. Mr Botan glanced up at the sea gypsies and then back at the television.

'Tess,' I said, indicating Rory and Keeva, but she shook her head.

'No,' Tess said. 'Let them watch.'

Mrs Botan said something to Mr Botan at the sound of our voices and he picked up the remote and began flicking through the channels until he found the news in English. There was a smashed beach and a British voice was reeling off statistics.

'The death toll in Sri Lanka alone has been revised from three thousand to . . . twenty-six thousand,' the voice said, and in his little pause I knew you could have all of the information in the world and still be unable to comprehend the scale of what had happened. 'Worldwide, deaths stand at an estimated two hundred and fifty thousand,' he said. 'The homeless are expected to number more than one and a half million.'

There was only one story, but it could be told in many ways, in many different places. A road washed away in Southern India. A train tossed across jungle in Sri Lanka. A village swatted flat in New Guinea. A hotel drowned in Thailand.

In the areas where the tourists were, you watched jerky footage of what happened when the water came, but in the poor places where there were no foreigners, no phones and no cameras, you only saw the aftermath. I felt Tess take my hand and hold it and not let go.

The scenes of devastation switched to the studio, where a man in a suit and tie was looking grave.

'London journalist Nick Kazan was on holiday with his fiancée in Phuket, Thailand,' he said, and there was Nick, standing by the side of the road somewhere to the south,

158

one of the tourist resorts, although it had been battered out of all recognition.

'I wasn't really sure what was going on,' Nick said, not addressing the camera but someone standing just to one side of it. 'We were – we were driving back to our hotel,' he said, and I saw there was a young woman with him, a pretty English girl with long blonde hair, and she had been crying, and Nick looked at her before carrying on, and I could see that he was trying very hard to do his job, to do what he was trained for, to be a hard-nosed reporter, telling it as it was, but it was tough for him. 'And the people came running up from the beach,' he said, and he looked out to sea.

There was a palm tree behind him.

Uprooted, smashed, flattened.

He was somewhere around Patong, because I recognized the name of the hotel they cut to, but the landscape was mutilated, unrecognizable, like the end of all things. Crushed cars. Smashed wood that had once been buildings or trees. Mud everywhere. As though the coast had been pulped.

'It's a terrible thing,' Nick said, and the urge to do a professional job fought with the urge to weep. 'An unimaginable thing,' he said, and he hung his head, shaking it, finally lost for words.

A voice said, 'On the beaches of Phuket, many people did not realize the power of the waves until it was too late,' and there was more rough footage of people running from the beach, and the water swirling and claiming whatever it could, and then a steady shot from later, the emergency workers cutting their way through the fallen trees that were everywhere. A man still clung to one of the trees, his arms and legs wrapped tight around the trunk, and it took me a bewildered moment to understand that the man was dead.

That was when I gathered my children in my arms and

turned their faces from the TV screen, and I realized that Tess was gone.

'I think she's on the beach,' Keeva said.

Tess was where the Almost World Famous Seafood Grill had been, just beyond the first of the casuarina trees, sitting on a footstool, an upturned wooden box in front of her. There were perhaps thirty small bottles of mineral water in front of her.

That was all she could carry.

Her head was covered with a large hat, and there was a light cotton scarf pulled over her face, and she looked like one of the gardeners who tended the grounds of the big hotels. As I came through the trees a woman and a small child approached her, and Tess gave them each a bottle of water, and they both received it with a deep *wai*.

I looked up at the sky. With the sun as high as it was now, there was not enough shade for her on the beach. I walked back to the house and I borrowed a machete from Mr Botan's shed. The four children were sitting on our porch, the dog capering between them, ecstatic at all the attention.

When I returned to the beach with the machete there was a white man standing by Tess' side. Crisp blue shirt, clean white trousers, and a tan the colour of money. A rich *farang* with his hands behind his back, like minor royalty at a garden party.

Tess sat on her stool, wilting in the heat, ignoring him. As I walked up I saw it was Miles, the Englishman who had got me out of Phuket Provincial. He looked over at me as I went into the trees, and when he heard me chopping branches from the casuarinas, he came and stood by my side. He watched me for a while and then cleared his throat.

'You're aware that this part of Nai Yang is a national park?'

he said, and when I gave him a look he smiled at me, and then at Mr Botan's machete, and after that he did not say anything else.

I hefted the machete and brought it down hard on a low branch. It came away and I looked at it, thinking how I could use the casuarinas to make a wall, but that I would need to find something else – some of those big palm leaves would be good – for a roof. Then she would not get burned. Because I knew that if she still had water to give away, Tess would not leave the beach.

Miles followed me to where Tess was sitting with the bottled water on Hat Nai Yang. He did not offer to help me carry the wood. Now more people were coming as the word spread. I began to work around her, jamming the casuarina branches into the sand, and covering them with the biggest palm leaves I could find. Two walls, a couple of metres high, covered with the thick leaves on top. It was enough for now.

A cooling shadow fell over Tess, and she turned her head towards me. Above the cotton scarf that covered her nose and mouth and below the rim of her hat, I could see that her eyes were smiling. I loved her so much that she filled up my heart and she knew it and she did not need me to say it.

'Thanks,' she said.

'Okay,' I said, and when I came close to her, making adjustments, making the shelter more solid, squinting up at the sky to judge the angle of the sun, she lightly touched my back as I passed her, and something was decided.

I stood back as an old man slowly came forward for water, and I looked at the shelter, thinking it would last a while. When I looked at Miles I saw that he was almost laughing.

'What's so funny?' I said, and my voice sounded strange, croaky and harsh, in the silence of the beach in the blazing midday sun.

'That's very impressive,' he said. 'You've built her a real little beach house, haven't you?'

I knew what he was saying.

Or I thought that I did.

But I did not reply, and I continued to work, pushing the branches deeper into the sand, covering the gaps that let sunshine through in the roof, and letting the silence between us grow.

I was angry with him. He thought he knew me and he didn't know me at all. I went into the trees one last time and I looked at him as I dragged more palm leaves back to the beach. He wasn't smiling now.

'I'm just saying,' he said. 'You're very good with your hands. For someone . . . You know.'

I stopped what I was doing and looked at him hard, forcing him to say it. But he would not say it. He was too much of the little white-trousered diplomat. So I said it for him.

'For a driver?' I said, mopping the sweat from my face. I looked at the shelter I had built for my wife and thought that I had done a good job. It would work. It would give Tess the shade that she would need if she was going to stay on the beach.

'Yes,' Miles said. 'For a driver.'

'I'm not a driver,' I said. 'I'm a builder.'

At the hospital there were people shouting in English.

They were angry that the Thai nurses could only speak Thai. They were angry that the lists of people who had been admitted to the hospital were only written in Thai, which they could not read. They were angry because they had lost things that could never be replaced.

There was a Christmas tree in the entrance of the hospital, and under it there were neat stacks of designer clothes, with more arriving all the time. It could have looked absurd

162

– responding to what had happened with clothes that had fancy labels. But people felt the need to do something.

I walked out of the hospital and saw a face that I knew from somewhere, a man in police uniform, and it took me a while to recognize Sergeant Somter. He did not look like a young man any more.

He was talking to a group of men in suits. They looked important, like men from Bangkok, some kind of government or health officials. But they listened silently to Sergeant Somter as he explained something to them. When the men got into their cars Somter put on his shades, flopped into the passenger seat of a patrol car and was driven away.

'Tom?'

I turned and looked at Nick Kazan. He was dressed in a polo shirt and chinos, a London journalist's idea of summer clothes, but far too warm for Phuket in the final days of December.

'I saw you on TV,' I said. 'A few days ago. The day after it happened. I thought you'd be gone by now.'

'Why would I leave?' he said. 'This is the biggest story in the world. My girlfriend went home, but my editor is all for me staying another week or so.'

I nodded and began walking as he fell into step beside me.

'Don't you get tired of sticking your nose into other people's misery?' I said.

'It's sort of my job, Tom,' he said. 'Sorry. What you doing?'

I stopped and stared at him.

'I was looking for a little boy,' I said, and when I said it out loud I saw that it was hopeless. 'A Norwegian boy called Ole.'

'A missing child?' he said. 'He might turn up. You never know. You hear all these stories. Incredible stories. Missing kids being found. Climbers who saw it coming in from miles away. Scuba divers that didn't know that it had happened until they came back to shore and found everything gone. Unbelievable stories. Like the one about all the animals surviving.'

'The animals surviving?' I said.

'Yes.'

'Look at that,' I said.

There was a pick-up truck by the side of the road and when a man in a white breathing mask moved to one side you could see that the back of it was full of dead dogs.

I heard Nick Kazan gasp as though he had been punched in the stomach and he saw that not all of the animals had survived, that it was just a story, a happy myth that had spread fast and was always believed. But it was not true. The dogs in the back of the pick-up proved that it was not true.

They were beach dogs like Mister, the scavenger dogs, the ones that clung to the beaches and the tourists, looking for scraps, unloved and unwanted. But the man in the mask carefully placed the dog he was carrying into the back of the truck as if he were putting it down for its rest, and I saw that the beach dogs were not treated like rubbish in death.

'That's no good,' Nick Kazan said.

Some tourists were looking at the dead beach dogs as though they were one of the sights, peering into the back of the pick-up truck, grimacing and chuckling with theatrical disgust.

A man with a sagging belly straining at the palm trees on his Hawaiian shirt was taking pictures and Nick Kazan stepped forward and took the camera from the fat man's hand.

'Hey,' said the fat man. *'Was machen sie denn da?* Give me my camera!'

'You should be ashamed of yourself,' Nick said, and the fat man reared back, shouting something in German, and soon all the tourists were shouting at Nick about the police. Then he hurled the camera as hard as he could at the ground and their jaws dropped open as it exploded. The fat man retrieved his broken camera and they went off to fetch a policeman.

'We should go,' Nick said. 'Your family must need you.'

'Yes,' I said, seeing he was right. 'I have to go home now.'

And that was the day Nick became my friend.

There were no fireworks on New Year's Eve.

But we went to our beach where the sand met the sea and we lit a candle inside a balloon made of tissue paper and we set it adrift on the night sky.

Many others did the same all along Hat Nai Yang, and on the beaches to the south and to the north, and on every other beach and hill in Phuket, and as the tissue-paper balloons became floating lanterns, soon the night sky was full of thousands of small, flickering flames, and we could not tell our one from the rest.

The floating lanterns with their trembling flames were like all the lives that you would never know, and we craned our necks and watched them drifting from the shore to the heavens, high above the Andaman Sea, all these tiny stabs of fire in the black and starry night, always drifting away from us, always going higher, and my family stood on our beach, our beautiful Hat Nai Yang, Tess and Keeva and Rory and me, and we held hands as we felt the soft white sand beneath our bare feet and we watched the night sky until the last of the lights were gone.

PART THREE

The Young Man and the Sea Gypsy

19

On New Year's Day Mr Botan's new second-hand longtail spluttered out of the still, sun-polished bay and into the choppy, deeper blue of open sea.

Mr Botan gave me some small foamy pink earplugs which I took but didn't use. The throaty rumble of the longtail's two-stroke diesel engine was loud, though not deafening, as we left the shore far behind. I loved that sound.

As the sun grew stronger I sat in the middle of the longtail, huddled under a little green umbrella that Mr Botan had erected for me. He was the colour of old teak, and apparently unaffected by even the fiercest heat. But the sun was not the only reason he wanted me to stay in the centre of the boat.

When I was on either side of the longtail, Mr Botan could not see where he was steering, for ahead of us the bow of the longtail curved dramatically upwards like the sharp end of a Viking ship. From his position at the stern, steering our course with a rudder attached to the longtail's old diesel engine, Mr Botan never had a clear view of what was ahead of us. Under the national flag of the Kingdom of Thailand, there were bright silk scarves of blue, pink and yellow tied around the top of the bow, and they fluttered and whipped like the flags of some forgotten army in the wind of open water, not for decoration, as I had always thought, but for warning. Like so much of Thailand, behind the delicate, decorative beauty there was a hard-headed, practical purpose. The silk scarves were our headlamps.

Mrs Botan had made us *Haway thawt*, an omelette stuffed with mussels, and when we stopped on open water, we ate it with our fingers for lunch.

He showed me how to weight a trap for lobster. The fishing was poor, but just when it seemed that we would have a bad day because we had set out late and missed the best spots, the nets he threw into the water were suddenly full of white snapper, squid and crab, so much crab that he was able to teach me the difference between blue crab, red crab and soft-shell crab.

He was in a hurry to get back, and I could not understand why, but when Hat Nai Yang was in sight I could see that some rough version of the fish market was operating, and the longtails were docking with their catch. There were even a few tables and chairs on the sand where the line of restaurants had once stood. The island was already rebuilding.

Tess was sitting beneath the shelter that I had made on the sand, ready to give bottled water to anyone who asked. We had brought down all the water that we had left in the shed, and it took up so much space that Tess and Rory and Keeva and Chatree and Kai sat in a semi-circle before her using the stacked pallets as seating.

When we were close to shore, Mr Botan killed the engine and we jumped from the longtail into the shallow water and began hauling the boat up the sand, our catch slapping in their baskets and flashing silver in the crystal sunshine.

I recognized some of the faces buying and selling fish. But I was aware that other faces were missing, and it made me think that what had happened would never really be over.

As Mr Botan displayed our catch I reached up to touch Jesse's chain of amulets around my neck, saying a silent prayer of thanks for my family's safety, and was stopped by the colour of my arm.

I had not noticed before.

My pale skin had turned brown.

Mr Botan did not sell as much fish as he would have wanted. Business had begun but it was far from normal. He had so much left that it would take both of us to carry it home. Our families would have a lot of fish to eat tonight. We started down the beach road to home.

'What did you build?' he asked me. 'In England?'

'I built homes,' I said. 'I built houses and flats.'

'You did this alone?' he said.

'No,' I said. 'I had men working with me. But that is what we built. Places for people to live.'

He nodded. 'Can you build a restaurant?' he said. 'If you only have me to help?'

I looked at him for a long moment.

'Yes,' I said. 'I can do that.'

Mr Botan and I walked up the green hill to home and the sun set in a firework display of red and gold over the Andaman Sea, so blue and unmoving on the first day of the New Year that it could have been a painting of the sea.

There was a big black BMW parked at the end of the yellow dirt road and from inside the Botans' house I could hear a man shouting in Thai and the soft reasoned response of Mrs Botan.

'My son,' Mr Botan said, and I thought of the man in all of the photographs. 'He wants us to go with him to Bangkok,' Mr Botan said. 'Too dangerous here, he thinks.' He nodded,

171

not moving, and I thought perhaps that he was reluctant to go inside and join the argument. He already knew the sound case that his son would make for quitting and he already knew that, no matter what his son said or how loud he said it, he and his wife would not leave their life in Hat Nai Yang for the city to the north.

'I can understand why your son is worried about you,' I said.

Mr Botan shook his head.

'This is our home and we are staying,' he said. 'Just like you.'

20

The next day we drove south towards the rain hanging over the distant hills.

Mr Botan was at the wheel of his pick-up truck. I was beside him and in the open back Tess sat between Keeva and Kai on one side, with Rory and Chatree on the other. Tess cradled the modest luggage of the *chao ley* – two overnight bags that reflected the passions of my children from a couple of years back.

Hermione Granger was looking stern in front of Hogwarts on one bag, and there was a baby snow leopard with big eyes on the other. The bags were small but not full. Chatree and Kai only had what we had given them. It didn't look like enough to start a new life and the sight of those small forgotten bags made my spirits dip.

'My wife wanted to teach them English,' I said, as much to myself as to Mr Botan. 'So they could have a better life.'

Mr Botan glanced in his rear-view mirror.

'They will be better with their own people,' he said, and nodded emphatically, as if there was no doubt.

I was unconvinced. 'But surely, if their English was fluent . . .'

'Your wife is a kind woman,' Mr Botan said, cutting across me. 'But the girl is too old and the boy is too wild.'

We were going south to find what was left of their family.

The journey took us from one end of the island to the other and Phuket unravelled before us. Back roads winding through forest suddenly opened up on fields of pineapples and banana groves, there were large temples and small mosques everywhere, and the rubber plantations seemed to go on forever. Sometimes you saw the creamy sheets of rubber hung out to dry on bamboo, but it was easy to forget the real purpose of these plantations for it was as if the island was trying to hypnotize you with the tall, thin rubber trees in their neat regimented lines and lull you into some false, dangerous sleep. As I did on the bike, I sometimes jerked my head away from the neat rows of rubber trees, and did not look at them again for a while.

We drove into the rain, the five of them in the back shrieking with laughter and huddling under one broken umbrella, and then we were out of the other side and driving down to the very end of our island, and the laughter stopped.

Kai and Chatree had relatives living at the settlement of sea gypsies on Ko Siray, a tiny island just off the south-east coast of Phuket. When we finally arrived it hardly felt like an island at all. It felt like an afterthought. We rolled across a small bridge and we were there.

I peered down and below the bridge there were ramshackle houses on stilts beside sick-looking water, tin shacks that seemed on the verge of collapse, but alongside there were stalls laden with fruit, overflowing with the endless bounty of Phuket, and the sight of these natural riches stirred the hope that Chatree and Kai would be all right here.

'Ko Siray famous for two things,' Mr Botan said. '*Chao ley* – and monkeys.' He gave me a wry smile that said – *Spot the difference, right?* I didn't smile back at him.

Just beyond the bridge the monkeys appeared. Hundreds of them. So many that I thought my eyes were tricking me. They were scrawny, cunning-looking creatures that ambled from the woods at the first sign of humans. Two young female travellers with backpacks were feeding them old brown bananas. In the back of the truck Rory and Keeva were delirious at the sight of the monkeys. Kai and Chatree were less impressed.

'Some monkey-seeing for your children?' asked Mr Botan, always the perfect host.

I shook my head.

'Maybe on the way back,' I said. 'Let's just get them to their family.'

We drove to the far side of Ko Siray and suddenly the settlement was below us. There were more than twenty longtail boats bobbing in the choppy sea, moored close together. They were not like the proudly maintained longtails owned by the fishermen at Hat Nai Yang. These were old, abandoned, falling to bits. There was no sign of their owners. The pick-up truck rolled slowly down into the *chao ley* village and I had never been anywhere that felt so much like the end of the line.

They had not been devastated by the water the way we had on the west side of the island. But something else had hit them here, and it was impossible to imagine that they would ever get up.

A solitary unmade road ran through the village past shacks on wooden stilts. The shacks had buckling wooden floors, rusty tin roofs, slats hanging loose. Everything about them looked broken. The entire village looked broken. You could see the people inside the shacks. They were all sleeping. Children wandered around, but all the adults seemed to be out for the count.

'*Chao ley* sleep,' chuckled Mr Botan mirthlessly.

These were people with nothing. The sense of crushing poverty was everywhere. No escape, no respite. Poverty as a time-eating, terminal illness. Tess looked at me and shook her head.

Through the shorn and scrappy trees I could see the beach. I had started to take for granted the white-gold sand of the beaches in our part of the island. But this was a different kind of beach, strewn with stones and rubbish and empty Coke bottles. There were giant cages, the size of Wendy Houses, for fishing that made Mr Botan snort with contempt. And everywhere, stirring in their sleep as the pick-up truck drove by, there were people with that flash of gold in their hair.

Mr Botan parked the car.

Kai and Chatree took their pitiful little bags and conferred. They were meant to find their uncle, the brother of their father, who was said to be expecting them. Keeva and Rory wanted to go with them. Tess said they would all go with them. I was reluctant to let my family wander off, but there was no menace in the air here. When the people rose from their sleep they stared at us with total blank-eyed indifference. Tess slipped her arms around the shoulders of Keeva and Rory. But no harm would ever come to us in this place.

They all went off to look for the uncle, including Mr Botan, and I went for a walk. We had quickly got used to seeing things smashed to pieces on our island, but the *chao ley* village was something else. Everywhere on Phuket that was ravaged by the water had begun rebuilding within days. But it was as if the *chao ley* were living on another island, and the fighting spirit of Phuket had been knocked out of them.

Mr Botan found me. He could tell I was shocked.

'It is perhaps not what you expected,' he said, producing a roll-up cigarette from his pocket.

Until the moment we entered the *chao ley* village, I'd had a romantic view of the sea gypsies. Free spirits, romantic nomads, untied by civilization. All of that. Now I laughed at myself.

'I thought they were hunting buffalo on the plains,' I said. 'Instead they're sleeping it off on the reservation.'

He nodded, sucking deeply on his cigarette, as though we had reached an agreement about something.

'We have found their family,' he said. 'But there is a problem. Your wife says you must come.'

The problem was that the uncle had problems of his own.

We walked to a rickety shack at the far end of the village where Tess and Rory and Keeva stood outside, pale and silent, as a chained-up bony dog barked at them. Tess held them more closely now. She looked at me, unsmiling, as I climbed the wooden ladder into the shack's one room. It was dark in there, but when my eyes adjusted I could see the old uncle kneeling by a mattress on the floor. On the mattress there was an elderly woman who was clearly close to death.

Kai and Chatree were pressed up against one wall, staring at the scene, clutching their overnight bags. The old man rocked back and forth on his knees, briefly looking up at me with eyes half-closed with exhaustion and grief, and then back at his wife. He had a wet piece of cloth in his hand and he soothed the old woman's forehead. She did not move and for a moment I thought that she was already dead.

There was also a young man in the corner of the room, chewing his thumbnail as he considered his parents. He was young, perhaps in his early twenties, but carrying the extra weight of a man in his middle years. The streak of gold in his hair gave him a rakish air.

He cleared his throat, murmured a few words to Mr Botan,

177

and then we were all leaving the shack. Outside he made a lengthy speech to his cousins Kai and Chatree. There was nothing but hardness in his voice. It was a grudging welcome, if it was any kind of welcome at all.

Chatree stared at him, as if trying to understand, and Kai kept her eyes down, staring at the unmade road.

'What does he say?' I said.

'He says it is not a good time,' Mr Botan told me.

I shook my head. 'It sounds like he said more than that.'

'They will have to work hard,' Mr Botan said. He looked at me. 'It is not a good time.'

And that was where we left them.

Our children muttered their awkward goodbyes and Tess fiercely hugged Kai and Chatree as they stood there, stiff and awkward. Chatree was a couple of years older than Rory and Keeva, and Kai somewhere in her middle teens, but the *chao ley* seemed to be grown up in a way that my children would never be.

I put my hand on Chatree's shoulder.

'Thank you for letting us stay,' he said.

I shook his hand. The skin was rougher than a child's skin should be. Kai smiled at me in bashful apology and turned away.

Then, as her cousin watched her with his dead eyes, Kai climbed the wooden ladder into the darkness of the tin shack, her second-hand Hermione Granger bag dangling from one thin shoulder.

21

We climbed to the top of the hill and the lagoon lay spread below us.

Down in the clear and shallow water, four figures clung to an empty kayak. Two of them were in diving gear, and the other two wore orange life vests. They talked quietly in Thai among themselves, as they considered an unmoving dorsal fin nearby. The fin shone bone-white in the morning sun. A family of monkeys, skinny and wild, watched with mild interest from the muddy shore.

Rory started down to the lagoon but I placed a hand on his shoulder.

'I don't know,' I said, shaking my head. 'That thing will take your head off.'

He looked up at me and sighed.

'It's a dolphin, not a shark,' my son said impatiently. 'Probably Indo-Pacific bottlenose.' He took off his glasses, cleaned them on his T-shirt and put them back on. He peered down at the lagoon. 'But how did it get here?'

Carried by the water. Picked up by the sea. We both knew that much. But there was no obvious way in or out. The lagoon felt like a secret place, shut off from the rest of the world. We made our way to the water, coming down the slope diagonally to avoid the monkeys.

When we reached the mud we took off our sandals and placed heavy rocks on them so that the monkeys couldn't steal them. Keeping our T-shirts on to protect our backs from the sun, we slipped into the water. The men glanced up at us as we approached the kayak, but merely smiled briefly in polite greeting and looked back at the fin. The water came up to my chest. My son had to swim. But he was getting better at it these days.

We could see the dolphin clearly now. Up close it was the lightest shade of blue, with darker flecks of colour on its belly, and its jewel-black eyes gleamed with terror. It was so still that it could have been dead. Only the glint in those black eyes told you that it was not dead, but waiting to die.

We all watched the dolphin for a while and then one of the divers made a motion towards it. With a tiny shudder of its tail, the dolphin moved away.

'They never live alone,' my son whispered to me, his head just above the water, flecks of wet on his glasses. He turned his head to the men. 'The Indo-Pacific bottlenose,' he said, slightly louder. 'They live in family groups. Five, ten, fifteen dolphins. It's been separated from its family.'

The men all nodded thoughtfully, although as far as I could tell they did not speak English. Rory moved slowly through the water in a gentle doggy paddle. This time the dolphin did not move away. My son placed a hand on the dolphin's beak, and a light flashed in those dark eyes. It was perhaps two metres long. My size, and the size of the Thai divers, but much bigger than my boy, who trod water as he continued to rest one hand on the dolphin's beak while his other hand stroked the top of its head. My son looked at me and smiled.

'Go on,' he told me. 'Touch him.'

I moved through the water, half-swimming, half-walking, until I was beside the dolphin. I placed the palm of my right hand on its side and it was like touching leather and silk all at once.

'He's beautiful, isn't he?' said my son.

I nodded and placed my other hand on the light blue skin of the dolphin. It was actually more like silk than leather, although it felt like the toughest silk in the world, silk that was built to last for journeys of a thousand miles.

Then the men were suddenly there, their voices low but excited, pushing the kayak under water and manoeuvring it beneath the body of the dolphin. On the shore the monkeys chattered with mad excitement. The dolphin did not resist or try to move away as we rolled, pushed and lifted it on to the kayak, and it was then that I felt the weight and the power of this creature, and I thought that it would be too much for us, just five men and a boy.

But after one final effort and a wild flurry of water, the dolphin was somehow on the kayak. One of the men placed a blanket over its head, and above its slender beak the black eyes shifted with surprise. On the shore the monkeys cheered, sounding as if they were clearing their throats.

The kayak moved slowly through the water, towards the corner of the lagoon, and the dolphin was infinitely patient and still, trying to be of help, trying to cooperate. From high above us, I heard the sound of applause.

Nick was sitting on a rock, smiling as he lifted a camera to his face and took a picture, and then another. He was still wearing his polo shirt and chinos. It was too much in this heat. But it did not matter much because he was going home soon.

'Lucky fish!' he called.

Rory's face was tight with rage.

'It's not a *fish*,' he hissed, trying not to raise his voice. 'It's a marine mammal.'

Nick nodded. 'Lucky marine mammal!' he called. 'Do you know how long they were staring at Flipper there before you two turned up?'

He said something else, but we didn't hear him as we were approaching the sheer wall of the lagoon. Then suddenly we were moving into it, through a half-submerged cave, and when one of the divers shone a torch at the ceiling we saw that the roof of the cave was covered in bats. Thousands of bats. It was as if the ceiling of the cave was made of bats.

'Fruit bats,' Rory said. 'Fascinating.'

One of the divers placed a finger over his mouth and Rory smiled and nodded. 'I understand,' he whispered. 'Mouths shut, right? Because of the possibility of bat poo.'

I cursed under my breath, but after that I kept my mouth shut tight.

The kayak moved slowly through the cave, the weight of its passenger pushing it low in the water. Above us the bats rustled and stirred, the sound as dry and lifeless as leaves.

Ahead of us we could see a semi-circle of light. Then suddenly we were out of the cave and in open sea, and for one moment we paused, our eyes adjusting to the sunlight's glare after the blackness of the cave. Now the men were at the back of the kayak, lifting it up and shouting encouragement, and I quickly pulled my son away as the dolphin slid and splashed into the sea. There was a flash of silver like underwater lightning, and then it was away and gone.

Rory trod water and stared out at the ocean as the men pushed the kayak back into the cave. The sound of their happy laughter echoed in that dark chamber and then faded away.

Rory continued to look out at the horizon. But of course there was no longer anything to see.

'Dad,' my son said. 'Can we come back tomorrow?'

'Sorry,' I said. 'Tomorrow I have to work.'

Later I sat on the sand of Hat Nai Yang with Nick, and as the children played with the dog down by the shore we watched the setting sun paint the sky in the exact colours of fire.

Behind us I could hear Tess telling a young aid worker that she did not have to pay for the bottle of water she was handing her.

Tess' *nam plao* stand had been going for a week. I had re-inforced and extended the shelter, so it was bigger and more cool and shady, and I had found a ping-pong table washed up on the beach and dragged it back to use as a kind of bar.

I looked at her and she smiled and gave me a thumbs up before tearing the cellophane off another twelve-pack of water. There were still quite a few left, but demand had slowed to a trickle. The shortages were over in days. There was water and food and electricity. What the island needed now was to rebuild.

Rory and Keeva wandered up from the shore, Mister yapping between them.

'So what happened to your girlfriend?' Keeva asked Nick. 'We saw her on television. She's very pretty.'

'She went home,' Nick smiled.

'Do you want to help me look for bottlenose dolphins?' Rory asked him. 'My dad's got to work.'

'I'm going back tomorrow,' Nick said. 'I've got to work, too.'

'Do you like our bar?' Keeva said, looking up at Nick.

'It's a great bar,' he smiled.

'It's a very long bar,' my daughter said. 'Because my dad got my mum a ping-pong table.'

Nick laughed. 'It's *the* long bar,' he said, and the name made me smile.

The long bar, I said to myself.

Tess would like that.

Rory and Keeva wandered off to help their mother and Nick pushed his bare toes into the soft white-gold sand of Hat Nai Yang. He lifted up a fistful and let it run through his fingers, and I heard him sigh. It was difficult to leave the beach.

'So the dolphin will be a story, will he?' I said.

He nodded. 'In my game they say, "If it bleeds, it leads,"' he said. 'Meaning there's nothing that the world likes better than hearing about someone else's misery. But it's not true.' He looked up at me. 'Most of all, people like stories that give them hope. The dolphin is that kind of story.'

There was almost nothing of the sun left now, just the fading red and gold smeared low across the sky.

'You all packed?' I asked him.

He nodded. He was leaving in the morning.

'There must be a thousand stories in this place,' he said. 'But the clear-up has kicked off and there are no more miracle survivors. You all right?'

I was thinking of the little Norwegian boy called Ole. I wondered if his father had found him. I would never know.

'I'm fine,' I said. 'So your editor wants you back?'

He nodded and as the last of the sun slipped away it was as if God had suddenly turned on the night.

'I could use a beer,' Nick said, turning to look at me. But he knew that we only had water. 'Don't you fancy a few beers, Tom?' he said.

I looked up at the hill. I could see no lights in the Botans' house. It was possible that they had already turned in.

'I'm getting up early tomorrow,' I said. 'But I'll drop you off somewhere on the bike.'

He thought about it for a moment.

'Thanks,' he said. 'You heard of this place – the Bangla Road?'

I drove him to Patong.

Before he had got off the Royal Enfield, a girl was out of one of the bars and on him.

'Oh, hello, sexy man! Oh, hello, my big, big honey! Oh, I want you happy-happy! Oh, I want to take care of you! Oh, I want you *so* happy-happy!'

She had him in the bar-girl full nelson – one arm wrapped around his waist, the other snaking around his arm. In this fashion, she eased him from my motorbike.

Laughing, he shook her hand and said he was very pleased to meet her. For his reward she gave him a wide white smile and an ecstatic squeeze, as though he was too adorable to believe. Then she tugged modestly at her tiny leather mini-skirt, as if anxious that he should not get the wrong impression about her. Nick tried to hide it, but I could see that he was very slightly overwhelmed.

'She acts like she's been waiting for me all her life,' he said, a big grin spreading across his handsome face.

'Yes,' I nodded. 'Don't get too carried away. She would act that way with the Elephant Man. In fact, I think I saw him just leaving.'

We shook hands and we said goodbye. I could not imagine when I would see him again.

But Nick Kazan slept very late the next day.

And his Thai Airways flight left for home without him.

185

22

At first light Mr Botan and I carried our tool bags down to the beach.

Already Hat Nai Yang was bustling with life. All along the beach, from where the seafront restaurants had once stood to the far end of the bay, the curving far end of the beach road where nothing had ever stood before, dark figures pulled back the tarpaulins that covered building materials to protect them from the sun.

The sound was exactly like sails out on open water being whipped by the wind, and it made my heart feel light and happy to hear it because it was the sound of work, and it was the sound of hope and it was the sound of all that had been taken away starting up again.

For the island. For the beach. And for me.

'Eat breakfast later?' Mr Botan said, his voice still gruff with sleep.

'Fine,' I said. 'I'm not hungry.'

'Then we begin,' he said.

And without saying anything beyond deciding on our immediate tasks, Mr Botan and I went to work.

*   *   *

Before, the Almost World Famous Seafood Grill had been just a few tables and chairs scattered across the beach, from the beach road at the top all the way down to where the sand met the sea.

Now we were planning to add a couple of open-sided shelters – hardwood tables and benches on raised decking where the roof would provide shelter from the sun or the rain.

Before, the only lighting had been a candle on every table with a few random lights hung in the trees plus the fairy lights strung around the entrance. Now Mrs Botan – who had a deep love of fairy lights, and a profound belief in their power – wanted every tree on our little part of the beach to have wreathes of tiny coloured lights running through their branches, which would mean rigging the electricity to reach to the very edge of the sea. The Almost World Famous Seafood Grill would be different this time. Bigger, better, brighter and with many more fairy lights.

'But still no bread,' Mrs Botan told me.

She brought me steaming Pahd Thai wrapped in wafer-thin omelette for breakfast and we laughed as I remembered the day we had watched the elephants come out of the sea. When she was gone I looked over at the little ramshackle structure that I now thought of as The Long Bar, and Tess raised her hand and waved to me, and she did it every time I looked over at her, until I felt that I should concentrate more on what I was doing, and ration the number of times that I looked at her.

Tess was watching me work.

The sun came up and the heat built but still we kept at it, me out on the sand cutting the wood for the two open-sided shelters, Mr Botan on the other side of the beach road, joined by Mrs Botan now, where the kitchen had stood before and where it would stand again, as they took delivery after delivery and attempted to make sense of the boxes of equipment that were continually arriving.

It was lucky that this was the coolest time of the year, the middle of the dry season. January meant days of blue skies, calm seas and a wind that was never more than a warm breeze. It meant that I could work for hours without stopping.

My first job was to build the two little wooden shelters that were already the talk of Hat Nai Yang. How could the other seafood restaurants begin to compete? Smiling to myself, I knelt next to the neat stacks of wood and, between measuring and cutting them to size, I let my fingers glide across their surface.

I loved the wood in Thailand. The look of it, the feel of it, the rich deep brown colour. Tropical hardwood that would have been much too expensive to build with back home was the same price as standard construction woods like pine and fir. I loved to smell it, to see those rich shades of brown, and to run my fingers over that glass-smooth surface. As I worked with it on that first day, I could not imagine a time when I would ever take its tough beauty for granted.

Our progress was good on that first day. It was early afternoon when the heat finally became too much, and all at once I was too tired to go on.

Mr Botan came across the beach road, a cold bottle of *nam plao* in each hand, and he nodded with satisfaction at my work.

The skeleton of the new improved Almost World Famous Seafood Grill was starting to take shape. Already the rough outlines of our two open-sided shelters were marked out with the wood that would build them, and I had also mapped out the area where the Almost World Famous Seafood Grill

188

had once stood with posts and string. It was as if Hat Nai Yang itself remembered what had stood here before the water came.

'Enough for one day,' Mr Botan said.

'Okay,' I said, taking the water gratefully as I crouched down and touched the wood for one last time today.

It was strong and beautiful and heavy.

It would last a very long time.

Tess was no longer alone.

Keeva and Rory were there, Mister going mental between them, and two slim young figures who I took for aid workers, going to or coming from the devastation further north in Phang Nga. But as Mr Botan and I got closer to The Long Bar they waved and smiled at me and I saw that it was Kai and Chatree.

'The *chao ley*,' Mr Botan said.

'But what are they doing here?' I said.

He laughed at the question.

'Still they wander,' he said. 'The *chao ley* – forever they wander.'

Chatree had picked up Mister and the dog was licking his face.

'Just visiting, I guess,' I said.

Mr Botan rolled his eyes, as if sea gypsies never did anything else.

As we reached The Long Bar I saw that Kai and Chatree were holding their childish overnight bags. Hermione Granger and the snow leopard. They smiled at me bashfully and I looked at Tess. It seemed a bit quick for a visit.

'They've had to come back,' she told me, and turned to look at them. 'Haven't you?' she said.

'What happened?' I said. 'What about your family in Ko Siray?'

189

They both smiled broadly, a sign of deep embarrassment.

'There's no work,' Kai said.

'No work for anyone,' Chatree echoed.

'No fishing?' I said.

'The boats don't leave the shore in Ko Siray,' Chatree told me. 'They fear the ghosts.'

I nodded, and patted the kid on the shoulder. It did not seem ridiculous to me. It did not seem far-fetched. I still spent time staring at the horizon. I could easily understand how you could be afraid of the ghosts who haunted that sea.

'Enough talk,' Tess said briskly. 'These children are hungry. And they need a place to stay.'

Mr Botan had been watching the *chao ley* without expression. At last he spoke.

'Your house is full,' he said, addressing Tess. 'But we have space.'

Tess nodded, and smiled her thanks, and there was nothing left to discuss.

A man strolled out of the casuarina trees wearing a straw hat and carrying a broken umbrella. He wore ragged khaki shorts, a stained polo shirt and the black leather shoes of some other life. He looked as though he had just got up. A butterfly the size of my hand flew past his face and he reared back in terror for a moment then carried on, grinning with embarrassment. It was Nick.

'Hard at it?' Tess said.

'Trying,' he said, giving us all the benefit of his sleepy grin. 'Decided to stick around for a while. I've been trying to write something all morning.' He took off his straw hat and scratched his bird's-nest hair. 'But it's strange. When I had been here for a day, I felt I could write a book about the place. Then when I had been here for a week, I thought I could write a short story.' He smiled and shrugged. 'And now I don't know what to say.'

'Well, you missed a beautiful morning,' Tess told him, and she introduced him to Kai and Chatree. They stared without expression at the strange sleepy Englishman with his straw hat and ragged shorts and broken umbrella.

But Nick smiled at them, and stroked the dog in Chatree's arm. He looked away, took off his hat and stared out at sea. Then he looked back at Kai with a goofy expression on his face.

And I got it then.

I had thought of Kai and Chatree as children, more grown-up and bruised by the world, but not so different from our own.

But Kai was almost a woman now and when I saw the way that Nick was looking at her, and then looking quickly away, I knew that Mr Botan was right.

She was too old for school.

23

I rode the bike north, taking it slow, watching for the last turning before reaching the bridge to Phang Nga, because the turn was easy to miss, and because I had Tess on the back.

She had one arm wrapped around my waist and the other cradling the food that Mrs Botan had prepared. I could feel the cardboard containers in the plastic bag warm against the base of my spine and the thought of what was inside made my mouth flood with juices.

After three weeks of work, the kitchen of what would one day be the new Almost World Famous Seafood Grill was still just a single gas ring in a room with no roof, but Mrs Botan had somehow prepared rice noodle soup with pork belly, a fish curry that would explode on the back of the tongue and her great staple, Pahd Thai in a blanket of wafer-thin omelette. She used the gas ring to feed Mr Botan and me while we worked. But this meal was for Nick.

We had seen nothing of him since that day on the beach, but a fortnight ago he had left a message that he had moved from his hotel in Patong to a beach hut in the north. There was nothing up there on the very end of the island, and Tess worried that he wasn't eating properly.

The road to his beach hut was the toughest turn on Phuket because if you overshot then you had to go over the Sarasin Bridge to Phang Nga, leaving the island, then swing back and then go through the roadblock of Royal Thai Police who waited unsmiling in their shades at the start of Phuket. I always preferred giving the police a wide berth, so we looked sharp for the turning.

'This is it!' Tess shouted into the wind.

The turning was a dirt-track road to the left that ran off into the casuarina trees, but if you followed it down far enough then you came to a barrier that was permanently raised. This had once been the headquarters of the Sirinath National Park – the beach on the far side of the trees was where we had seen the turtle lay her eggs – and the land was still protected, although it had long ago been abandoned by the authorities.

The only sign that they had once been here was the raised barrier and a small settlement of beach huts under the trees by the beach. They were nothing fancy, just basic bamboo and thatched palm-leaf huts, but they were cheap and popular with travellers. This was where Nick was staying.

'Which one is it?' Tess said.

I thought his message had said that it was the hut closest to the beach, but now I wasn't so sure. There was a dinky moped parked outside and I could not imagine Nick renting something like that. But I thought that was his hut, and I nodded towards it.

'Looks like he's making friends,' Tess smiled, and I felt my spirits dip.

I parked the bike next to the scooter, Tess with the food in her hands, and already steeling myself for the worst.

But it was worse than that.

The door opened and a young woman came out. She was pale and skinny in a little leather skirt and spike heels. When she threw back her long black waterfall of hair, her eyes were raw and shining from where she had been crying.

I risked a glance at Tess.

She was not smiling now.

The girl climbed on the passenger seat of the dinky moped and buried her face in her hands. Then the door to the beach hut opened again and another young woman came out.

Her clothes were less obvious than the first. This one was in bar-girl mufti – T-shirt, jeans, flip-flops – but what made her career choice obvious was her complexion – she had the ghostly night pallor of the bar life, and the diamond-bright sunshine of midday made her vampiric. Even in her unassuming street clothes, she looked like a creature of the night.

This one was dry-eyed but unsmiling and grim. She said something to the girl sitting on the back of the scooter, and her words crackled with a hurt and anger that threatened to explode. I couldn't look at Tess now.

One of these girls would have been bad enough.

Two was too many.

The girls exchanged a few words and arranged themselves on the scooter. Then the door opened again and I looked up expecting to see Nick, sheepishly grinning in khaki shorts and straw hat. But, amazingly, it was yet another girl, whose breast-enhancement surgery gave her the look of a pouter pigeon. I stared in wonder at the door. It began to seem like a debauched magic trick, an attempt at some sick world record.

Just how many bar girls can you get into a beach hut?

The third girl squatted on the handlebars and the middle girl eased the moped into life.

We watched them go, puttering off into the trees and the road south. Then I turned to Tess, awaiting her decision.

'Shall we just . . .'

My voice trailed off, and I gestured towards the open road, and home.

But Tess nodded at the door.

'Knock,' she said, very quietly.

'Tess,' I said. 'He's a single guy. More or less.'

'It's wrong,' she said. 'You know it's wrong. Knock,' she said. 'There's something I need to tell your friend.'

So I knocked. Nick came to the door. I quickly scanned the room over his shoulder, worried that there might be a few more stray bar girls lurking in there. But the room was now empty. Tess edged me to one side and shoved the plastic bag of food into his midriff. He caught it with a shock of breath.

'Here,' she said. 'Dinner is served.'

'Thank you,' he said, with his most winning smile, lifting the bag to look at it.

Tess did not smile.

'Don't thank me,' she said. 'It's from Mrs Botan.' She turned to go, and then turned back. 'Personally,' she said. 'I hope it chokes you. Men like you are what ruin this island. And this country. And this planet.'

He looked sheepish.

'I can explain,' he said.

'I don't think so,' Tess said. She had not erupted yet, she had not gone volcanic in the way that I knew she could, but she was getting there.

'Bad timing,' he said.

'Bad something,' she said.

'May I just say something?' he said.

'You may go fuck yourself,' said Tess, who never swore, unless you pushed her to breaking point. Then she looked him in the eye. Because this was what she wanted him to remember, this was what she wanted to say. '*And stay away from that girl*,' she said.

195

'What girl?' he said.

'You know what girl,' she said, her green eyes fierce, furious slits, and he stepped back. 'Just keep right away from her. Okay?'

'All right,' he said, and I thought of the way he had looked at Kai on the beach, and the way that she had not even noticed.

Then Tess was gone.

She got on the Royal Enfield and took off, giving it far too much throttle, so that the front wheel rose dramatically and the bike kicked up a billowing cloud of yellow dust that quickly rose and slowly fell on the dirt road.

I looked at Nick and shook my head.

'Well,' I said. 'Hello, my big, big honey. Hello, you sexy man. That looks like it was some party you had last night.'

He shook his head, unnerved by Tess' anger. 'More like a wake,' he said. 'They only want me for my laptop.'

I had to smile at that. 'Your laptop?' I said. 'Is that what you call it?'

He stood back and gestured for me to come in. I looked at the road, thinking of the long walk I had ahead of me back to Hat Nai Yang. I went inside and there was a small table with his computer on it, the Apple sign throbbing white in the half-light of the beach hut.

And there were letters. Dozens of letters. Letters with *par avion* envelopes with stamps from Australia and the United States and Germany and Switzerland and India. Stamps from everywhere.

And there were other letters that were waiting to be sent. These were letters on cheap writing paper that was often decorated with hearts or bears or some unspecified cute creature with giant Manga eyes in envelopes bearing the beautiful stamps of Thailand – His Majesty the King and bright tropical flowers and characters from that ancient Sanskrit epic, *The Ramayana*.

'These girls get letters,' Nick said, flopping down in a chair. 'They get letters and they write letters.'

'What's wrong with email?' I said.

'You can't put money in an email,' he said. 'Oh, they like email too – especially when funds are being sent to them and they need the MTCN – the Money Transfer Control Number – but they are the last of the great letter writers. Love letters, begging letters, all sorts of letters. Some of them just want money wired to them at Western Union. Some of them think they're in love. And maybe they are in love – these girls, and the men they meet in the bars.'

I nodded, picking up a letter to a man in Rotterdam. 'But these girls,' I said. 'They all speak English.'

And I thought how incredible it was that all these young women, many of them uneducated and from farms, were such brilliant linguists.

'It only takes them so far,' Nick said. 'The English they have. It takes them up to – wham-bam-khawp-kun-karp-ma'am. Then it fails them. When they become lovers. When the man goes home but they stay in contact. When the guy is revealing that he is married, or he wants to bring her over to Melbourne or Manchester, or he is worried that she is not really in love with him.' He laughed. 'All the mysteries of the human heart. And that's when their words run out and I come in. For a small fee, I translate for them. Put their feelings into words. Help them to express themselves. Read the letters they receive, explaining why the man is not coming back, or why he will always love her, or none of the above.'

I shook my head.

'Those three girls are from the Bangla Road, right?' I said.

'Yes,' he said. 'They're all from the No Name Bar.'

197

'It's the sex industry, Nick,' I said. 'It's a business that came into being to separate sailors on shore leave from their pay packet. That's all. Love doesn't come into it. Love doesn't drink at the No Name Bar.'

He sighed. 'Sure,' he said. 'But it doesn't always end with the money handed over, and it doesn't always end with the sex. Most of the time, yes – but not all of the time. The Bangla Road is the romance industry as well as the sex industry.'

'Boy meets girl,' I said. 'Boy pays girl. What's romantic about that?'

'But they make connections,' he insisted. 'Some of them. Human, emotional connections – whether it's mad or not. Whether it's moral or not. Whether you – or Tess, or me, or the world – approves or not. The girls. The men. Sometimes the bond – the love – is faked for the sake of business. Not always. Sometimes they spend weeks together – they think of the other one as their lover. You know it happens. You see it all the time. The guy pays her bar fine for a week or two, and suddenly they're dating.'

'I've seen those dates,' I said. 'They always run out of conversation.'

He shook his head. 'It starts off that she's the one with youth and beauty and he is the one with cash and credit cards. And then – some of them – they end up needing each other. The women want to be saved and the men want to be loved. It's sort of the opposite to the real world. Is that wrong?'

'A rich foreigner with a poor Thai girl is never going to be one of my favourite sights on this island,' I said.

'What happens if they fall in love?' he said.

'That's even worse,' I said. 'And these people – the men, the girls – can mess up their lives without you lending a hand.'

I leafed through the letters while he got us a drink. Love letters, I suppose you would call them. But if they were love letters, then they were love letters full of doubt and fear, a hard-nosed reality, love letters with the shadow of the No Name Bar falling over them. I picked up one with a crying panda on the top right-hand corner.

My darling,
I will never forget the night you came to the No Name Bar
or the two weeks we spent together. Thank you for asking
– me and my baby are fine. The money arrived at Western
Union – thank you. The Thai baht is very weak right now.
When will you come back to me? Did you get the divorce
from your wife? Do you love me still?

He came back with two bottles of water from the small yellow cube that was the beach hut's fridge.

'It's better than the stuff you wrote about me,' I said. 'You're getting better.'

'That's how she feels,' he said, a bit defensive. 'I just help her to express it.'

'I hope she's not holding her breath for that divorce,' I said.

'It happens,' he said. 'You'd be surprised. But of course, you're right – sometimes it doesn't happen. Maybe most of the time.' He didn't look me in the eye. 'That's what makes my job even more important.'

Your job, I thought, and picked up a letter from the UK.

My darling,
I bet you are surprised to receive a letter from Portsmouth in
England. Do you remember me? I never forget you. Darling,
I do not like to think of you going to work in the No Name
Bar every night. Please be careful in that world . . .

Men who had met some girl in a bar. Men in every corner of the developed world with jobs, lives and money – at least, compared to our island. The letters from the men were full of practical details – about sending money to Western Union, about when they planned to come back, about why life was hard. And there was plenty of the other stuff – the fear of their beloved going to work in a string bikini and a pair of high heels in a place where everything was for sale, including her.

'You sleeping with these girls?' I said.

'No,' he said. 'I got sick of the Bangla Road after one night. That was enough to last me a lifetime.'

I believed him.

'Nick,' I said. 'You didn't lose your job, did you?'

He closed his eyes and sighed.

'I stayed too long in the sun,' he said. 'Overdid it on the first day. Typical tourist, right? I should have gone back with Sarah,' he said, and I guessed that Sarah was the pretty blonde English girl we had seen. 'I should have been at my desk three weeks ago,' he said. 'But I couldn't leave. Can you understand that?'

Through the insect net on his window I could see a patch of stainless sky and the polished blue sea and the empty beach, its colour somewhere between white and gold.

'Yes,' I said. 'I can understand that.'

'I thought I could file more stories from here,' he said. 'I *know* I can file more stories from here. Great stories.' He looked out the window and I couldn't tell if he was thinking about the great stories or the perfect blue sea.

'My editor thinks I should try going freelance for a while,' he said. 'Did I tell you it's a dying industry?'

'What about your fiancée?' I said.

'She's not my fiancée,' he said. 'Not any more. She called me after she had been back for a couple of weeks. Thinks we should try it apart for a while. There's been some guy sniffing around – some old boyfriend . . .' He shook his head, having enough of it, not looking at me. 'It's really okay – all of it.'

'What are you going to live on?'

'I have some money put aside. Not much, but I don't have many expenses here. And the girls pay me what they can.'

'So this is your writing career? Being an Agony Uncle for bar girls?'

'It's not really how I imagined the future. Where do you see yourself in five years? Oh, ideally, I would like to be writing letters for prostitutes.' His face clouded. 'I shouldn't call them that. You know, most of them are good girls. Sounds ridiculous, but it's true. There's goodness in them. This is not the life they want. They want work, marriage, children – same as everyone else. If those three girls had been born in England, they would be decent women.'

His eyes got a faraway look as he thought of the Bangla Road.

'It's not for me,' he said. 'Not that side of it. I've seen it and it's a dead end. For me, at least. In the bars – those kind of bars – you think you have found yourself. But really you have lost yourself.' Then he smiled. 'Besides, as a poor free-lance, I can't afford it, can I?'

Suddenly he was aware of the bag of food sitting among the piles of letters.

'Join me?' he said.

'Sure,' I said.

He looked for plates.

'I'll have to buy some chopsticks,' he called from the tiny kitchen.

How little he knew. 'Thais don't use chopsticks, you dumb bastard,' I called.

He came back smiling with two bottles of Singha from the little yellow fridge and watched me unwrap the food. Fish curry. Gway jaap, rolled rice-noodle soup with pork. Pahd Thai, in its bright yellow blanket of wafer-thin omelette. A pile of bite-sized spring rolls with a chilli dip made from sugar, shrimp paste, lime juice, thinly sliced shallot and chillies – especially chillies. And a bag of fleshy, pale yellow fruit.

'Grapefruit?' he said, frowning.

'Pomelo,' I said. 'For dessert.'

It was not like any Thai food he had eaten in London, or even in the restaurants he had been to on Phuket. This food was full of competing flavours, and made no concessions to timid Western taste, and the chillies made it seem as if it was on fire.

It was a simple meal. But I knew that it would be the best meal Nick had ever eaten in his life. This was, after all, the best food in the world.

After the first mouthful of fish curry, he broke out into a sweat, smiled, and gave me a wordless thumbs up. Then he choked, controlled himself, and smiled again. He could not speak.

And all at once I tasted garlic and lime juice and lemon grass, the sour and the sweet and the sharp, the salt and the sugar, the pungent tang and the searing heat.

This was the food of the island. So many flavours pulling in opposite directions, but somehow you were aware of them all at once.

And perhaps that was the island too.

Then Nick croaked out something that I didn't get.

'What?' I smiled.

'I said – it *hurts*,' he managed. 'Jesus Christ, Tom. It's *hot*.' I nodded.

'But good,' I said. 'And Tess is right. You should keep your

202

distance from Kai. She's not like the girls you meet down on the Bangla Road.'

'I told you,' he said, dragging his fingers through his thick black hair. The sweat was making it stick to his skin. 'I'm sick of the Bangla Road,' he said.

24

There had been no day of rest from the building on Hat Nai Yang and for those early months of the year we worked seven days a week. But now it was March and the cool season would soon be over. The breezes would be gone and the weather would become hotter, wetter and more humid. The work would be harder.

I stood on the sand with the Botans. On the far side of the beach road, the kitchen needed a roof and the small bar was still missing. But on the beach itself, halfway between the road and the sea, the two open-sided shelters were completed. I had just put up the curved wooden archway of the entrance at the edge of the sand, the door with no walls, and when Mrs Botan wrapped it with palm leaves and decked it in fairy lights it would once again look like the front door of the Almost World Famous Seafood Grill.

The little patch of Hat Nai Yang where we worked had stopped looking like a building site on the sand and started looking like a beachfront restaurant. We would have to complete the final touches in the hot season, and we would need to hire more men to get the big roof on, but we were nearly there.

'We need to decide about the roof,' Mr Botan said.

'The choice is wood or steel,' I said. 'Wood looks better, but steel is faster, cheaper and doesn't get eaten by insects.'

'I still like wood,' he said.

'Me too,' I said.

'Enough for now!' Mrs Botan told her husband in English. 'Let the man spend some time with his family,' she said.

So on the first Sunday of the new month, I took a day off and Tess and Keeva and Rory and I walked between two waterfalls. It was a hard walk. Between the Ton Sai and the Bang Pae waterfalls, there was nothing but virgin rainforest.

At the visitor centre of the Khao Phra Thaew National Park they had told us that it would take maybe three hours of serious walking. But with two children in tow – Keeva pushing on ahead with Tess, Rory lagging behind with me, his glasses steaming up in the day's growing heat – we walked all the morning and we still had not reached our destination.

Rory paused to sit on a fallen tree. Up ahead I could see Tess and Keeva. Far more athletic than her brother would ever be, I saw my daughter jump on a trunk barring the path, strike an ironic ballerina pose for a moment and then she was gone. Ahead of her, Tess had disappeared from view, but now and then I could hear the *thwack-thwack* sound of the machete that Mr Botan had urged us to carry.

I looked at Rory with concern. It was too far to go back. All we could do was push on to the Bang Pae waterfall.

'You all right, kiddo?' I asked him.

He nodded and smiled. His face had that soft, squinty look that he always got when he removed his glasses.

'It's worth it,' he said, and looked around with satisfaction. 'There were elephants here once. And tigers. And rhinos. And Malayan sun bears.'

I watched something rustling in the thick undergrowth.

'And it's still quite busy,' I said.

Then we lifted our heads because we heard the sound of a gibbon singing – that haunting, owlish hooting – coming from somewhere up in the trees.

'Come on,' Rory said excitedly, putting on his glasses and jumping up. 'It can't be far now.'

The walk was steep, and it felt as if we were always climbing. The canopy of trees was perhaps sixty metres above our heads, and it was like a thick green roof, shutting out most of the sunlight. We had been told that the floor of the rainforest was clear, but in places there was dense growth underfoot, and there were times when the track – which we had been assured was always obvious – seemed to taper off into a thick green nowhere, containing hundreds of trees, all of them different.

But there was water close by. As Rory pushed on, making slow progress because I would not let him take the machete, I crouched beside a small stream that ran over rocks worn smooth and burnished the colour of old gold. I cupped cold water in my free hand and threw it on my face. Then I heard it again and it sounded more like a musical barking, sharp single notes, like a flute from another world.

The song of the gibbons.

And still we could not see them.

'They avoid humans,' Rory said, pausing to catch his breath. 'And I don't blame them.'

Something stirred close to our feet and I took his hand. Neither of us moved.

'Cobras are nocturnal,' he whispered. 'They don't harm humans unless threatened.'

'That's really comforting,' I hissed.

'The thing about cobras, the thing about cobras . . .'

He was babbling now. I gripped his hand tighter. Up ahead I heard Tess call his name and then mine. We did not reply. 'Females,' he said, then swallowed hard. 'Female cobras lay up to forty-five eggs in a clutch. They hunt birds, other snakes, toads and—'

A black creature stuck its snout out of the thick green bush and stared at us with its beady little eyes. I breathed out – it wasn't a cobra. It had a muzzle so long that it almost touched the ground, and a powerful body supported by strangely spindly legs. For a moment neither of us moved. And then it shot back into the dense undergrowth and was gone.

Rory grinned happily.

'Wild pig,' he said. 'I wonder if it was a male or female?'

'Let's not ask,' I said. 'Come on.'

We walked on and within minutes we heard the sound of the Bang Pae waterfall. We had crossed the rainforest. Tess and Keeva were waiting for us in a small clearing by the side of the fall.

'Look,' Tess said.

There was high wire mesh fencing among the trees. It was the first of the cages. But these cages at the top of the Bang Pae waterfall were so huge, so high – the very last stop before gibbons were returned to the wild – that they seemed to reach all the way to the canopy of trees and beyond, so that they did not seem man-made at all, but as if they were part of the rainforest.

We walked down the track that led to the gibbon rehabilitation centre and, standing outside one of the smaller cages, there was a young man holding a bottle of baby milk, looking up into the trees. He took off his baseball cap to wipe his face with the back of his hand, and I saw the familiar shock of white-blond hair.

'It's our friend,' Rory said.

He was right. It was our friend. I called his name and Jesse turned towards us, and I could see the changes. He was lean, fit, serious. He looked older.

'They let you back in?' Tess said.

He grinned with embarrassment.

'I wasn't blacklisted,' he said. 'So they let me back in.'

'You *work* here?' Rory said, looking from the bottle of baby milk to his face.

'It's temporary,' he said. 'Until I get a real job somewhere. But I get board. And I get to see my friend. And it's a good place. You know?'

'I know,' Rory said, and Tess put her arm around him.

'I want to do it a bit differently this time,' Jesse said, looking at me. He felt the temperature of the baby bottle and whistled up into the trees. 'You know what I mean? Do it right this time.'

I knew what he meant.

Then a skinny baby gibbon ambled out from under a small climbing frame. Its face was pink and hairless, shockingly human, and its fur a pale crop. Its wet black eyes were huge in its tiny head. It draped a hand over the lowest bar on the climbing frame but made no attempt to scale it.

'Come on,' Jesse said, waving the hand that wasn't holding the baby milk. 'Come on, you dozy little bugger! Climb! Climb!'

But the baby gibbon would not climb. Instead it swung on to the fence, its eyes on the bottle of milk. It glanced our way, then back at the milk, hopping a bit further up the cage and pushing its mouth through the mesh. Jesse held the teat to its mouth and it sucked on it hungrily. As he fed the gibbon, Jesse held one small paw between his thumb and his index finger, and he gently rubbed it as the baby gibbon suckled.

'So you're back, Jesse,' I said, really pleased to see him. 'You're back and you're here.'

Jesse smiled. 'I just volunteer here,' he said. 'But it's something I want to do. At least until the money runs out.'

'What are your duties?' Rory asked, as if volunteering was something he would like a crack at.

'I help the animal keepers preparing food and feeding. I talk to the tourists about our work here. I work in the gift shop. I sell T-shirts and souvenirs. I clean the cages. You want to feed her?'

Rory frowned. 'But aren't we supposed to limit human contact? So that they remember they are gibbons? So they don't need us?'

'Well, that's right,' Jesse said, suddenly blushing.

'I'll feed her,' Keeva said.

'No, best not to,' Tess said, putting her arms around her, and cutting off disappointment and further debate with a look.

'You can both help me with my chores,' Jesse said. He unfurled a hose and showed Rory and Keeva how to fill the water containers that were attached to the side of the cages.

'Where's Travis?' Rory said. 'Is he here? Is he back in the wild?'

Jesse didn't look at us.

'No,' he said. 'He's not back in the wild.'

'Where then?' Rory said.

'You'll see.'

We went to a higher cage, halfway up the Bang Pae waterfall. There were a few gibbons here, languidly swinging on climbing frames before disappearing into the trees, but I recognized Travis immediately – the soft brown fur with a snow-white trim around a jet-black face, and those unforgettable black eyes – round and moist and bottomless. He was sitting quietly, contemplating another gibbon. Smaller, golden and – I was guessing – female.

Rory gasped with excitement.

'Travis found a mate?' he said.

Jesse shook his head. 'He's still looking for a date,' he said.

We watched Travis watching the small, golden girl gibbon.

'What's her name?' Tess said.

'Paula,' Jesse said. 'Her background is very similar to Travis. Hunter killed her family when she was a baby.'

'Oh,' said my daughter, her hands flying to her mouth. 'Oh.'

'Sold her to some beach photographer down on Hat Patong,' Jesse said.

'I hate Hat Patong,' said Rory.

'The beach photographer was getting grief from the cops, so he sold her to a bar,' Jesse said. 'They gave her things to keep her awake, which didn't do her a lot of good.'

'But now they can mate,' Rory said. 'Now they can start a family and go back to the wild.'

'Well, that's the idea,' Jesse said. 'They're taken in. Remember to be a gibbon. Find a partner. Learn to be part of a family. And released, when they can survive in the forest.'

'He should sing to her,' Rory suggested. 'Travis should sing her a few songs so Paula will get to like him.'

Jesse looked pained, and I wondered what was coming.

'It doesn't work out for all of them,' Jesse said. 'There are three kinds of gibbons in here. Babies and juveniles who are learning to be gibbons. The ones who are looking for a partner so they can eventually be released – like our mate Travis here. And then there's the third kind, who can never be released because of some disability or illness – like Paula.'

'But Paula seems fine,' Rory protested.

Tess shot me a look.

'Look at Paula's front paws,' Jesse said.

And immediately we saw that her hands were mere stumps where the tops of her fingers had been chopped off.

'She was in the bar,' Jesse said. 'It was late. Some man decided that it would be funny to dance with her. She

210

scratched his face. So they chopped off her fingers. And now she can never go back to the wild.'

'What?' said Keeva. 'Never?'

But my son did not speak. Because he already understood. We were silent for a while, watching the darker, larger gibbon admiring the smaller, lighter gibbon, who completely ignored him.

Travis sang. He had a high, sweet singing voice with a trembling quaver in it, as if he was still getting the hang of the whole singing thing.

But the female gibbon looked away, unimpressed, and contemplated her mutilated hands, as if she knew that this would never work out.

'Gibbons need to be part of a family,' said Keeva, looking up at her mother. 'They're a bit like us.'

'No, darling,' said Tess. 'They're exactly like us.'

When the four of us walked into the half-built kitchen it was still early, but near the end of Sunday's daylight.

At one end of the bay the sky was inky black with cloud and night and at the other end the sky was streaming with pink and orange and red.

Then, as we collected our plates of fish curry from Mrs Botan and carried them down to the beach, real night suddenly fell, and all you could see out on the water were the parking lights that some of the longtails had, pulsing red or green in the sudden darkness, while further down the bow-shaped bay the lights of the restaurants and bars and massage shops all came on at once, a shining arc of white and gold.

Hat Nai Yang was bigger now, much bigger, with a strip of new small businesses at that far end of the beach. There was music drifting in the night, lots of music, mostly Thai pop songs but with the odd big Western hit, and all the different kinds of music bled into each other.

But there were still no jet skis and no hotels and no banana boats, I thought. Hat Nai Yang was open for business, but it was not open to the modern world.

We ate our fish curry in one of the two dining areas that I had built, the dusting of the Milky Way close enough to reach out and touch, and the feel of the new tropical hardwood and the memory of the long days spent working made Mrs Botan's fish curry taste even better.

Tess smiled. 'Looks good,' she said, and her face became serious as she touched the collection of cuts and welts on the palms of my hands. 'Oh, your poor hands,' she said, and the way she said it made me feel loved.

I grinned proudly and looked up at the restaurant, seeing the figures of Mrs Botan and Kai moving about in the roofless kitchen on the far side of the beach road. When you were eating at the Almost World Famous Seafood Grill, it felt as though it ended and began on the beach. But when you stopped and took it all in, from the kitchen and the bar on the far side of the beach road, to the tables that reached all the way to the edge of the sea, you could see that it was a big place that felt small. There was a lot to do.

Kai and Chatree seemed very happy living with the Botans, and although our neighbours were kind people – despite Mr Botan's prejudice against the *chao ley* – I suspected that the main reason they got along was because Kai and Chatree were both used to working.

There was a small catch of fish on ice outside the entrance, that gateway with no sides and no walls and no purpose other than to make you feel as if you had come to some special place, and to make you feel welcome, and the leafy arch of palm leaves was now covered in fairy lights, though they were dark tonight. There were also fairy lights in the trees, and there were more lights strewn across the roof of the shelters I had built, but none of them were turned on

212

because the Botans did not want to give the appearance that the place was already open.

But two young Swedes came up the beach, watching our family tuck into fish curry. A boy and a girl. They had both been recently patched up from a motorbike fall – the girl had one arm in a sling and the boy had lost a lot of skin on both arms – but this was such a common sight on our island that they did not look unusual.

'Family,' Mrs Botan told them, coming down to meet them, wiping her hands on a dishcloth. 'Only family tonight.'

The two young Swedes nodded and walked away and the girl reached out her good hand and the boy took it as they stared at the beach, and the bay, and the white gold lights that glittered in the soft warm night. They stared at Hat Nai Yang and I felt that I saw it through their eyes. The stillness, the beauty, the quiet untouched glory of the place. They breathed in the air, very deep and slow, really noticing it for the first time, and they were thinking that it seemed sweeter and cleaner and lighter than any air they had ever known.

That's what they were thinking.

And they were right.

Then suddenly they were all there. Mrs Botan with more food, grilled prawns the size of lobsters, the fat pink and white flesh and charred black shell, and Kai carrying a tray bearing plates and cutlery and the book she had been reading, and then Mr Botan sneaking a quick roll-up before he sat down, and finally Chatree bringing up the rear, his head completely covered by an old black crash helmet he must have found in the shed. He played it straight, sitting at the far end of the table by himself and reading a book through the helmet, elaborately turning his head as he enjoyed our laughter. And even Mr Botan had to laugh at the sight of a sea gypsy in a crash helmet.

A figure came out of the darkness, drawn by the scent of

fresh seafood, and I saw that dishevelled *farang* silhouette of baggy polo shirt and cargo shorts before I realized that it was Nick. Mrs Botan stood up and I expected her to say that it was family only tonight, but her husband said something to her in Thai and she greeted him with a small *wai*.

'Please,' she said, indicating the table where already we were reaching for the giant prawns, and we all shuffled down to let him sit. He found himself sitting next to Tess.

He smiled around the table, shaking his head with wonder at the food, and nodding at the books by Kai and Chatree's plates.

'So,' he said. 'How are the lessons going?'

Tess seemed to soften a little.

'These two like poetry,' she said, indicating Kai and Chatree. 'Much more than my two. I don't know. Maybe it's easier to learn a language when it rhymes.' She stood up and reached across the table and banged on Chatree's black crash helmet. 'You like a bit of poetry, don't you?' she said, and we all laughed.

Chatree whipped off his helmet.

'*Bobby Shafto's gone to sea*,' he chanted, reaching for a giant prawn. '*Silver buckles on his knee – he'll come back and marry me – Bonny Bobby Shafto!*'

He took a large bite of prawn and bowed gracefully, acknowledging the table's wild applause.

Nick was looking at Kai.

She was wearing one of Tess' T-shirts, too big for her, and it slipped off one shoulder and revealed her shoulder blade in the creamy moonlight before she pulled it back in place. She was smiling with shy feline grace, knowing it was her turn now.

'*And the sunlight clasps the earth*,' she said, very quietly, screwing up her eyes in memory. She stopped and looked at Tess. My wife nodded encouragement.

'It's good, Kai,' Tess said. 'You know it now.'

'*And the sunlight clasps the earth,*' Kai repeated. '*And the moonbeams kiss the sea – what are all these kissings worth – if you don't kiss me?*'

'That,' Nick said, and shook his head, words failing him. He had completely forgotten about the giant prawn in his hand. 'That's . . . that's . . . God.'

'That's Shelley,' Tess said briskly. 'As I say, they like poetry. What's that Roger McGough you like, Chatree? *Summer with Monika?*'

'*Ten milk bottles standing in the hall,*' Chatree laughed. '*Ten milk bottles up against the wall.*'

'Such a little Englishman,' Mrs Botan said.

But Nick was still looking at Kai.

'Wow,' he said. 'You know Shelley. 'Love's Philosophy', right? *What good are all these kissings . . .* I'm impressed.'

Kai gave a modest shake of her head and her hands flurried in denial.

'No,' she smiled. 'No, no, no. I don't know it at all. I only know the words.'

'Less talking,' Mr Botan said gruffly, reaching for the rapidly shrinking stack of giant prawns. 'More eating.'

But I was full.

So while the others kept eating I ran my hands over the table I had built, enjoying the way the wood felt both soft and strong, and I thought of Jesse up at Bang Pae with the gibbons, and how without a family to hold you to the ground you could not survive here for very long, and the hardwood was cool and smooth under the cuts on my hands as Tess watched the faces of Nick and Kai, looking at each other across the table, and smiling in the darkness.

25

I came out of the fish market pushing a stained wad of baht into my pocket, a huge plastic bag of ice held in my other arm, and I looked around for the dog, calling his name.

I was just about to give up when Mister trotted out of a massage joint on the other side of the road, surrounded by smiling middle-aged women, holding his ratty brown head high, and looking very pleased with himself.

'I'm not hanging about for you any more,' I said. 'If you keep wandering off, I'm not waiting for you, all right?'

He looked away, feigning indifference, or perhaps genuinely indifferent, settling down on the unmade beach road to give his testicles a good lick. But as I started back to the restaurant, holding the ice in both arms now, he sprang up and trotted along beside me. To our right the sun beat down on the glassy sea and the light was so bright that I had to look away.

The hot season was here and by now Hat Nai Yang was no longer just a beach. On the sea side there were restaurants and bars running all the way from the fish market to the shadow of our hill, and on the other side of the beach road there was a ramshackle strip of open-fronted shops advertising

216

elephant rides, boat trips to the islands, snorkelling, fishing, motorbike rental, car rental, longtail rides, money exchange, Muay Thai tickets and laundry – often all in one big glass window.

Even in the baking air of mid-afternoon, traffic was heavy; mostly bikes and scooters, but with the occasional rented jeep bumping slowly down the beach road, and I had to lift Mister up and put him on the pavement to keep him from walking in the road.

The dog was still half-wild. He came and went from our home at his leisure, relishing the attention and regular meals that he got with our family, but jealously guarding his independence. He was still a Thai beach dog, despite the smart collar and name-and-address tag that Rory and Keeva had proudly hung around his neck.

I watched him peel off and saunter into one of the new beachside bars.

Mister, I thought. What kind of dumb name is that for a dog?

But I stopped and waited for him, looking up as I heard the roar of engines in the sky. A big jet came out of the sun and seemed to fly in a flat line across the sea and then disappear into the trees north of the bay. I felt the bag of ice slick and cold against my chest and walked on, knowing that Mister would appear again when the mood took him.

There were motorbikes everywhere at our end of the beach because all of the seafront restaurants were open again, apart from the Almost World Famous Seafood Grill.

There were also children everywhere. They seemed to belong to no one and to everyone. Safety was gently administered. When someone – a waitress, a massage woman, one of the men who lounged by the ancient taxis – saw a toddler staggering too close to the stream of bikes and scooters in the road, they were tenderly shooed out of danger. The place teemed with life and yet I had never felt so safe. Despite all the changes, it was still a place of cool hearts and easy smiles. I brought the ice to Mrs Botan and watched her pour it into a large plastic box. Then she packed it with a dozen prawns the size of old-fashioned telephones. This is what we had kept back from our catch to feed us tonight.

'There are men outside,' she said.

'Men?'

I looked out at the beach. I could see Nick sitting alone at the nearest table, his straw hat pulled low over his face even though he was in the shade of the casuarinas and, in one of the open-sided shelters, there were dark figures hunched around the table.

'They think we are open,' she said. 'Because they see Nick eat. I tried to explain but my English is very bad.'

'There's nothing wrong with your English,' I said, putting my arm around her. 'I'll tell them.'

I walked out to the beach, exhaling with the heat, noting the three hired Harleys parked outside the palm-leaf entrance to the restaurant. Nick had the remains of a pair of giant prawns in front of him and a bottle of Singha in his hand. He did not look at me as I went past him. He was watching Kai clean the tables.

I walked up to the shelter. There were three of them. Bikers. I took in tattoos, goatees, and shaven heads. Muscles and beer guts. The island was full of men like that, but they usually stayed a lot further south.

'Three Singhas,' one of them told me, the accent southern English.

I laughed.

'Sorry, lads, we're not open yet,' I smiled. 'Come back soon and we'll be happy to serve you.'

They looked at me as if I was a liar. Pale blue eyes in a big pasty face turned towards me. There was something wrong with his face. He had a bristling red beard on his chin but nothing on his upper lip.

'What about him?' the man said, nodding in the vague direction of Nick. 'Because it looks like you're open for him.'

'He's family,' I said, and I wasn't smiling now, because it was no good smiling at them.

The man looked at his friends and laughed. 'He doesn't look like he's family,' he said.

'Just bring us three beers,' one of his companions said. He was smaller, nastier, every inch the bully's apprentice. 'Cold ones from the fridge.'

'The fridge hasn't been delivered yet,' I said, turning away. 'Come back when we're open.'

Nick was watching Kai as she placed steaming bowls of rice noodle soup before Rory and Keeva. I stood by his side, but all Nick saw was the girl.

'Do you know you've got your mouth open?' I said.

He tore his eyes away and blushed.

'I've never seen anyone like her,' he said, not to me but to the remains of his giant prawns. 'I've never met anyone like her. She's completely unspoilt. When she's around me, I feel like the sun has come out. And when she's not there, it's like – I don't know – some plug has been pulled.'

I looked at him for a while.

'Kai's a lovely girl,' I said. 'But would you feel the same way if you met her back home?'

He shot me a fierce look. 'Of course,' he said. 'What's that got to do with it?'

Everything, I thought. But I said nothing more.

A tall man came out of the shadows of the trees. Before I saw his face I recognized the baseball cap – the yellow badge on the green hat, the Chinese dragon in dark glasses. The Foreign Correspondents Club of Hong Kong, it said.

'The old place has come back to life,' James Miles smiled,

shaking my hand as he looked up and down Hat Nai Yang. 'Remarkable.'

The last time I had seen him had been when I built Tess the shelter on the beach. It felt like longer than a few months.

'This is Nick Kazan,' I said. 'He's a writer too.'

Miles shook Nick's hand and asked him a few polite questions about who he worked for, and how long he was staying. Nick's replies were equally polite, but vague and slightly defensive. When Miles said goodbye and walked off down the beach road, Nick watched him go with an amused expression on his face.

'Who's the spook?' he said.

I had no idea what he was talking about.

'That's James Miles,' I said. 'He helped me out when I got into some trouble. He's a travel writer. He writes – you know – guide books.'

Nick laughed. 'A travel writer? In jeans that have got creases? That would be a first. I bet he speaks the local lingo, right?'

I nodded.

'What books did he write?' he asked me, and I shrugged.

'Maybe he did knock out a couple of books,' Nick said. 'And maybe not. But I've met his type before. Run into them all over the world. Well-spoken Englishmen. Keeping an eye on British interests on foreign shores. Usually while drinking themselves to death – although not that one, by the look of him. The man's a spook if ever I saw one,' he said.

'A spook?' I said.

'He's British Intelligence, Tom,' Nick said. 'And you don't get a lot of that in Phuket, do you?'

I heard Keeva's voice and looked up to see her chasing Mister across the sand. The dog – who never cared for the way my daughter held him – scampered up the three steps and into the shelter where the bikers were still waiting to be served.

Keeva stopped dead at the bottom of the steps, looking up. There was a man at the top of the steps, holding our dog in his hands. He was the third biker, the one who had not spoken to me.

I saw a powerfully built man who had drunk a lot of beer, smiling at my daughter, her dog held high in just one of his giant hands. Heavily muscled arms poked out of his black vest, and a huge belly sagged over his khaki shorts. The dog's ears were pressed flat against its head in terror. I heard the sound of laughter, male laughter, coming from behind him. The man stood stroking the dog, holding it too tight, smiling down at my daughter.

I was moving towards them, walking as quickly as I could without running and then, just as I reached Keeva, the big man with the belly came slowly down the three steps and handed my daughter the dog. It fell to the sand and took off, and Keeva went after him.

There was more loud, dumb laughter from inside the shelter. The man went back to his friends. I went back to Nick and sat down with him, my hands shaking.

'You all right?' Nick said.

'I'm fine,' I said.

They will go away, I thought, they will get on their bikes and ride south, to the bars and the beer and the girls, because Hat Nai Yang will be too boring for them.

But they did not go away for a long time. We let them sit in the shelter, and we said nothing, and I said nothing even when I saw them putting their feet up on the table, even when I saw that they were smoking out there, and I knew there were no ash trays, and they would have to stub their dog ends out on the beautiful tropical hardwood.

'Are you all right?' Tess asked me, when she came with homework for Keeva and Rory, and I stood in the kitchen that now had a beautiful wooden roof, and I watched the men on the beach.

'I'm fine,' I said.

The trouble started when they were leaving. Just when I thought that they would ride back to the Bangla Road and we would never see them again. That's when the trouble started. Because they decided to take Kai with them.

Or maybe they were just pretending to take Kai with them. I don't know. It was hard to tell if it was a bad joke or a bad plan. It didn't matter.

Night was falling fast and they were heading towards the archway covered in unlit fairy lights when Kai came through, carrying a tray with her dinner on. Fish curry and steamed rice and an apple juice.

The small one, the bully's apprentice, took away her tray while the one I had seen holding Mister picked Kai up as if she weighed nothing and threw her over his shoulder. The third one – the great big barrel of lard and lager who had spoken to me first – laughed himself red in the face. Then all at once I was in front of the man holding the girl. He looked at my face and frowned.

'Come on,' I said, my throat tight. 'Put her down.'

He did not put her down.

He patted her butt thoughtfully.

'I don't think so,' he said. 'What are you going to do about it, little man?'

I would wait for him to speak again and then I would hit him as hard as I could in the mouth. I had resigned myself to a beating. Probably any one of them could have taken me. But I knew that I could do enough to get him to put Kai down and leave her alone. I was sure of that.

Then Nick was by my side.

'Now you bloody listen to me,' he said, and the short one, the bully's apprentice, kicked him full in the face.

It was the kind of kick that you only master after a lot of practice. He twisted the ball of his left foot into the sand and swung his right leg on a hinge that began at his hip, continued with his knee and ended at his ankle. I heard the sharp crack that a bone makes when it is breaking and Nick was down on his knees, the blood from his nose already flowing.

The big man put Kai down and it was only now that I saw she was crying, more from fury than fear, and in the same instant I saw that the Botans and Chatree had arrived from the kitchen and they were standing either side of me. Mr and Mrs Botan each had a carving knife in their hand. Chatree was looking at his sister and weeping with rage, and when he flew at them I caught his arm and would not let him go. I could hear Keeva and Rory quietly sobbing and that made me want to kill these men.

'Ah,' the big man said. 'There's plenty more where she came from. Come on, lads.'

They ambled out of the Almost World Famous Seafood Grill and got on their rented Harleys, their leering commentary drowned out by the sound of the bikes. They tore off and we stood there for a moment, not knowing what to do.

Then Kai and I took Nick up to the Botans' house and we sat him on the edge of the bath with his head held back, an entire kitchen roll in his hand. Tess came in and said that he should lean his head forward to clot the blood and he did as he was told. Kai sat beside him, one hand lightly resting on the back of his neck. I stood there watching my friend until my wife pulled me away. She pulled me out of the bathroom, out of the house and on to the balcony.

'Maybe I should take him to the hospital,' I said.

She kissed me hard on the mouth.

223

'Leave them,' Tess told me. 'Just leave them to it, all right?'

'But . . .' I said.

Then she kissed me again.

And so we left them.

Later, when Tess was sleeping in my arms, I touched the amulets that still hung from my neck as the night closed in around the two houses at the top of the green hill above Hat Nai Yang, and our little part of the island was silent apart from the constant buzzsaw of bikes on the highway, the sound of our breathing, and somewhere out there in the dreaming night, the lonely barking of a beach dog.

26

Nick and Kai were married the day we opened the Almost World Famous Seafood Grill.

The sun was just losing its heat when the bride and groom knelt on a pedestal with garlands around their necks, their hands pressed together in a gesture of prayer and connected with a small chain of flowers. Mrs Botan stepped forward holding a conch shell and poured water from the shell over their joined hands. I turned to Mr Botan for an explanation.

But it had been a long day, and a long wedding ceremony, beginning last night when nine shaven-headed monks in their saffron robes walked from the local *wat* down our dirt-track road to prepare Nick and Kai for the wedding – 'Asking blessing from the ancestors,' Mr Botan had told me at the time, with a bit more enthusiasm than he could work up now.

I smiled sympathetically at him, knowing he was getting tired of talking me through it all. A Thai wedding ceremony lasts longer than a lot of marriages back home.

'Happy ending story,' he said briskly, his old Chinese face nodding once, as if that was the end of the matter. I thanked him and turned to watch the young couple on their pedestal.

They kissed.

Nick and Kai became man and wife on Hat Nai Yang and they kissed. Or at least – Nick kissed, pressing his lips awkwardly on her face, partly on her mouth, partly on her cheek, and Kai squeezed her lips together in shy response, but did not quite touch his face.

And then she sniffed him.

Kai put her face close to her new husband's face and inhaled – briefly, deeply, softly, but unmistakably – and I did not need Mr Botan to explain this gesture of understated adoration. But he explained it anyway.

'*Hom kaem*,' said Mr Botan. 'Called *hom kaem*.' He was smiling again. We were all smiling now. Tess and Keeva and Rory. Mr and Mrs Botan. Chatree. The cousin and uncle who had come up from Ko Siray. The owners and chefs and waitresses and waiters from the neighbouring beachfront restaurants, and even a few of their early-evening diners. Nick's family and friends from Liverpool and London.

Nick kissed Kai and Kai sniffed Nick, as proud and bold as a war bride, and every single one of us saw it and smiled.

'Nice-smelling kiss,' Mr Botan said. 'Like animals. Sniffing the other animal.' He looked down at Rory and touched him gently on his back. 'Humans are just more animals, no?' he said.

'That's right,' Rory said, as though he had never doubted it.

Rory was wearing a silk smock jacket like the white one that the groom was wearing. Most of the men and boys at the wedding wore them. The jackets buttoned all the way up to the neck and had a high collar with little upright lapels. There was an Indian tailor on the Hat Nai Yang strip who had made a job lot for us. Peter Suit International, it was called, run by Mr Peter himself. Exclusive Ladies and Gents Custom Tailor, it said on his card. *Daman und Herren*

Masschneider Shraddare. We all got to choose our colour. Mine was green. Rory's was gold. Mr Botan's was red. I had no idea if this was correct form – if you could choose any random colour for your wedding jacket. But that is what we did. The only warning we had been given was that we could not choose black. 'No black at a Thai wedding,' said Mr Peter of Peter Suit International on Hat Nai Yang, his dark eyes flashing with amusement. 'Black is very bad luck for the Thai marriage.'

I reached Nick and Kai and took my turn pouring water on their clasped hands. Nick's hands looked huge next to those of his bride. I could not work out if her hands were really so small or if my friend had huge hands and I had just never noticed before. And he was so pale and she was so dark. And he was so tall and she was so small. Everything about them seemed totally different, apart from the joy in the smiles they wore.

It had been a hurricane of a courtship and there had been many moments in the weeks leading up to the wedding when I had doubted the wisdom of all this – but not now.

Today I felt nothing but happiness for the pair of them. There was no trace of cynicism or doubt inside me. They each seemed to be the missing half of the other. They fit together. It was as simple as that. Tess looked at me and smiled, and squeezed my arm as I stepped away from the pedestal, and I knew that she felt it too.

I had seen flashes of doubt on the faces of the wedding party during the long and various steps of the ceremony – nothing much, just the odd muttered comment, the quiet shaking of a head, the long cool look at the grinning Englishman and his Thai bride. But the misgivings and disbelief seemed to fade with the heat of the day.

The wedding guests were a mixed crowd. A few of Nick's

friends from London in their late twenties, most of them with partners, one or two toting small babies, and his divorced parents from Liverpool, both with their new spouses. All of them were reeling with jet lag and the heat. Then there was us – the Hat Nai Yang people, our family and the Botans, and of course Chatree, proudly carrying around Nick's camera, and taking charge of the endless photography of a Thai wedding ceremony, for it felt like every moment had to be captured. And finally there were two *chao ley* from Ko Siray – the cousin and the uncle, awkward and apart, as if working out what it could all possibly mean. Aside from the nine monks from the local *wat*, who had joined us for the wedding on the beach, improbable and exotic in their bright saffron robes, the two sea gypsies were the only local men who were not wearing one of the silk smock coats. They wore the sleeveless shirts and baggy trousers of the island's fishermen.

A police car stopped on the beach road and the cousin and uncle lowered their heads and spoke among themselves, watching it warily out of the corner of their eye. Sergeant Somter got out of the passenger seat and leaned over the open door, watching the wedding from behind his shades.

'You should go and talk to him,' Tess told me. 'I don't know if they cleared all the paperwork for today.'

I nodded. On Hat Nai Yang there was always a grey area between what we had permission to do and what we just did. I walked over to the police car as Nick and Kai posed for more photographs.

'Those *chao ley*,' Somter said, not looking at me. 'They are a long way north.'

He meant the cousin and the uncle, not Kai and Chatree. At least, that's what I think he meant.

'They're family,' I said.

'Family?' he said, almost smiling.

'The bride's side,' I said. 'Fishermen from down south. Why does everyone seem to hate them?'

He inhaled deeply.

'There was once bamboo all over these islands,' he said, looking around, as if remembering the bamboo. 'The *chao ley* cut it all down. All the bamboo in these islands – chopped down by *chao ley*.'

I had heard this one before. It was one of the reasons that the sea gypsies were considered second-class citizens, or not citizens at all.

'To make homes,' I said. 'The *chao ley* chopped down the bamboo so that they could build homes.'

And Sergeant Somter looked as though he had heard that answer before. He nodded, unimpressed.

'Home,' he said, turning his dark glasses in my direction. 'I told you to go home, didn't I?'

We looked at each other for a while.

'I went home,' I said quietly, and he laughed.

He took off his glasses and looked at me – really looked at me – for the first time today.

'No, you did not go home,' he said. 'And now it is too late for you to go home.'

'What's your problem with me?' I said.

'You do not take me seriously,' he said.

'I do take you seriously,' I said.

He held up a hand, and shook his head. He wasn't having it.

'The Westerners in Thailand do not take the law seriously. Not until the moment you are crying for your mother or your embassy or your lawyer.'

'Oh well,' I said.

He smiled grimly. 'One day I think you will take me seriously,' he said.

I kept my mouth shut. He got back into his car and nodded

to the driver. As he pulled away, I walked back to the wedding party.

'Is it all right?' Tess asked me, and I put my arm around her and kissed her cheek. Nothing was going to spoil today.

The ceremony was nearly over. The day was nearly done. The sun was sliding into the glassy sea. The timing was perfect. The candles shimmered and shone on the tables of the Almost World Famous Seafood Grill. We were ready to open.

There was a large plastic box packed with ice in the entrance to the restaurant. Mackerel, snapper, grouper, giant prawns and fish that I had never learned the names of. And, off to one side, in the misty water of a massive glass case, the lobsters moved in slow motion.

The bride and groom were posing for their final photographs just as the sun went down with its usual dramatic light show over Nai Yang bay, and on the horizon low clouds that looked like a distant mountain range were smeared with red and gold. I could smell the fresh fish being grilled and my mouth flooded with hunger as I released a breath that felt like it had been held forever.

Then from out to sea there was the rising whine of a fast, powerful engine, coming closer.

It was not a sound that we heard very often on our beach, where we were more used to the dignified diesel growl of the longtails. I looked up to see a speedboat curving around the bay, coming from the south, heading directly for Hat Nai Yang.

Chatree grinned at me and then back at the speedboat.

'*Poo-yai!*' he said, turning away from the bride and groom and rushing down to the water. '*Poo-yai!*'

As it got closer to the beach the engine was cut, and the speedboat drifted in between two longtails, the old boats of the fishermen bobbing in its wake.

There was a white man standing on the bow of the boat

in a black T-shirt and black jeans and I remembered the warning about not letting anyone wearing black approach the wedding party, and I thought it would be better if he could have landed further down the beach.

But it was too late now.

Bad luck, I thought, but then I remembered the laughter in the eyes of Mr Peter the Indian tailor when he had told me of the superstition, and I dismissed the thought. The boat was drifting towards Hat Nai Yang, with the last of the sunset directly behind the man in black, making the sky look as if it was on fire.

The man on the boat was Farren.

Chatree laughed happily.

'*Poo-yai!*' he said, and took a photograph.

I looked at Mr Botan to translate. He ignored me, watching the longtails rock in response to the speedboat, and one of them was his own.

'*Poo-yai!*' the boy said again, as Farren jumped off his boat and waded ashore and on to our beach. He walked past without looking at me, heading for the bride and groom.

Mr Botan's lips curled with distaste. At the end of a long day, he had finally run out of words. But he made one last effort.

'*Poo-yai,*' he said. 'Head of family. Big shot. Big man.' His old Chinese face gave away nothing. 'The boss,' he said.

I heard the sound of laughter and somewhere a switch was pulled, and the thousand fairy lights of the Almost World Famous Seafood Grill all came on at once. There was applause, more laughter, and the lights were all around.

Farren hopped on to the little pedestal and kissed the bride, and my fingers flew to the amulets around my neck.

Black at a Thai wedding, I thought.

What rotten luck.

PART FOUR

Song of the Gibbons

27

The real heat came in April and the old Royal Enfield kicked up clouds of pale yellow dust on the back roads of the island.

The heat was always there, of course, but the heat that came in April was the hard stuff – the air bone-dry and still, the trees unmoving, and as I rode towards Nai Yang village and home, the entire island seemed to shimmer in the haze.

At the sound of the approaching bike, a girl in her teens stepped into the road. She was grinning and holding a plastic orange saucepan of water. As I passed her, she threw it in my face.

I steadied the bike, water streaming down my visor and the girl in fits of giggles behind me. Then there was a young man with a blue plastic bowl ahead of me, waiting. I steeled myself for the inevitable and as I reached him he threw the contents of the blue plastic bowl at me. His aim was not as true as the girl with the orange saucepan and the water hit my chest and lap and bike. I looked down anxiously as I heard the elderly engine splutter and cough with shock. But I kept going, nodding and forcing a good-natured smile that I did not really feel. I was coming back from Phuket City with some parts for the bike, and people had been throwing water at me all the way.

Then, just as I was leaving the village, there was a pick-up truck rumbling behind me, the back full of young men and women. They all had buckets and they all emptied them over the head of the young man with the blue plastic bowl. He stood there, stunned and dripping.

And that did make me smile.

This was Songkran, the Buddhist festival of the Thai New Year. At the local *wat*, Buddha images were purified with water for good luck. Children poured fragrant holy water over the hands of their senior relatives. And everyone else had a water fight. They seemed to particularly like soaking a *farang* on a motorbike.

As I came out of Nai Yang village and started up the hill to home, my eyes were stung by a drifting cloud of thick black smoke. It was coming from the edge of the football pitch where the water buffalo grazed. Some of the villagers were burning piles of rubbish. It was the time of year when all that was old and dirty had to be burned.

The way Mr Botan translated it for me, Songkran meant change. The Thais loved to chuck around water to wash away old sins – it was where the national spirit of *sanuk* was at its most widespread – but the piles of garbage that were quietly burned were also part of the festival. If you took the unclean with you into the coming year, it would bring you bad luck. Everyone knew about the water, but there was also the black smoke of the small fires.

And that was Songkran too.

I had the bike up on my bench in the shed so that its name was at the same height as my face. I turned on the engine and let the bike warm up, thinning the oil and getting all the rubbish into the bottom of the crankshaft. The humidity of the island left condensation on the crankshaft, and there was a lot of crap in there.

I liked clean oil. I was no mechanic, but changing the oil was cheap and easy and always made me feel better. The bike liked it too. Nothing kept the old Royal Enfield running sweeter than fresh oil.

Outside there was the sound of laughter and shouting as the children chased each other through the trees with water pistols.

I let the engine run for five minutes, circling the bike, preparing my gear, careful not to touch the exhaust with my bare arms. It was getting hot now.

Keeva appeared in the doorway of the shed, toting a white plastic AK-47 water gun, her hair and T-shirt flattened with many soakings.

'Where's Mister?' she said.

I laughed. 'Probably hiding from you.'

She stayed in the doorway.

I turned off the bike. The oil was ready to drain now. 'Why don't you stay and help me, Keev?' I said. 'I'll show you how to change the oil on a motorbike.'

'Nah,' she said, waving her hand. 'I've got to find that dog.'

'Okay, kiddo.'

Then she was off and gone and I turned back to the bike.

I took off the drain plug with a spanner. Mrs Botan had given me a five-litre tin that had once held cooking oil and I drained the bike's oil into that. The oil was very hot from where I had warmed up the engine and although I tried to be careful some of it splashed on to the palm of my hand and left a darker stain where it burned my tanned skin.

When I had finished, the cooking oil tin was more than half full and I knew that was exactly how much oil I had to put back. I gave the Royal Enfield three litres of fresh oil and I turned on the bike. Then I stood back and watched it, rubbing at the burn on my skin with an old oily rag. The bike purred with contentment.

I felt someone in the doorway of the shed and I looked up, expecting to see one of my children in search of their dog. But the shadow was the shape of a man, and the man was Farren.

'Tom,' he said, and he came into the shed, and shook my hand, and my palm was slick with oil and still stinging with the burn. 'Let me look at you,' he said.

I was barefoot, stripped to the waist and wearing a baggy pair of green fisherman's trousers.

He laughed at me.

'You went native, didn't you?' he said.

I turned off the Royal Enfield.

He was groomed – shaved and clean and spruce, sprayed with something sweet that was out of place in my oily little shed. He only stopped smiling at me when I got my sore hand around his throat and banged him up against the wall. I pushed my face close to his face, shaking my head.

'You dropped me in it, didn't you?' I said.

I let him go almost immediately. I was afraid of the police. I was afraid what they might do to me and my family if I hurt him.

'That cop,' he said. 'Somter. He had me down as running a boiler room. I was never running a boiler room – you know that, don't you?'

'You sold property,' I said. 'And you sold land. Even though foreigners can't own land in Thailand.'

He snorted with impatience.

'There are ways around that,' he said.

'Yeah,' I said. 'The client gets his Thai girlfriend or Thai wife to put it in her name. Then one day – a week later – ten years later – she comes home and finds him in bed with

238

some other woman. But the land is still in her name. That always works quite well, right?'

He shook his head and laughed, as if I didn't get it, and I never would, as if it was all a bit too complicated for me to understand.

'Got a job for you,' he said. 'A real job.' He looked around the shed, smirked at the baggy trousers. 'Great days are coming,' he said. 'This area is so beautiful. The coastal forest. The empty beaches. The stillness of the place. I'm going to build a bar on Hat Nai Yang. A proper bar. Not one of these hole-in-the-wall joints.'

'You mean like the No Name Bar,' I said. 'That kind of proper bar?'

'The world is going to come to this place, Tom. I'm putting it on the map. This island is still the richest province in Thailand. The beaches up here are the most untouched on the island. There's real money to be made. And we can sell it without spoiling it.'

I touched the exhaust with the tips of my fingers. It was still hot.

'When we were in Phuket Provincial,' I said, 'someone told me that you would end up running a bar. I didn't believe him.'

'Who told you that?' he said. 'Miles? That burned-out old spook? That sad case – he lives with his boyfriend in Ko Surin – did you know that about him? He was in Bangkok and the Brits kicked him out because he couldn't keep his hands off the boys and the Kathoeys. James Miles was an *embarrassment* in Bangkok. He can speak the lingo – I'll give him that, the old fag. See, Tom, you don't know everything. Just because you've got yourself some fisherman's pants – it doesn't make an old hand.'

'But he was right,' I said. 'All the big talk and you wind up running a bar on a beach.'

The first flash of anger.

'That's just a start,' he said. 'A cash cow to get me on my feet. Don't you want a future? For yourself? For your family?'

'I want to stay out of jail,' I said. 'And I'm not looking for a job. I already have one.'

He nodded, his gaze drifting to the back wall where all of my tools were lined up. Bookended by two twenty-litre jerrycans – one for petrol, one for oil – there were tools for maintenance of the bike. Pressure gauge, feeler gauge, screwdrivers, spanners, ratchets, a socket set, an Allen wrench. Then there were my general tools for building that had been given to me by Mr Botan. A paint-stained old spirit level, second-hand saws dappled with rust, ancient hammers and chisels. And in pride of place, on the bench in front of the back wall, there was a glinting 127-piece toolkit in an aluminium case that Tess had bought me for Christmas. Slotted screwdriver, cross-point screwdriver, long-nose pliers, diagonal cutting pliers, combination pliers. I always left the lid of the aluminium case open and the tools displayed in their regimented lines because I thought it looked so beautiful.

Farren was grinning. He nodded at the case.

'And what's all this?' he said.

'My tools,' I said.

He laughed and shot a quick look at me, as if we had some secret understanding.

'Your tools,' he smiled, and the way that he said it made it seem ridiculous.

Then Tess was in the doorway, holding one of the water pistols.

'We don't want you here,' she told him.

'*Suk-san wan Songkran*,' he said. 'Happy Songkran day.'

'Just stay away from us,' she said.

He went off, still smiling.

I reached for her but she stepped away, shaking her head, and I could not touch her. Outside I could hear the laughter of the children.

'You bring so much trouble to this family,' she said, and my face flushed with shame. 'I know you don't mean to, Tom. But you do.'

Mr Peter of Peter Suit International was standing in the doorway of his shop, surveying the strip. Behind him, the half-made, hand-stitched business suits on the mannequins seemed to be dreaming of some other life in some northern country.

I pulled up next to him and he stepped forward, grinning at me, his white teeth shining in his smooth young face. Like many of the businesses on the strip, Mr Peter's shop was brightly lit but seemed to cast no light beyond its entrance. Take one step away from it and you were in the natural darkness of Hat Nai Yang, lit by nothing but the Milky Way and moonlight.

'Many people come now,' he said.

'Yes, they do,' I said, raising my voice above the throaty rumble of the traffic.

The traffic on the beach road was different now. Not just heavier, but different. In the days before the water came, when there was just a strip of seafood restaurants on the sand, there had always been a puttering procession of small bikes and scooters that went on past midnight. But now the bikes were bigger, and the faces of the riders were whiter, and when they got to one end of the Hat Nai Yang beach road, they turned around and came slowly back, as if they were looking for something.

'Now there are many opportunities,' Mr Peter said.

'Let's hope so.' I smiled.

Mr Peter rubbed his hands with glee, but behind him his shop was empty, and his bespoke tailoring ignored.

I pushed off for home, and there was a lizard on the wall of a massage shop where the women kneeled in front of their clients, digging their thumbs into the feet of travellers, and something about the light made the shadow of the lizard massive. In the past the women in the massage shop would call out a greeting to me, and perhaps offer me a cup of the ginger drink that they supped constantly, but they were very busy now and they did not notice me.

The music was different too. The various songs no longer bled into each other, that strange night soundtrack of Thai pop and sentimental ballads and big hits from the West. All of that was shouted down by the music coming from the big bar that was not even built yet but already open for business.

There was a long straight shaded bar on the beach, serving on both sides, and on the beach road in front of it were a line of bikes outside a door with no walls. There was a sign above the door that they must have found on the beach. THE LONG BAR, it said, and the writing was mine, because it was from the shelter where Tess had given out the bottles of fresh water.

I could hear someone on a microphone, and the laughter of the crowd, and I caught a glimpse of some kind of coronation. It was a girl in a string bikini on a plastic chair flanked by two more girls, all of them grinning with bashful pride.

'Miss Songkran,' said the voice, and there were cheers and more laughter.

I rode on, away from the strip, and in this part of the beach road, between the strip at the far end and the line of restaurants at the other, there was only the stars and the moonlight, a beautiful silvery-white light that seemed to wash over everything, and to touch and bless it all. The tall casuarinas were bright with moonlight, and the same silvery-white light splashed across the rough road, and dappled the black surface of the Andaman Sea, and lit up the dead beach dog in the middle of the road ahead.

He had been hit by a large bike. Other bikes had gone over him, before or after he died, and I remembered the respect that the Thais had shown to the dead beach dogs after the water came, and how they had been handled with care and gentleness, and I knew that I could not just leave the dog there. I stopped the bike and until the moment I reached out to pick him up, I did not realize that the dog was Mister.

I stepped back, almost crying out, and I sat down beside the road and just looked at him, knowing it was our dog now, wondering how I could have thought that it was any other. Then I heard some bikes driving fast in the distance, and I walked into the beach road and picked him up. He was a broken bag of fur and bones and dirt. He weighed next to nothing.

'Oh, Mister,' I said out loud. 'What kind of stupid name is that for a dog?'

I got back on the bike, cradling him in one arm, and I drove up the green hill to home very slowly, knowing that I had to deliver his body to the care and custody of my son and my daughter.

28

The longtail moved out of still water into the open sea and as the wind whipped our faces I wrapped my arms around Rory, still red-eyed and breathless from grief, while Tess sat behind us with Keeva and Chatree, the pair of them pale and silent, all five of us huddled in the centre of Mr Botan's longtail, lessons cancelled for a day of mourning.

I turned to look back at Hat Nai Yang.

Towards the south, on the right-hand side of the beach, our side, there was the line of seafood restaurants with their jumble of tables and chairs, apparently identical to each other apart from the little wooden huts I had built on the sand in front of the Almost World Famous Seafood Grill. Towards the north, to my left as I looked back at the beach, I could see the businesses of the strip, the dive shops and beachside bars and massage shops and motorbike rentals.

And separating the two ends of Hat Nai Yang, like the bridge between the past of the beach and its future, they were building The Long Bar.

It was a huge air hangar of a place, squatting across the beach road and Hat Nai Yang itself like some giant black toad. Even this early in the day I could see a few solitary foreigners nursing their Singha beers at a bar that ran around an empty stage. Young women who looked as though they had been wearing high heels for about a week tottered around them, stuffing fresh bar chits into the cup that sat before every man.

Then Keeva was on her feet.

'Look!' she cried.

There was a sea turtle by the side of the longtail, only a couple of feet below the surface.

It was huge, the shape of a giant teardrop, powered through the water by massive front flippers that looked more like wings than fins. Its mouth was a giant maw, set in a ferocious stern line, and the black eyes in its huge spotted head slanted down, making it look as if it was permanently squinting. I was so shocked by its sudden appearance that I did not notice it had no shell until Rory pointed it out.

'Leatherback!' he said, jumping up, and I held his arm as he shouted above the noise of the longtail's engine. 'See? Look, look – no bony shell on its back! Just his skin!'

His skin looked like the thickest leather coat in the world.

Rory sat back down, settling into my arms, while Keeva and Chatree leaned over the edge of the boat, laughing wildly, reaching out to touch the sea turtle. The old leatherback shot them a warning glance.

'Oh, no, no,' Rory said, wringing his hands. 'They have to come to the surface to breathe. If you frighten them then they will stay under water and might drown.' Mr Botan made a slight adjustment to the longtail's course and we edged away from the sea turtle. Rory smiled gratefully at Mr Botan and the old man nodded in acknowledgement. Then, as we watched, the leatherback dipped his head and, with what seemed like one smooth movement of flippers that were as big as a man, drove itself into the deep of the Andaman Sea, far away from Keeva and Chatree.

I looked at my son and, for the first time that day, Rory smiled.

The longtail passed the curve in the bay and Hat Mai Khao lay spread out before us, an endless expanse of un-developed, untouched empty white sand, and the giant white beach at the end of our island looked like the beach at the end of the world.

The huts were set back from Hat Mai Khao, making the most of the shade and invisible from the sea, but the longtail knew where it was going, and Mr Botan glided to a halt towards the northern tip of the beach, where the casuarina trees gave way to thick mangroves. As we approached land there were fishing nets ahead of us, and Mr Botan lifted the engine from the water so that we could clear them. Suspended by the corroded metal pole, the blackened diesel engine was like an anti-aircraft gun from some rusting planet, and Mr Botan covered it with stripy tarpaulin and then heaved an anchor into the water that looked as though it had once been owned by Long John Silver.

Chatree slipped over the side, weighting the anchor further with stones that were stored on the deck. We splashed ashore and the sand was so hot that we ran for the trees, crying out with appalled laughter.

Chatree burst into his sister's home and we followed him. The beach huts at Hat Mai Khao only had two rooms, a living room and a bedroom, and the sound of raised voices came from the other room. I had never heard Kai angry before.

'*Kliat maak!*' she screamed. '*Moh hoh khun!*'

Mr Botan grunted to himself, shaking his head as if this was just what he knew would happen, and headed back to his boat without a word. The door opened and Nick came out.

'She hates it,' he said. 'I make her angry.'

Kai followed him into the room, fighting back the tears. 'Yes,' she said. 'Yes.'

'Go and play outside,' Tess said. 'The three of you.'

'But we came to see Nick and Kai,' Keeva said.

I tried to silence her with a look, the way that her mother could, and it just about worked. The three children went outside and soon I could hear their subdued voices talking to each other under the trees. I looked at Tess, wondering if we should just leave too.

'It's amazing how poor you can be when you have a cheap life,' Nick said, scratching his head. He looked awful. Pale, puffy, as though he had just got up. I could smell the wine on him. And then someone else came out of the other room, the cousin from Ko Siray, and he flopped into an old rattan chair, surveying the proceedings with his wary eyes. He looked at me and then away.

'Sorry,' I said. 'It's a bad time.'

'Him? He's always hanging around,' Nick said. 'You marry a Thai girl and you marry her family. They are very fond of me, though. They say that I am the nicest cashpoint machine they have ever met.'

Kai laughed bitterly at that. 'Tap, tap, tap,' she said, gesturing at the laptop glowing on the coffee table. 'Tap, tap, tap, all day long. And still no money in this machine.'

'My angel, you do not understand the vagaries of the freelance existence, I'm afraid,' Nick said. He looked at me. 'I'm trying to sell a story about the Chinese quarter of Phuket City. Have you seen it? Fascinating place. The Chinese came over to mine tin and some of them stayed to build houses of incredible beauty.'

'I've seen it,' I said, remembering when Mr Botan had taken me there. It was not even a Chinatown. It was too small for that. Just a few Chinese streets in Phuket City, a reminder of the thousands of Chinese who had come to the island to sweat in the tin mines. It was a beautiful old neighbourhood and Mr Botan and I had drunk coffee there once when we were buying equipment for the kitchen of the Almost World Famous Seafood Grill. But even I could see that it would be hard to sell a story about it to the outside world.

Tess touched my arm, not even needing to look at me.

'Nick,' I said. 'We're going to go.'

Kai wiped her eyes. 'Sorry,' she said, too ashamed to look at us. 'Oh, so sorry.' There was a corner of the room with a sink and she began to fuss with a kettle and a couple of chipped cups.

'It's fine, Kai,' Tess said, quickly embracing her, and placing a kiss on the gold streak in her hair. 'But we're just going to go.'

I gave her a squeeze and the cousin looked at me as if he wanted to cut my throat.

Nick and Kai looked at each other then, and it was as if there was nobody else in the room. I could hear the children outside, their voices louder now.

'*Chan rak khun ja dai,*' Nick said quietly, and she came to his arms and he held her. '*Chan rak khun ja dai,*' he repeated.

The cousin got up and went into the bedroom. Tess was looking from the doorway.

'Yes,' I said. 'You don't stop caring about each other because of money. Tell your wife you love her.'

'*Chan rak khun ja dai,*' Nick said. 'It means more than that.'

And I thought to myself – But what could mean more than that?

I took a deep breath and left, only to find there was chaos on the beach. Keeva was screaming, Rory was crying and, standing up in the middle of his longtail, Mr Botan was shouting angrily in Thai.

248

Tess ran down to where the sand met the sea, and began to jog along the shore, trying to keep up with the two locked figures out in the shallow water, who plunged below the surface and then rose to gasp for air, and then plunged once more below the water, as Chatree clung to the blunt, splotchy head of the leatherback sea turtle that fought so hard to throw him off.

It had been a long day, and not the day that any of us had wanted, so when we walked between the two waterfalls we did so in silence, all alone with our own thoughts, not even really looking at each other until we paused, and heard the song of the gibbons.

In the high rainforest above the Bang Pae waterfall, you could hear the gibbons long before you ever saw them.

We stepped on to the trail that led down to the waterfall, listening to their songs, and Rory's face lit up with happiness.

'Listen,' he smiled, as the strange music drifted through the canopy of trees. He lifted his head and his spectacles were covered in a thin film of mist.

Ahead of us, Keeva slashed impatiently at the under-growth with a machete. 'Let's just get down there,' she said, mopping her face with the back of her hand. The five of us were limp with the heat, our T-shirts clinging with sweat.

'Just listen,' Rory said. 'That's him. That's Travis.'

I knew what he meant. In the strange symphony of the gibbons, that hooting music that sounds like owls pretending to be penny whistles, or penny whistles pretending to be owls, one call seemed to stand out. The song was high and sweet with an almost comical trembling note in it.

'Maybe,' said Chatree. 'Maybe not.'

'No, that's him,' said Rory, and we continued down the trail, past the Bang Pae waterfall, completely deserted in the middle of the hot season, and the first of the giant cages rose up before us. This was the halfway house, the cage between rehab and the rainforest.

Rory was right. The trembling warble belonged to Travis. He swung across between the trees with an effortless grace, his long arms seeming to have all the time in the world as they reached out for the next branch.

Below him, Jesse busied himself filling the water supply with a hose. But apart from Jesse, the big cage was empty. We stood with our faces pressed up against the wire mesh.

'Where's his friend?' Rory called. 'Where's Paula?'

Jesse continued to fill the water container.

'Paula didn't make it,' he said.

I watched the smile fade from Rory's face.

'She didn't make it?' Rory said.

Jesse turned off the hose and came across to us. Above us the gibbon continued to make his way through the trees at the top of the cage, and then, when he reached the limit of his freedom, he would turn round and come back, and all the while he sang in the high, wobbling vibrato that was his singing voice, and now I thought that it sounded as though there was something in it that I had not noticed before.

Jesse looked at Rory, and addressed him alone.

'I came into the cage last week and Paula was dead,' Jesse said.

Rory shook his head. It wasn't that he was sad. It just didn't make any sense.

'But these white-handed gibbons – they live until they're thirty or forty,' he said. 'Paula was – what? Six? Seven?'

'Paula died young, okay?' Jesse said. He looked at Tess and me. 'Hepatitis B,' he said.

'Hepatitis B?' Rory said.

'It's a disease that humans get,' I said.

Keeva and Chatree wandered further down the trail to where there were more gibbons.

'I don't understand,' Rory said, looking up at Tess.

'Do you want me to explain it to him?' Jesse said.

I shook my head, crouching down so that I was the same height as my son. He was soaking wet from the walk between the waterfalls and now he took off his glasses and polished them furiously.

'They probably gave Paula things in the bar,' I said. 'Drugs. To keep her awake or to keep her quiet. And they must have used a bad needle. A dirty needle to give her the drugs.'

My son nodded and put on his glasses. 'Okay,' he said. 'Okay.'

He was beyond crying.

Above us Travis crashed hard into the wire mesh and pressed his face against it, and for the first time he looked as though he was in a prison and he kept on singing his broken song, and now I saw that it was a song of loss and grief.

He was singing to someone he would never see again, a young female gibbon who had the tips of her fingers chopped off for scratching the face of a drunk tourist.

'I'm sorry, kid,' Jesse said to Rory.

'You should be fucking sorry,' my son said.

Tess grabbed his wrist and pulled it hard.

'Hey!' I told him. 'Watch your mouth, young man!'

Travis went to Jesse then.

The gibbon dropped from the wire mesh and hopped up into Jesse's arms, burying his face into a T-shirt that said, WE ARE WILD – DO NOT PET US. Travis drooped one of his long arms around Jesse's neck. The sight seemed to sicken my son to his stomach.

'How many gibbons do they have to kill before they can capture one?' Rory said. 'They shoot the mother in the tree

251

and she falls holding her baby. Most of the babies die in the fall. But not all of them. And the rest of the family try to protect the baby that survives, and so the poachers have to kill them too.' He swallowed hard, his eyes not leaving Travis resting his head against Jesse's chest. 'And the really sad thing is – the saddest thing of all – is that they think whatever human bastard takes them in is their family.'

'I'm sorry,' Jesse said.

'They love us and we kill them,' my son said. 'That's the saddest thing of all.'

Travis took to the trees.

'I want to show you some new arrivals,' Jesse said.

'I'm not interested,' Rory said. 'I'm going to sit by the waterfall.' He glanced at Tess through his steamed-up glasses. 'Come and get me when you're ready to go home,' our son said.

We let him go and walked down the trail with Jesse to where Keeva and Chatree were watching a mother suckling her baby. The mother was dark brown with a white, heart-shaped trim around her face, and the baby had hair so short that it looked as though it had been cropped, and a face that was hairless and bright pink.

'If we walk a bit further down,' Jesse said, 'we've got some young ones who arrived this week.'

I nodded at the dark-brown gibbon with her pink-faced baby.

'What's the story here?' I asked.

Jesse shook his head.

'The father of the baby was another one who didn't make it,' he said. 'He was kept in a bird cage as a baby. When he started growing, they still kept him in the birdcage. So his arms grew bent backwards. Even if he had lived, he would never have been released into the wild.'

'So who does she sing to?' Tess said.

Jesse looked at the mother with her baby.

'She doesn't sing to anyone,' he said.

We walked down our road as the pale light of sunset became the cool shadows of twilight.

There was a police car outside our front door and a middle-aged woman I did not recognize sitting on our veranda.

As we approached our home the woman came forward and began speaking angrily to Chatree in Thai. He froze on the spot, paralysed in the presence of authority.

'What's going on?' Tess asked the woman, but there was no reason on earth why she should speak English. The door of the police car opened and Sergeant Somter got out. He leaned against the top of the passenger door and looked at me. The woman was still talking, still very angry, but Somter made it easy for us.

'This *chao ley* child should be in school,' he said, and he looked at Tess. 'She says – a real school.'

'We have schools,' the woman said, breaking into sudden English.

'I know,' Tess said. 'Of course you have schools.' My wife looked down at our dirt-track road. 'Sorry.'

29

Chatree stood awkwardly on next door's veranda as Tess did up his top button. He was dressed in the uniform of the local school children – white polo shirt, dark shorts, white socks and black leather shoes. Neat, clean, old-fashioned. He looked at us and then looked away, grinning with embarrassment.

We stood watching him, the children and Mrs Botan and me, as Tess tried to smooth down his shock of black hair with its golden streak. But it refused to be smoothed and so she pointed him in the direction of the outside world and gave him a gentle shove. Mr Botan appeared in the doorway and murmured something gruffly in Thai. The boy responded with a short affirmative and headed off down the lane. He did not look back.

My family fell into step beside him.

Chatree walked with the heavy steps of a prisoner making his way to the gallows. He was to get a ride to school at the end of our lane, where it met the road down to the village. We waited in silence until a Songthaew appeared, the two rows on the open-sided truck already full of school children. They stared at Chatree with open curiosity as he climbed on

254

board. He did not look at us as the bus pulled away in a cloud of dust.

'He looks a bit different,' Keeva said.

'He is a bit different,' Tess said. 'It's his first day at school.'

The children ran on ahead and it was only then that Tess let her eyes sting with tears.

'He'll be all right,' I laughed. 'Look at the size of him.'

'Not him,' she said, nodding towards our son and daughter as they disappeared into our house. 'Those two.'

We stopped. 'They're fine,' I said.

She shook her head.

'No,' she said. 'They're great kids. But Keeva's half-wild and Rory has a head full of animals.'

'They're smart, kind, funny,' I said. 'And you do a great job with them.'

'I'm at my limit,' she said. 'I'm at my limit with them, Tom. The island is the best place in the world for a nine-year-old. I believe that with all my heart. But they're getting older. And so are we. So are we, Tom.'

'What are you talking about?' I said.

But I knew exactly what Tess was talking about. She was talking about home.

I hung my head and I felt my throat close tight with misery. The sun was on my face as I thought of the life we had left behind and the life we would be losing.

'It would be better this time,' Tess said.

I shook my head. 'No,' I said. 'It would be the same. It would be the bloody same, Tess.'

'It would be better,' she insisted, and she took my hands and she ran her fingertips over the cracked wounds. 'And we wouldn't be going back for us,' she said. 'We would be doing it for the children.'

Then she took my ugly hands and she placed them against the thin cotton of her T-shirt, where it hung flat against her belly, and she guided my hands to make that gesture, that three-part gesture that she had made ten years ago, up and down and up again, a movement that covered a few inches, and a life.

'Tess,' I said, understanding at last.

A child, I thought. Another child! Our child . . .

Already I longed to hold that little bundle in my arms and to know again that feeling like no other, that feeling of limitless and unconditional love. Our baby. I had never dreamed that I could be so blessed.

But even in that moment when I was almost drunk with happiness, I thought of going home, and England, and starting over, and it was a weight that I could hardly carry.

I thought of the mountains that I would have to climb, the daily Everests that I would have to get up and over just to survive, just to put food on the table and a roof above our heads. For a moment – one shameful, terrifying moment – I did not know if I could do it.

But then I looked into her face, the undeniable and beautiful reality of her, my wife, my Tess, and she filled me up, that is the only way I know how to describe it – *she filled me up* – and I knew that in the end I would always gladly go where she wanted to be, and then I would climb any mountains they put in front of me, because my home would always be wherever this woman called home.

She laughed and smiled and gently removed my hands from her belly and the tiny life inside her, this little life we had made, shaking her head as she looked at the wounds, fresh and old, that scored my palms, my fingers, my cracked broken nails.

'Your hands,' she said.

When the day's heat was dying the four of us walked along the beach where the warm water touched the white-gold sand and we saw the green hill of Nai Yang start to grow a darker shade of green above the bay, and the shadows of the hundred-year-old trees reached out across the sand, as if stretching with weariness at the end of another long, hot day.

In the hot season, nothing moved if it could help it. I had never seen the sea so totally clear and peaceful. It could have been a mirror made of gold-flecked glass, and the longtails that were moored along Hat Nai Yang were as still as statues.

Far ahead of us, where the bay began to curve, a lone figure rose from a table at the front of The Long Bar and came towards us. It was still a shock to see how big and brash the strip had become, and Farren's bar rose black and silent behind him, still waiting for the night. The man's skin was pale, almost white, and even this late in the afternoon he wore a baseball cap pulled low over his face to shield him from the unforgiving sun. But when he got closer I recognized the T-shirt.

WE ARE WILD, it said. DO NOT PET US.

'I want to show you something,' Jesse said to Rory. 'Near the Ton Sai waterfall.'

'I don't want to see it,' Rory said.

Jesse looked at Tess. She smiled at our son.

'Let's go,' she said, taking his hand.

And so we went.

The waterfall was a trickle now.

We followed it uphill over slick wet stones at the start of the Khao Phra Thaew National Park, where the ground rose steeply until the real rainforest began. Then all at once we were in a green world where the trees were suddenly rising, and the light of the day was gone, hidden by the thick canopy above us. Jesse led the way, but he had to stop every few minutes to find the trail that weaved in and out of thick undergrowth.

Then we were going downhill, an easier trek but more dangerous, with the ground falling away sharply to one side. The trail took us to a small wooden bridge and Jesse stopped to get his bearings. He seemed suddenly uncertain of himself, looking for something that there was no sign of, waiting for a sound that never came.

We all heard it at once.

The calling of a solitary gibbon. From somewhere high in the rainforest. I had heard their songs many times by now, but that strange hooting music had never sounded so haunting. This was the sound of a gibbon in the wild and it made me shiver.

Then there was another, responding call, much further away, so that it sounded like a train whistle heard in the middle of the night, and there were more of them, up the hill ahead of us and to the right of the trail. Jesse was off and moving as fast as he could, and we hurried to keep up, climbing again, sometimes bending to avoid the branches that crept low across the trail, sometimes using them for support, sometimes climbing over the fallen trees that blocked our path. And the only sound was our voices – Careful here – Watch your face on that branch – It's slippery here – and the ghostly symphony high in the trees.

Jesse stopped. He looked back at us and smiled. He held out his hand to Rory. My son hesitated for a moment and then came forward, taking his hand. Jesse's smile grew wider and he nodded to a clearing in the undergrowth.

It was the dark brown gibbon with the trim of white fur around her face. She turned to monitor some noise high in the trees and we saw the baby in her arms. It was no longer the crop-haired little foetus that we had seen at Bang Pae. Already the fur was growing, to the same deep brown as its mother, and the pink old-man face that we had seen was much darker, though not yet the jet black of the mother. The short fur on the baby's arms made its limbs seem impossibly long and bony.

There was a trembling hoot close by, and suddenly Travis was with them, ambling across the clearing to mother and child and then stopping to have a relaxed look round.

'They get up at first light,' Jesse whispered. 'The female leads the family to some fruit trees for feeding. Then they listen to some singing. Then they respond to the singing. After that, they groom and rest for a bit. They like the rain – they like playing in the rain. It really makes them happy. There are some other families nearby, and Travis stares at the other males on the edge of their boundary. The males chase each other while the females and the babies hang back. Then they feed again, go for a swing through the rainforest and turn in early. The baby sleeps with the mother, and Travis sleeps nearby but alone.'

'Yes,' said my son. 'That's what they do.'

We watched them until the light was gone.

Once, just before they left us, Travis – although of course that was not his name – stole a shy glance in our direction and then looked quickly away, as if he knew us but could not quite place us, like a good friend from some other lifetime.

Mr Botan was coughing hard, despite the fact that the cigarette in his hand was unlit. His old Chinese face creased with discomfort.

'I am old,' he said, nodding at me, and then Tess. 'I am old and I will be gone.'

I laughed at him.

'I reckon you're good for a while yet,' I said, and I looked around the restaurant. The Almost World Famous Seafood

Grill was packed. The far end of the beach road, the new businesses thrown up on the strip, were all busy, but somehow that just seemed to increase our custom. For the first time ever, Hat Nai Yang was a place that foreigners came to.

'But there's no *tables*,' Keeva said.

'Come,' Mrs Botan said, and Tess and the kids started following her towards the kitchen. But Mr Botan held my arm.

'One day,' he said, holding my gaze. 'It's true. One day I will be gone.'

I wasn't laughing now. 'You're fine,' I said.

It had been a long time since there had been anyone resembling a parent in my life. I did not want to be reminded that they always left you in the end.

'Getting too much,' he said. 'All of it. The fishing. The business. You see how long it takes me to get my old body in the longtail. What kind of fisherman can't get in his own boat?'

'Mr Botan,' I said. 'We all get old.'

He nodded. 'Already – your children – so big,' he smiled. 'They were like little children when you came.'

'It goes fast,' I said. 'Time passing. And nothing measures it like your children.'

I thought of the third child, the unknown child, the baby growing inside my wife, and I thought of the years ahead, and how it takes so long for them to grow up, although at the same time it all goes so fast, and the only thing that I could think of, the only thing that I wanted in the world at that moment, was to live long enough to see that unborn, unnamed child fully grown.

'We want you to have it all,' Mr Botan said. 'My wife and I. There is not much – this restaurant, the boat. But when I can't work any more, we want you to have it. The house – we keep the house, and when we are both gone that goes to my son in Bangkok. But not the business. That is for you.'

'Mr Botan,' I said, and in his gruff old face I saw such beauty and kindness that for a moment I could not speak. 'I don't know what to say.'

'We will make it legal,' he said. 'All in writing. No problem. Never any problem.'

'You honour me greatly,' I said.

'You know many things,' he said, and his face lit up with humour. 'Although not how to hit a nail without first hitting your hands.'

'Nobody was ever so kind to my family,' I said, choking on the truth of it. 'Nobody was ever so generous to me. Thank you.'

He smiled, and the sight of it pulled my heart, and I thought that I would wait a while before I told him. But there was no good in waiting.

'We're thinking about going back,' I said in a rush. 'Going back to England. There is another baby. The children need proper schools. There's . . .'

There were a million tiny reasons, I suppose, but none of them sounded like enough to refuse his offer. He frowned under the fairy lights, turning away.

'Big shot,' he said. 'Just like my son. The big shot does not want to do simple work.'

'It's not that,' I said. 'You know it's not that. Thank you—'

'Big shot!'

It ripped at my heart to refuse his great kind gift, which was everything in the world that he had to give, although I could do nothing else. The best part of me would always be with him, and out on the longtail, and in the small house on top of the green hill, and in the restaurant on the beach, and I would remember his face and his kindness on my dying day, but I did not have the words to explain any of this or to make him understand. All he knew was that we were leaving soon. I wished that I could tell him that he had been more of a father to me than any man I ever knew. I would somehow find the words.

But he had turned away, and it was too late, and he was heading for the kitchen where my family were gathered around a small table helping themselves to an enormous plate of lobster noodles. Mrs Botan looked over at me, smiling, but then she saw her husband's face as he shook his head, just once, and her smile faded, like that sweet imagined future that I, too, had wanted to believe in.

I loved the old man but I was not his son and he was not my father and all the wishing in the world would make no difference.

Nick was celebrating. From the way he was walking down the beach road, he looked as if he had been celebrating for quite a while.

He came into the Almost World Famous Seafood Grill, raising his hand in salute and somehow got his arm entangled in the fairy lights that adorned the entrance. It took a few minutes to fish him out.

Flushed and grinning with embarrassment, he staggered between the crowded tables to where I sat with my family at the edge of the sea, brandishing the newspaper he carried.

'Rejoice,' he said. 'Rejoice.'

Then he saw the children and placed a theatrical finger to his lips. Rory was asleep with his head on his arms, while Keeva was drowsily spooning noodles into her mouth, her eyes almost closed.

'They're beat,' I said. 'But you look happy.'

He sat down and spread the newspaper on the table.

'They printed it,' he said. 'My piece on the Chinese Old Town. Look.'

It was the newspaper he had worked for in London, open towards the back, at the travel section. There was a photo of the walled garden at the China Inn Café on Thanon Thalang and an article spread over two pages, with his name on it. In the picture an attractive young couple were smiling at each other over a shared Thai salad. I looked at the date at the top. The paper was almost a week old now.

'Congratulations,' I said, and I started reading the piece.

'They chopped it down,' he said, somewhere between angry and apologetic. 'There was a lot more history in there. About how the Chinese came to the island and worked the tin mines.' He shook his head. 'How they built Taoist temples even as they were converting to Buddhism.' His face looked stressed and sweaty under the fairy lights. 'They even cut my line about the Shrine of Serene Light.'

'You got your story printed,' Tess said. 'That's the main thing.'

He brightened. 'Yeah,' he said. 'I did, didn't I?'

Keeva placed her fork on her noodles and slid sideways into my arms. She was almost asleep.

'Let's have a drink,' he grinned.

I only hesitated for a moment. 'Sure,' I said. 'Let's have one to celebrate.' I looked at the travel story before me. 'How much they pay you for something like this, Nick?'

He didn't hear me, or he didn't want to think about it, because he waved his hand in the air to attract attention and a waiter I did not recognize came over.

'Two Singha,' Nick told him. 'What was the question?' he said.

'Kai not here tonight?' I said.

'Ah,' he said. 'My wife got a job at the other place.' Halfway down Hat Nai Yang, where the strip exploded into light, we could hear ten-year-old Western music booming from The Long Bar. 'That's where I want to have a drink,' he said.

From somewhere deep inside the Almost World Famous Seafood Grill, someone turned off the fairy lights.

The strip was still busy at this end.

The beach road was a noisy procession of bikes and scooters, with the odd taxi carefully inching along, and crowds of *farang* moving between the darkness of the road and the brightness of the shops.

Mr Peter was inside the dazzling interior of Peter Suit International, showing a man in shorts and a singlet that said *Suck My Deck* a swatch of pin-striped grey flannel, while his girlfriend took a seat and frowned at her mosquito bites. The middle-aged women in the massage shop were kneeling before a line of reclining customers and in the middle of the strip, one of Bon Jovi's greatest hits was coming from The Long Bar. The first person I saw inside was Farren.

He stood alone at a table, a huge chunk of ice in a champagne bucket before him as he hacked and stabbed and struck at the ice with a vicious-looking ice pick. I guessed that the ice had come from the fish market next door and wondered if this was the first time their ice had ever been used for something other than cooling fish. He didn't stop working on his chunk of ice when he saw us.

'This is a courtesy to you,' he told me. 'Because we're friends. Your pal was here earlier, embarrassing himself. Did he tell you that?'

I looked at Nick and he laughed and shook his head. He gripped my arms briefly and set off towards the bar.

'Get him out of here before someone gets hurt,' Farren said.

As Nick fought his way to the bar, I looked at Farren's

place. Bars in Asia must have looked like this for fifty years, bars that were originally designed to separate American GIs and British sailors from their pay packet. The business model still held, even after all those American GIs and British sailors had died of old age. The Long Bar was gripped by a fever and it was the fever of shore leave. It had the sweaty urgency of R and R. Good times, with the time running out. There were men, beer and girls everywhere. It resembled a bar like the No Name that you might have found on the Bangla Road, but it was bigger, because we were so far north, and because land was cheap up here. There was a long, oval-shaped bar around a central stage. Behind it, four Thai bartenders, two men and two women, struggled to keep up with the orders.

Every one of the bar stools was occupied by a foreign man, and most of them had a local girl or two hanging from their arms like human bracelets. There were more girls on stage, swaying with a kind of absent-minded lethargy to the music, and pausing now and then to adjust their pants in the wall mirror, or to check their mobile phones, or to chat with their friends. Mostly they just swayed and stared into the distance, their mind anywhere but here.

At the back of the bar it opened out on to the beach, so that you could not really tell where the bar ended and Hat Nai Yang began. In the gloom, away from the stage, there were more high tables and bar stools, and they all had the men and the girls and the cup sitting among the drinks where bar bills were stuffed by the waitresses. I could not see Nick. And I could not see Kai. But I knew she must be a waitress, and my eyes went to them, looking for one with a golden streak in her hair.

In a place full of people wearing few clothes, in a place so full of naked flesh – the tiny brown-skinned girls dressed for the beach or bed, the larger, paler men with their bare white legs and fleshy, tattooed arms – the waitresses looked almost demure. They wore a sort of parody of a male evening dress – black bow tie, white shirt, short black jacket. It looked like the work of Peter Suit International. They did not wear high heels. The waitresses all wore flat shoes so that they could move quickly.

Kai was sitting at the far end of the bar, playing Connect Four with an expression of shy good humour on her face. She looked as if she had been playing Connect Four all her life.

'The customers like her,' Farren said, still furiously pummelling the ice. 'She's got that sweetness you don't see a lot of in the bars. You know what I mean, Tom?'

'She just got married,' I said.

He laughed at me.

'To a loser,' he said. 'Who can't even support his new wife.'

His face was sweating from the exertion. A spray of ice flew out of the champagne bucket and across the bar.

'I offered her more money,' he said. 'Seems to work every time. Look, your pissed friend can stay if he doesn't make a scene.'

'What did he do?'

Farren shook his head, unable to believe the stupidity of it all.

'He wanted to play Connect Four with her,' he said. 'But you play with everyone or you don't play at all.'

I moved through the bar. Kai caught my eye and looked away, and it was only when I was almost next to her that I recognized the men she was with. Even then, I wasn't quite sure – with their shaven heads and bad tattoos they didn't stand out from the crowd. But I knew them from the Harleys parked outside – the three from the Almost World Famous.

The bully's apprentice.

The fat bastard.

And the big man with the bald head and the goatee. He was the one to watch, I thought. But it was the one with the goatee who held out a meaty paw.

'We didn't realize you were so tight with Farren,' he said. 'No hard feelings, mate.'

I smiled pleasantly and nodded.

'I'm not your fucking mate,' I said.

I turned away, looking for Nick, and felt a hand on my arm. A long-haired Thai woman of about fifty shoved her face into mine. She was dressed all in black, as if trying to fade into the shadows, but I knew that this was the mamma-san and that she ran the place. Her skin was like the surface of the moon.

'Lindsay is busy now,' she whispered confidentially.

'Lindsay?'

She meant Kai. Lindsay was the bar name that she had either been given or chosen because she liked the sound of it. It was a ridiculous name for a *chao ley*.

'But Lindsay will see you later,' the mamma-san told me. 'Until then, we have many nice girl.'

I shook her off and went out to the beach. It was cool now and the open air kept the numbers down. I found Nick sitting alone at a table closest to the sea, struggling to light a cigarette. I took it out of his mouth and threw it away.

'You don't smoke,' I said.

He frowned in the vague direction of the cigarette. Then he looked at me. 'You want a beer?' He waved a hand in the air. He seemed drunker now, this close to his wife. 'Two Singha!' he said.

'Let's just go home,' I said, standing up. 'Enough for one night.'

Two Singha beers appeared before us. I sighed and took

267

a swig. It was sharp and cold and it made me shiver in the late-night air.

'I've had enough to last me a lifetime,' he said.

'She's a waitress,' I said. 'That's all.'

'You know what happens in these bars?' he said. 'You know about the bar fines? About the medicals the girls have every fortnight?' He laughed bitterly. 'The whole country is one big knocking shop.'

'That's not true,' I said, taking his bar bill out of the cup on the table. I added up the chits and began counting out the money. 'It's there if you want it,' I said. 'Or you can walk away.'

'But I can't walk away,' he said. 'I have to watch my wife. To make sure . . .' He shook his head and covered his face in his hands. I looked around, not wanting him to cry here.

'Nick,' I said.

'To make sure she's *safe*,' he said. He looked at me with desperate, wet eyes, and shrugged. 'Just to make sure.'

'I understand,' I said. 'But this is no good. Sitting here. Watching her. It's not healthy, Nick.'

'I'm not watching her,' he insisted, and he drained his beer in one go. 'I just want to sit here and be close to her.'

But that wasn't an option. A bouncer came out to us and stood by the table, his hands by his side. His body language almost apologetic, but I knew that it could change in a moment. If Nick knew he was there, he gave no sign.

'You hear about these Thai women who marry foreigners when they have already got Thai husbands,' he said. 'You hear about that all the time, don't you? And they say it happens because they don't think we're really human. So we don't really count, right?'

I thought about the cousin from Ko Siray and then I forced myself to stop thinking about him.

'That's the Singha talking,' I said. 'That's not you.'

'If anyone hurts her in here, I'll kill them,' Nick said, turning his head and shouting now.

'Hey,' I said. 'Don't go all *Lord of the Flies* on me.'

The bouncer put a thick hand under Nick's elbow and lifted him out of his chair. The Thai had the moves. With very little effort he had lifted Nick up and, still by doing nothing more than elevating his elbow, he was pointing him towards the exit. I stood up and, across the table, shoved the bouncer in the chest as hard as I could. He looked at me and then smiled. He thought he could take me and he was probably right. But he wasn't totally sure. Because this drunken Englishman mattered more to me than he did to him.

'We're going, okay?' I said, and he let Nick go.

Now I took Nick's arm and walked him back towards the bar. He was smiling to himself.

'Do you know the legend of Orpheus and Eurydice?' he asked me.

'Let's just go home, okay?' I said. 'You can crash at my place for tonight.'

'Orpheus went to collect his wife Eurydice from the underworld,' he said. 'She had died on her wedding day. A satyr attacked her and she fell into a nest of vipers. But the music that Orpheus played to mourn his lost wife was so beautiful that the gods wept.'

Nick began weeping himself.

'I think I saw the movie,' I said. 'Let's go.'

'And Orpheus was told that he could collect his dead wife from the land of the dead and take her back to the land of the living on one condition – he must not look at her until they had both reached the land of the living.'

We stepped off the beach and into The Long Bar. It was even more crowded now and our progress was slow. I saw that Kai was still playing Connect Four with the bikers. One of them, the small, ratty one, had placed a familiar hand on her arm. Nick didn't look at them. Nick was trying his best not to look at them. He was Orpheus in the underworld.

He stared at the stage where, after some shouted commands from the mamma-san, the listless go-go girls had been replaced by a two-piece Filipino band, a male guitarist and a girl singer. The guitarist went into the opening to 'Hotel California'. He was very good. The girl began to sing about a dark desert highway, and she was very good too.

'I think if I can leave here without looking at her, then we will be all right,' Nick said. 'I really believe it, Tom.'

'I'm sure that's right,' I said.

A young blonde woman – very pretty, very drunk – climbed on stage and began bumping and grinding and laughing. The Filipino musicians smiled good-naturedly, for they had seen it all before. They kept smiling even when she seized the microphone and began to sing along to 'Hotel California', even though she was from somewhere in Eastern Europe and was clearly no expert on the Eagles.

'I love her, you see,' Nick said.

'I know you do,' I said.

We pushed through the crowds.

The stage invader's enormous boyfriend attempted to join her in a duet but he was too fat and drunk and the steps to the stage were designed for nineteen-year-old Thai dancers, not forty-year-old East European gangsters. He collapsed halfway up the stairs and threw in the towel, screaming at me in some unknown language as we passed him. I think it may have been something about his girlfriend's wonderful voice.

We finally reached the door.

Nick turned and looked back.

He could just not help himself.

The game of Connect Four had finished and Kai was at

the bar, shouting an order at one of the bartenders. He had looked back before both of them had reached the land of the living.

'Black at the wedding,' Nick said. 'Did you see the black at our wedding?'

On the other side of the beach road there was a shop like a glass box. It was one of those vague businesses where you could rent a bike, book a tour, change some money, buy Muay Thai tickets or get your laundry done. There was nobody in the shop apart from a baby in a wooden playpen who was practising her standing up. I was watching the baby and wondering where her parents were, and I did not see the motorbike until it almost ran us over.

I stepped back and the bike raced up the road. It had a sidecar with a metal freezer. The rider was so young that he was still wearing his school uniform. I watched the bike stop further down the street outside one of the massage shops. The rider removed a handful of ice cream tubs from the sidecar and handed them to one of the women in return for a fistful of baht. I had not noticed the blond streak in his hair when he nearly ran me down.

So it was not until he was stuffing the money into the pockets of his school trousers that I realized the midnight ice-cream man was Chatree.

I went to get a sleeping bag from the house and brought it out to the shed. Nick was attempting to light another cigarette and this time I took the entire pack away from him. There were jerrycans full of oil and petrol in here, as well as the bike. He made no protest. The night had worn him out.

'I was glad that you were at the wedding,' he said. 'My family – they didn't get it. But I knew you understood. Kai is special – every man thinks that about his bride, I know.

There's a magic about her.' He looked at me and he did not seem quite so drunk now. 'My wife is unspoilt,' he said.

'Try to get some sleep,' I said. 'The pair of you will work it out.'

I really believed it. He would sell more stories and there would be more money and they would work it out. I moved to the door and waited until he had settled himself inside the sleeping bag before I turned off the light, and it was as if for just that moment I was his parent and he was my child. Then I killed the light and there was only the pale glow of the stars and what was left of the moon.

'There's this thing that we say to each other,' he said sleepily, talking to himself now. *'Chan rak khun ja dai,'* he said. *'Chan rak khun ja dai.* We say it all the time.'

'I know you do,' I said.

And I still did not know what it meant.

Tess woke me in the middle of the night.

'Smoke,' she said. 'Smoke!'

I was out of bed and pulling on my trousers and already I could smell it, this thick, acrid smoke filling the night, and the back of my throat. I headed for the door, hearing my wife calming our waking children behind me. Mr and Mrs Botan were already on their veranda. Chatree appeared by their side, rubbing his eyes. Mr Botan raised his hand and pointed.

'On the beach,' he said.

Far below us the bay curved like a perfect crescent in reverse, and all was dark now but for the fire that raged and burned in the middle of Hat Nai Yang. It must have been burning for a while, because some of the flames were as high as the tallest trees.

In the black of the night the fire cast a sickening light, illuminating the casuarinas, and throwing enormous shadows that grew and danced with wild abandon across the sleeping sea. The thick black smoke drifted up from the beach and it blotted out the stars and the moon and it burned my eyes.

I ran to the shed, shouting his name aloud as I threw back the door, although I already knew that I would find it empty.

30

In the pearly light of morning Tess climbed on to the back of the bike and we rode down to the beach road to look at the blackened hulk of The Long Bar.

There were many people on the beach road, staring at the wet black ruin, noting the twisted metal stools and the drifts of broken glass and the long bar itself looking like a boat that had been set alight, sunk, and pulled sodden and ravaged to the surface.

Behind me on the Royal Enfield, Tess pressed her face against me.

'Oh, God,' she said. 'What has he done?'

But the inhabitants of Nai Yang did not linger. Destruction held no great fascination for them. The people of Phuket were not the kind who slow down to look at traffic accidents. They saw it all the time – the mess that human beings so casually make. So a burned-out bar wasn't much. They had all seen a lot worse in recent memory. It would be torn down and levelled and its presence would soon be a fading memory when it was replaced by whatever the strip threw up next. Besides, there was a living to earn, and children to pack off to school and fish to catch, and early-morning travellers to approach with the promise of elephant rides, foot massage, cooking lessons and trips out to the neighbouring islands. The Long Bar had burned all through the night but the next day life went on without pausing for breath all down the sandy white curve of Hat Nai Yang. The Royal Thai police were sealing off the smoking ruins of the bar, and their yellow crime-scene tape extended halfway across the beach road on one side, and down to the edge of the sea on the other.

'Where is he?' Tess said. 'Where is he, Tom?'

'I don't know,' I said. 'He's just running.'

There were five of the maroon-and-white pick-up trucks they used for police cars parked on the beach road and this seemed like a lot for a fire in a beach-front bar until I saw the three body bags laid in a neat line at the boots of the cops in their brown uniforms.

A cop bent over one of the bags, pulling up the long zip at the front. Before it closed I caught a glimpse of what remained of the face. I did not recognize it. But I recognized the three rented Harleys that still stood untouched on the beach road.

The cop stood up and looked over at us. It was Somter, and though he made no move towards us, I knew that I was not free to leave. I would have to answer his questions, even if he already knew the answers. Then I saw the tall figure next to him, the green baseball cap with its gold crest pulled low over his face.

'Why is Miles here?' I said.

'They must have been British nationals,' Tess said. 'The people in those bags. That's why he's here. Because they were British nationals.'

I could see it. Too drunk to ride south. Crashed out on the floor of The Long Bar. Nick would not even have known they were there.

And when I saw Farren in the wreckage, raging and cursing and weeping, I remembered that none of the businesses on Hat Nai Yang were insured. When what you had was taken – by fire, by water – then it was gone forever.

'We have to find them,' Tess said. 'Nick and Kai. We have to find them before anyone else does. I don't know what he might do, Tom.'

'And do what?' I said. 'Smuggle him across the border? Nick hasn't overstayed his visa, Tess, he's not doing dodgy land deals.' I nodded at the body bags as they were carefully loaded on to the back of a maroon-and-white. 'He can't get out of that.'

'I don't mean the police,' Tess said. 'I mean Farren.'

There was a motorbike with an ice-cream sidecar parked outside their beach hut. Chatree had come looking for his sister. He came out looking dazed when he heard our bike. He was wearing his school uniform and he had his rucksack with him, but he held it mechanically with one hand and let it drag across the ground.

Tess said his name and he looked away, trying not to cry. It was the first time I ever thought he looked truly young.

'She didn't come home,' he said.

Tess put her arm around him and together the pair of them walked through the trees towards the mangroves, stopping when they reached the picnic tables that were relics of the old national park. They talked for a long time, but when Tess came back, she came back alone.

'He doesn't want to come with us,' Tess said. 'He wants to stay here. He wants to wait for her.'

'He'll be all right,' I said, not believing it.

I saw Chatree walking through the casuarinas down to the empty white sand of Hat Mai Khao. I watched him remove a book from his rucksack and send it skimming across the pure blue water. He did it again.

Then he stopped, as a smooth muscle seemed to appear in the Andaman Sea, and then another, and then more, as the heads of the elephants broke the surface and began their slow, dramatic march to the shore.

The boy on the beach stood motionless, a new exercise book forgotten in his hand, as he watched the great grey beasts rising out of the water, their huge heads nodding as if confirming that this was not a dream, their eyes with lashes like a spider's web blinking away the streams of water that ran down their ancient faces into that bottomless maw of a mouth, with more water flying off the ears, running down the vast expanse of their grey hides, and dripping from the bodies of the men on their backs, the mahouts, with their bare feet pressed behind the ears of the elephants, and the silver hook in their hands glinting in the sunlight.

But you always looked straight through the men. All you ever saw were the elephants coming out of the empty sea.

And then we turned away and walked back to the bike, and I saw no more.

I followed the girl through the house.

It was a traditional house in the Southern style, built to accommodate the heat and the rain. It faced a river, the long sloping *Panya* roof extended over the front stairway, and inside it was a place of cool shadows and empty space and polished wood. When the girl's bare feet touched the floor, they made no sound.

'Please,' she said, and she looked away as she smiled and I thought how unlike most Thai women she seemed. The ones I knew, from Kai to Mrs Botan, all had a clear-eyed confidence about them. They looked you in the eye as if they had no reason to do anything else. But there was a self-consciousness about this young woman, and I thought that it couldn't be explained by the fact that I had come to this place uninvited.

It was a home with no children. All was calm, there was no clutter, and what furniture there was – a heavy, claw-foot coffee table in front of a cane sofa upholstered in red silk, antique wooden figurines of gods that I didn't know – looked as though it was on display. There were sliding shuttered walls on every side, and they were pulled back now to catch the breeze of early morning.

James Miles was on the veranda of the walled garden. He was wearing a white cotton robe, sitting at a small table for two and reading a faxed copy of that morning's *Times*. I had never before seen him without his FCC hat, and it lay at his side next to a skinny grey cat. He was quite bald.

'Your friend,' the girl announced, smiling into the distance, and as I thanked her for her kindness I saw what was different about her. It was her Adam's apple.

'Tom,' Miles said, too much of a gentleman to express surprise or displeasure at my appearance, and in one smooth movement he stood, shook my hand and placed the green baseball cap with its dragon crest on his head. He adjusted his robe and I caught a glimpse of his body, and was surprised how toned he looked for a man of his age. If he had once been a drinker in Bangkok, there was no sign of it now. The skinny grey cat squawked in protest at being disturbed.

He was drinking ginger, like the women in the massage shops on Hat Nai Yang, and he poured me a glass. He played the perfect host. It was almost as if he had been expecting me.

'You have a beautiful home,' I said.

'Isn't it?' he said. 'Thank you. We have been here for a number of years.' He paused, as if debating whether he should tell me the name of the girl with the Adam's apple.

He apparently decided against it. 'We've been very happy here,' he said.

He sighed and looked out at the walled garden. What was unusual about it was that nothing was planted in the ground. The tiles were covered with potted plants. There were clusters of terracotta pots holding purple flowers and red-leaf plants, and there were the giant wide-rimmed dragon jars – *mangkorn*, Thais call them – bearing everything from what looked like lilies floating on water to small, spiny-stemmed trees. But nothing grew in the ground.

'My neighbour,' I said, sipping my ginger, 'Mr Botan, he told me that the Thai love of potted plants is based in Buddhism. Things planted in soil seem more permanent. Something planted in a pot reminds us everything passes in the end.'

'Your neighbour is right, Tom,' Miles smiled. 'Although there is also the practical consideration of a people who sometimes have to move home quickly. You can take a potted plant with you.' He was warming to the theme. 'And then there's the Thai obsession with *riab roi*. They place great value on tidiness.' He took a drink, not looking at me, and the mask seemed to slip. 'You know you shouldn't have come here, don't you?'

'I didn't know where else to go,' I said truthfully.

He shook his head.

'But I can't help you,' he said. 'Your friend is in a lot of trouble. You know that.'

'Tess told me to come to you,' I said. 'My wife. It was her idea. I know you don't think much of me, and I don't blame you. But I think you respect her.'

He was silent for a while. We could hear the island sound of light motorbikes and scooters buzzing by, but they seemed very far away. In the end he tugged at the rim of his FCC hat and shook his head again, and there was a finality about it now.

'You have to leave,' he said, courteous but firm. 'I'm very busy.'

'Do me one favour,' I said. 'Please.'

'I can't do anything for you,' he said.

'You're a travel writer,' I said. 'You know things about this place. You have contacts.'

'Yes,' he said. 'I'm a travel writer.'

'All I'm asking,' I said, 'is that you help me to find someone.'

'Very well,' he said. 'But your friend should turn himself in immediately. Anything else will make it far worse for him in the end.'

'It's not Nick that I need to find,' I said. 'It's his wife.'

'What's her name?'

I looked at him for a beat.

'Lindsay,' I said. 'Her name is Lindsay.'

Inside the house I saw the girl moving through the hushed shadows, carrying some clean laundry into what must have been the bedroom, and as her bare feet fell softly on the dull gold of the hardwood floors, they made no sound at all.

In the heat of the middle of the day, I walked past the great houses built by the Chinese who had made their fortunes in tin and rubber on the island more than a hundred years ago.

There was nobody else on the street and it was not just because of the heat. The old Chinese quarter of Phuket town was not a place that many travellers sought out, and it was of no interest to the Thais with no Chinese blood. So the streets belonged to me – and with my T-shirt stuck to my body like cling film, I walked past the great homes of Thanon Thalang, Thanon Romanee and Thanon Deebuk as beyond the black, wrought-iron fences the great houses seemed to be sleeping behind their closed shutters. The houses were cream and yellow and blue, and they were so lovingly cared for that most of them looked newly built. I looked up at their balconies and half-expected the hard, smart, self-made Chinese men who had built them to walk out.

There were alleys in the quarter. I ducked down one of them and felt the fire before I saw it. It was coming from an oven, and an old woman was burning counterfeit money – hell notes – to prepare her way in the next world. In the tight little alley I had to squeeze myself against the wall to get past her, but she made no move to get out of the way, just kept on feeding the hell notes to the fire, as if one of us was already a ghost.

There was a temple next to the alley. Mr Botan had taken me here and told me that, although the Thai street signs called the temple Kwanim Teng, its true name – its Chinese name – was Pu Jao, dedicated to Kuan Yin, the Taoist god of mercy.

I went inside, and stepped immediately into a thick fog of incense and hell money burning in huge stone drums. It was too much – a lung-clenching, mind-warping perfumed smoke, and combined with the hundreds of small sacred statues, it made the temple an hallucinogenic experience. At first I thought I was just imagining him. But it was really Nick – standing motionless as an elderly Chinese man shook bamboo sticks to find out what the future would bring.

Nick looked at me and smiled weakly. 'I didn't think anyone would find me down here,' he said.

'This is the first place I've looked,' I said.

Our eyes watered in the holy smog.

'Oh,' he said. 'How stupid I am.'

'Not so stupid,' I said. 'It could be worse.'

He laughed bitterly at that.

'You didn't run,' I said, and I touched his arm. 'You didn't try to get across the border.'

'I thought about it,' he said. 'I did, Tom. I couldn't make up my mind between Laos, Cambodia or Burma. Figured I would get a tug in Malaysia – as I would landing at Heathrow. I also thought about topping myself.' He laughed. 'But I couldn't decide between sleeping pills and jumping under a *tuk-tuk*. And then I realized that I couldn't do any of these things because I love my wife.' He choked on his sadness and his love and picked up some bamboo sticks. 'Do you know what you do with these things?' he said.

'You shake them and read the number they give you,' I said. 'Then you go into the other room and find out your fortune. But I don't think it's in English.'

He gave the bamboo sticks a tentative shake. 'Shall I do it?' he said, attempting a smile. 'See what the future holds?'

'Nick,' I said. 'I found her. I found Kai.'

He looked at me, waiting, the bamboo sticks still in his hand.

'It's a place for rich Thais,' I said. 'Foreigners can't go there.'

He tossed down the bamboo sticks.

'I'm going there,' he said. 'What's the address?'

'Nick?'

'What?'

'It's not a good place,' I said.

'It doesn't matter,' he said angrily. 'It doesn't fucking matter that it's not a good place. Do you think it matters what kind of a place it is?'

The perfumed smoke of the backstreet temple filled my eyes, my throat and my lungs.

'No,' I said. 'I don't think it matters at all.'

31

Without taking my left hand from the bike I could see from my watch that it was close to midnight. I could hear Nick breathing behind me as we looked up at the house.

'It's almost time,' I said.

We were on a quiet residential road in the heart of the Old Town. It was a short, terraced street of what they called Chinese shop-houses. These were not the great colonial mansions behind the black iron fences. This was where, a hundred years ago, a family had a business on the ground floor and a home above – long, thin buildings, narrow at the front but going way back. They all had three shuttered windows on the first floor. Most of the street was in darkness. But in just one of the old Chinese shop-houses, now among the most expensive properties on the island, all the lights were blazing.

'You understand that we can't just walk in there,' I said, without turning round. 'They don't want us in there.' Nothing from the back of the bike. I turned my head and spoke more sharply. 'Are you listening to me?' I said.

'Yes,' Nick said quietly, not taking his eyes from the house with the lights. 'I'm listening. I am.'

We took off, nice and easy, just another motorbike moving through the city, and I rode to the night market that sits off a side street on the Phang Nga Road.

The night market operated in shifts. In a few hours the vendors selling fresh produce would be setting up their wares and the cooks and their helpers would be arriving to buy fruit and vegetables in the cool time before dawn. Later there would be food stalls selling soup and noodles for the hungry people who got up early or stayed up late. But right now the market was a giant car boot sale selling clothes, craftwork, bootleg DVDs and everything else that would raise a few baht. Thai pop music was blasting everywhere.

'How do you know about this place?' Nick said.

'Tess ordered water from here once,' I said. 'When we first arrived.'

I parked up the Royal Enfield and we started roaming the stalls. After five minutes I found what I was looking for – a man selling soft drinks wholesale, drinks he had either got from businesses that had gone bust or stuff that had fallen off the back of a *tuk-tuk*. I bought two dozen big bottles of *nam plao* in four shrink-wrapped packs of six.

'Mineral water?' Nick said. 'But why are we—'

'Listen,' I said. 'Just shut up and trust me and everything will be fine. Okay?'

He looked at me in the harsh yellow light of the night market and for the first time since we met, he no longer looked a young man.

'Okay,' he said.

We rode back to the street of the Chinese shop-houses. As we turned into it, I heard Nick curse behind me. At the end of the road there was a maroon-and-white from the Royal Thai Police with its lights off. Even in the dimly lit street, it was clear that there was only one man in the car.

I stopped the bike across the road from the house with all the lights and turned to look at Nick.

'It's Somter,' I said. 'He'll be waiting for us when we come out with Kai. Waiting for you.'

At first he couldn't speak. Then his face twisted with anger.

'You called him?' he said. 'You *called* him?'

'It's the only way,' I said. 'You have to face it – what you did. You can't run, Nick. If I thought you could run, I would let you run.' We both stared at the maroon-and-white at the end of the street. Somter was unmoving at the wheel. 'I trust him,' I said. 'He's not a barbarian. He's a good man. He is going to give us fifteen minutes.'

Nick hung his head. And then he laughed. The bike was heavy with all the water and I suddenly wondered if there was some other way.

'Maybe this is a stupid idea,' I said, wanting him to tell me that he would walk down the street to Somter now.

Nick shook his head. 'No,' he said. 'It's not a stupid idea. It's a good idea. Everybody needs water. Let's get it over with.'

We both took a six-pack of water in each hand and walked to the door of the Chinese shop-house. There was a metal buzzer and intercom to the left of the shuttered door. A Thai voice crackled through the speaker.

'*Nam plao*,' I said. 'Delivery. *Nam plao*.'

'Isn't it a bit late for a delivery?' Nick murmured.

I did not reply. I could hear Thai voices discussing the matter and just when I thought that my plan had not worked the door opened and a large Thai man in his thirties stood there, staring at us out of the darkness. Then he stood to one side and indicated the staircase.

'*Khawp kun karp*,' I said politely, dipping my head as I made for the stairs. Nick fell into step behind me.

The man laughed.

'*Yindee tawn rap!*' he said.

Welcome to Thailand.

The old concrete stairs were in darkness but light poured from the first floor. The door was open and a mamma-san was saying goodbye to a couple of men in their thirties. This place was different but she looked like every mamma-san on the Bangla Road. The hair of a very young girl and the face of a very old woman. One thing about her was different from all the other mamma-sans. She did not smile at a pair of white boys. Her smile faded and died as she looked at us. She jerked her head and we went inside.

I had never seen anywhere like it.

Men were lined up against one wall, standing and drinking and smoking. Women – ten, fifteen, twenty years younger than the men – were on the other wall, sitting and not drinking.

The girls were all in what looked like pretend evening dresses – silky, cut low at the front, slit at the sides, a mamma-san's idea of sophistication and class. There was some kind of little karaoke system set up in the middle of the room, and one of the girls was singing a Thai love song.

And that was Kai.

'Hey!' someone barked at us.

It was the mamma-san. She was indicating the bar in the corner of the room where the young Thai barman frantically chopped at a champagne bucket full of ice with a long silver pick.

I carried my dozen bottles of *nam plao* over to the bar. He didn't look at me. And why should he? I was nothing. A nod of his head told me to stick it under the bar.

Kai had finished singing. There was polite applause. One of the men left the wall and placed a garland of paper flowers around her neck. I noticed for the first time that the girls sitting against their wall all had garlands of paper flowers around their necks.

So that's how it works, I thought.

The girls trade the garlands in with the management at the end of the night. And then, as I looked up from placing the *nam plao* under the bar, I saw that it wasn't much about the paper flowers.

I watched the man who had placed the garland around Kai's neck take her hand and, blank-eyed and unsmiling, lead her towards the door on the far side of the room. And I knew that we had to get to her before she went upstairs.

'I don't believe it,' Farren said behind me.

Nick was standing in the middle of the room, in the no-man's land between the women and the men, still holding his dozen bottles of water, paralysed at the sight of his wife. The English words seemed to wake him from a dream.

'Kai!' he said.

She turned, and saw him, and pulled away from the man and I saw the faces of the other men twist with confusion and disbelief, and then anger, but before they could make a move Somter was standing there, small and neat in his brown uniform, although it was not yet fifteen minutes, listening with a stern, neutral expression as the mamma-san and the man who let us in spoke urgently to him.

Then Nick and Kai were standing at the bar and Farren was moving towards it as if he was going to order a drink and I was still on the other side, the barman by my side, although he had stopped smashing the ice with the pick, and Nick was crying a bit as he looked at the neat white marks on the brown skin of Kai's wrist where she had hurt herself.

'Ah,' he said, as if every mark was cutting into his flesh too. '*Chan rak khun ja dai*,' he said. 'What did you do to your beautiful arms, Kai?'

287

Farren was laughing.

'I really don't fucking believe it,' he said, but he placed the palm of his hands on the bar and he made no move. The sudden presence of the small sergeant from the Royal Thai Police had put fear into the room.

'You are in big trouble, Nick,' Kai said, and there was a dull light in her eyes, and I did not know if it was from lack of sleep or drugs or something else.

Somter was listening to the pleas of the mamma-san and the large man. He looked up and caught my eye and nodded.

'Get her out of here now,' I told Nick. But he couldn't move either.

'I'll face it,' he said. 'But come home. *Chan rak khun ja dai.*'

'You will go to jail,' she said.

'*Chan rak khun ja dai,*' he smiled.

I came out from behind the bar and gave him a shove. One of the Thai men had crossed the floor and was making his case to the policeman and a few more followed. I pushed Nick again, harder this time, and Kai began to move, leading him away. I followed them. The mamma-san grabbed Kai's wrist as she passed.

'Lindsay!' the old woman said sharply.

I placed my hand on the mamma-san's arm and she whirled to look at me.

'Her name is Kai,' I said. 'Not Lindsay.'

I indicated Nick and I tried to remember the Thai word for wife. But it was just out of reach and they did not need to know much English in here. It was a private world. 'She's his *wife*, okay?' I shouted, as the old woman refused to let go of Kai.

The mamma-san shook her head.

'*Mia noi, mia noi, mia noi,*' she said, jabbing a furious finger in Kai's face, and I saw that it had been heavily made up

288

to make her dark skin look lighter. '*Gik! Gik! Gik!*' the mamma-san said, and some of the men began to laugh at the observation – *fuck buddy* – and then the old woman's open palm slapped hard against Kai's face.

Suddenly there were people shouting and hands pulling at me and I caught a blow on the back of my neck and a kick high on the thigh and the mamma-san's fingernails clawed at my eyes. I lashed out wildly but Somter raised his voice and they all fell silent and still. Including me.

Only Nick and Kai kept moving, heading towards the door and the dark staircase beyond. They had almost made it when Farren stepped in front of them and punched Nick once in the chest.

And as Farren stepped back, there was the clatter of metal falling on a hardwood floor as the ice pick hit the ground.

Then Nick was on his back, the shock on his face and his wife trying to lift him up with one hand and stop the blood with the other. But the blood was already everywhere.

'*Chan rak khun ja dai,*' she told him, as he had told her so many times.

I love you to death.

The beach huts at Hat Mai Khao were all empty now. After Nick's death Kai had never gone back. I knew that Nick's parents were briefly at their son's home with their respective partners when they came to take his body back to England, but Tess and I steered clear until Mr Botan told us that the national park were sending in a cleaning team.

The world had been leaving us alone and that was how we liked it. But the season was changing. Now that the long rains had come to an end, it would soon be the best time to visit the island – a time of cool breezes, low humidity, when every day felt like the best day of summer. The national park was hopeful of renting out the beach huts under the casuarina trees, even though few travellers ever ventured this far north. A young Swedish couple who came to the Almost World Famous Seafood Grill every night for three weeks were briefly in one of them, but they had moved on to Ko Kood on the other side of the Gulf of Siam, seeking a triple-tier waterfall and an island that the world had not yet discovered. I never heard if they found it.

So when we knew that the national park would be throwing out anything that remained in the beach huts, Tess and I took Mr Botan's pick-up truck and we went to take one last look. We did not think about taking the old Royal Enfield. Tess was too far along with the baby for that.

There wasn't much in their little home. A few light clothes for both a man and a woman. Some newspapers with his old stories, including the one about the day we rescued the dolphin. A cardboard box full of more stories, maybe the ones that had never been published, the sides of the box already rotting from the humidity. On the small dresser on one side of their bed was a carved wooden figurine of a monk, his palms pressed together in prayer.

We packed it all up and loaded it on to the back of the pick-up truck, even though there was nothing to do with it and no one to give it to and in the end we would only throw it all away. But somehow leaving it there for a team of cleaners did not seem right.

There was a hole in the wall in the shape of a heart. Someone had punched it, or thrown something heavy. The walls of the beach huts were thin and cheap and you would not have had to hit it very hard to make a hole. I watched Tess go over to it and reach inside. She showed me what she had found. A band of gold in the palm of her hand. A woman's wedding ring.

'We must give her this,' Tess said, and her hand closed around it.

290

The beach hut was empty now. There was no clue that they had ever lived here. I could hear the traffic on Highway 402 heading for Sarasin Bridge and the end of the island. It was time to go.

Tess climbed into the driver's seat of Mr Botan's pick-up and I told her that I would follow on in a few minutes. I thought it unlikely that I would return to the beach huts any time soon and I wanted one last look at Hat Mai Khao. I watched her drive away and take the road south. Then I walked through the trees and on to the beach. The sight of it robbed me of my breath.

No beach could ever match its lonely beauty. The wide, white, sloping expanse of sand stretched south for as far as the eye could see, before it came to a gentle bump in the coastline. Hat Mai Khao looked more like a desert than a beach, and more like a mirage than a desert. The sand was white and fine and endless, and your bare feet seemed to sink into it in a way that they did not on any other beach. The sea was wilder here than on the beaches further south, and crests of white formed and fell on the smooth blue muscles of the waves. I pulled off my T-shirt and waded in.

It wasn't like our beach. It wasn't like Hat Nai Yang where you could wander into the sea and feel that you had stepped into some huge God-made swimming pool, warm and shallow and safe no matter how far behind you left the shore. On our beach you could swim far out and, if the mood took you, stand up, the water reaching your chest, smiling to yourself at how far away the shore looked. Hat Mai Khao was not like that – you went into the water by that long, empty beach and you knew immediately that you were in the sea. I began to swim parallel to that beautiful beach, looking at the trees beyond the beach, noticing how they became a darker green when the casuarinas gave way to the mangroves, and that was when I felt the current. It was like a change of mood in the sea, as undeniable as that, and it began pulling me backwards.

I looked at the spot where I had thrown down my T-shirt, the faded blue vivid against the white dune of sand, and I swam hard for that. But the sea took me in exactly the opposite direction – away from the T-shirt, away from the shore, away from the soft white sands of Hat Mai Khao.

I watched the beach grow more distant by the moment, and with each passing moment I felt my strength sap and my panic rise. I was very frightened now.

There were good reasons why this beach looked the way that it did. There were good reasons why Hat Mai Khao made you feel like you were the last person left alive in the world. They could not build here because of the turtles that had chosen this one beach on the island to lay their eggs. They could not build here because it was part of a national park and the Thais, no matter what the world might think, were good at protecting the best of their country. They could not build here because it was so far north. And they could not build here because of the current.

I fought against the current and it beat me without effort, and it beat me immediately. I fought it and then very quickly there was no fight left in me, it was too strong, and then I didn't fight it at all. And it pulled me south along the great white stretch of Hat Mai Khao, too far from the shore to feel anything but raw terror. But after a lifetime it dragged me beyond the gentle bump in the coast that marks the end of Hat Mai Khao, and I felt the sea suddenly release me from its grip.

I was looking at the horizon, the white clouds like a distant mountain range, and after I had brought up a gutful of salty bile, I trod water, steadying my breathing before I turned round.

And when I turned around, there was Hat Nai Yang.

I was still too far from the shore to feel no fear, but the sight of our beach was enough to convince me that I would not die today.

There was the beach road. There were the longtails. There was the strip of restaurants that ended with the Almost World Famous Seafood Grill. And above it all, there was the green hill that rises above Hat Nai Yang.

I filled my lungs with air. The water was warm and still and so clear that I could see a school of bright yellow fish gliding across the sandy bottom.

I began to swim towards the beach.

Home, I thought, and now there was no room in my heart to think of anything else but that.

Home.

32

We had a small house on the green hill that rises above Hat Nai Yang.

Our home stood at the end of a yellow lane of hard-packed sand, and when the long rains came in September and October the road darkened to the colour of buried gold. It was almost empty now. Our belongings, such as they were, had already been shipped back to England. We would follow soon. The baby would be born in London, in winter.

On the island the long rains turned the back roads to mud and made the main highways slick with danger. Down on the beach road that ran next to Hat Nai Yang the water was sometimes up to your shins, and yet I loved the long rains because of their savage beauty.

Called by the rolling thunder, I would stand in the doorway of the shed where I worked on the Royal Enfield and watch the summer lightning split the sky in jagged flashes.

Life went on as it always would. In the over-lit shops selling everything from foot massage to handmade suits to rides on the elephants, and in the strip of restaurants on the beach selling fish that had begun the day in the Andaman Sea, they never closed. Sometimes the long rains made the people of Hat Nai Yang run for cover, and then we were caught and soaked to the soul. But Hat Nai Yang always went on. There was always a living to be made, and a meal to be eaten, and work to be done. There were always small children wandering about long past anything remotely resembling bedtime, their solemn brown eyes shining in the night. As always, the children seemed to belong to no one or to everyone. Safety was gently administered, and I never saw one of them allowed to come to any harm. Hat Nai Yang was a wonderful place to grow up or, for Rory and Keeva, to have spent a part of their childhood.

As the long rains neared their end, I could not remember when I had last heard the thick green coastal forest of our island home dripping with water. I would come out of the shed to look at the last of the lightning flashing over the horizon.

More often than not Mr Botan, my neighbour and my friend, would be out on his veranda watching the white light cut the inky, blue-black sky, and because I valued his opinion on these matters, and because weather forecasts on our island were always a strangely hit-and-miss affair, I would ask him if he thought that there might be a storm coming in later.

He would think about it for a while as he contemplated the distant lightning and his features, which I had once thought were more Chinese than Thai, but now simply thought of as him, would frown with concentration. And then, before we both went back to our work or our rest or our meal, he would give me his verdict.

'It hasn't rained since yesterday,' Mr Botan would say.

There was a gift shop on Ko Siray now.

Not really a gift shop – more of a stall with a tin shelter from the sun and the rain, and it sat in the middle of the

unmade road that ran through the *chao ley* village. But Rory
and Keeva treated it like a gift shop, chattering with excitement as they counted out the few baht they had stuffed in
their jeans and examined the things for sale.

They were beautiful things – giant wind chimes made
from hundreds of sea shells, wind chimes such as I had never
seen, intricate and elaborate and the result of endless hours
of work, each shell chosen for its special shape or colour, all
hanging down on thin pieces of string from a coconut shell,
and softly jangling like the sigh of the sea. They were very
cheap. Rory and Keeva bought one each, and the old woman
on the stall began to carefully fold the shells into the coconut.
Tess smiled at me and I thought I knew what she was
thinking. The wind chimes of Ko Siray would live in their
bedrooms in London and the wind outside would never
disturb them.

The village of the sea gypsies had not changed. The tin
shacks on their stilts stared out at a rubbish-strewn beach
where ancient longtails rocked in a choppy sea. Some men
were on the beach, repairing the giant cages they used for
fishing. People slept. And everywhere you saw that flash of
gold in the hair that marked the *chao ley* out as people from
another tribe, another place and perhaps another time.

It still felt more like another planet than the other end
of an island. We were the only visitors, and I wondered if
there would ever be a time in our lives when we would
come back. Or perhaps Keeva and Rory would come back
here one day, together or alone, all grown up, teenagers
travelling with a rucksack and a year to burn, or older, with
their partner and perhaps even their children, just to show
them, just to tell them, just to know.

This was our island.

Kai appeared in the open doorway of one of the tin shacks,
wearing her expression of shy good humour, lifting one hand

296

in salute while the other self-consciously rubbed the baby growing inside her. She came down the stilts slowly and heavily and when she reached the bottom we were waiting for her. Tess and Kai embraced, laughing, and it was a moment shared only by these two women, and the babies that grew inside them.

I looked up at the shack and I saw the unreadable face of her cousin. Then he disappeared into the shadows.

'Here,' Tess said, and she held something out in her hand.

The wedding ring glinted in Tess' palm and Kai took it, holding it up to the light and smiling, as if it was a particularly beautiful shell. But she did not put it on, and we did not expect her to.

Chatree slid down the shack's wooden ladder like a fireman responding to a call. He was in a rush, and he wanted us to know it. My children demanded that he come to the beach, to play with them the way they had under the casuarinas of Hat Nai Yang. But he was done with playing.

'Fisherman now,' he said, banging his fist against his broad chest. 'Now that my aunt has died, my uncle is fishing again.'

'Cool,' said my daughter.

'Chatree,' Tess said. 'We are leaving soon. We are going back to London. We have come to say goodbye.'

He nodded, a small gesture, almost nothing, as if she had made a remark about the weather.

'Everyone goes home in the end,' he told us.

Tess stepped forward and hugged him. He fiercely returned her embrace and then broke away. He began to run to the beach. My children chased after him. I looked at Tess, holding Kai's hand, as if reluctant to let her go, and then I went after them.

There was an old man on one of the longtails, and I recognized him as the uncle who had silently watched his wife dying, and silently watched his niece getting married.

Now, for the very first time, I heard him speak – shouting a brief command at Chatree as he splashed into the sea and waded to the old wooden boat. The boy hauled himself aboard as my children stopped on the shore, holding the coconut shells that held the wind chimes.

'Chatree!' Rory said. 'Wait!'

But Chatree could not wait for them. He was busy stashing the anchor and the weights that held the anchor. The old man yanked the diesel engine into life and the longtail began to move away from the stony beach of Ko Siray. The boy and the old man changed places, and we watched Chatree steering with one hand as his uncle prepared the lobster pots. And as they moved further out to sea, the old man and the boy were black shapes in the blinding sunshine. Keeva called the boy's name once. With one hand still steering the longtail, he raised his free hand in farewell, and that was when I knew he was gone.

The night before we left the moon rose full and white over the island and it was the time of Loy Krathong.

Rory and Keeva had spent the entire afternoon making their baskets. Mrs Botan had given them each a lotus-shaped section of a banana tree. The wood was soft enough to press in their small candles, incense sticks, banana leaves, coins and flowers, but strong enough to keep them there.

'Good,' Mrs Botan smiled, and her husband nodded, the unlit cigarette in his hand moving like worry beads.

When the full moon lit up the sky we walked down the green hill, Mr and Mrs Botan and Rory and Keeva and Tess and me, and we passed in single file through the fairy lights at the entrance of the Almost World Famous Seafood Grill and on to the beach. It was still very early, but already the glassy black surface of the sea was swarming with tiny lights.

All along the bow-shaped sweep of Hat Nai Yang parents and their children stood and crouched at the edge of the water and, at the beachside tables of the restaurants, travellers who had never before seen the November festival of Loy Krathong paused with their forks halfway to their mouths, stunned at the sight of the night sea suddenly blazing with what looked like ten thousand fireflies.

We knelt by the water and Tess lit the incense sticks and the candles of the children's baskets – tiny candles in pink and blue such as you would put on a birthday cake.

Keeva immediately launched her basket with a shove, spinning it across the surface of water with such enthusiasm that for a moment I thought it might capsize. But my daughter's basket seemed to recover from the shock of the launch and steady itself, twirling very slowly as it made its way out to sea.

Rory was different. He held the basket in both hands, staring at the beautiful jumble of banana leaves and candles and coins and all the rest, and I knew that he was reluctant to let it go. He wanted to keep it forever – as I wanted to keep our island, as I wanted to keep this time. But it was impossible, of course, so all at once he laughed and crouched down beside his sister, gently sending the basket on its way, shaking his head as if it had been silly to think there was anything else that could happen.

We stood on the soft sand of Hat Nai Yang and we watched our baskets drift away until they were lost among all the others, all those flickering pinpoints of fire on the water, and in the end all you could see were the tiny flames beyond counting, dancing in the darkness as they were carried faraway to sea.

Read on for one of Tony's short stories
from *Departures*:

No Tower for Old Men

Through the smoked glass of the control tower, the Jumbo 747 first revealed itself to Spike as if it were a star above a distant manger, a glittering point of white light in the ink-blue sky.

It was the hour before dawn on a midsummer's day and Spike loved this moment.

Because the star was always getting bigger, and getting closer, and the naked eye of the young man in the Air Traffic Control tower could make out other stars, other bright pinpoints of light stacked up behind it, and he knew that these lights were the first arrivals of the new day, the night flights from Hong Kong, Singapore and Bangkok.

There was a bank of screens before Spike but his eyes were on the sky, and the pinpoints of light above the distant London skyline.

There were three 200-ton planes up there – twenty-five miles away, twenty miles away and fifteen miles away respectively – their nine hundred passengers coming awake to see the sprawl of London beneath them. Three giant aircraft, heading this way at the end of their journey through the night.

And young Spike was going to land them all safe and sound before he had his morning macchiato.

Now he looked at the bank of screens. The Jumbo from Hong Kong appeared as a flight number – BA26 – an altitude – 9000 feet – and the ID of the airport where it was landing – LL for Heathrow. Just a bunch of letters and numbers on a screen, moving with the jerkiness of some video game from the last century. Spike looked at it, and he registered the information, but it was almost subconscious. The most important screen, Spike always said, was the window.

And now a shadow passed across it.

Spike ignored the shadow.

But Earl, Spike's lighting operator, stirred at the sight of the shadow falling across the window. Earl was sitting on the lower level of the tower, the perimeter, and from up on the podium Spike heard his lighting operator chuckle to himself.

'Final approach,' Spike said calmly to the pilot of the 747. It was no longer a shining light in a summer sky but a recognizable wide-body four-engine aircraft capable of flying 345 people across 8000 miles at over 600 miles an hour without once touching the ground. 'Speedbird 26 established on Instrument Landing System,' Spike said. 'Continue approach, clear to land. Wind speed thirty knots at fourteen hundred feet. Stand eighteen. Follow the greens.'

The 747 came out of the sky. Earl had lit up a string of green lights that would guide the pilot safely to his aircraft's designated stand. These were the greens – a unique lighting system that meant that nobody was going to hit the 747, and he was not going to hit anything.

'Left on Bravo, hold on Link four-one-seven,' Spike said. 'Follow the greens.'

'The shadow's back,' Earl said. 'Check it out, Spike.'

Finally Spike looked at the shadow on the glass.

There was a window cleaner on the outside of the Air Traffic Control tower. Some skinny youth in his early twenties who had been there for most of the week, making their massive smoked-glass window spotless, clipped to a hydraulic lift with massive squeegees attached to his wrist. The cab at the top of the tower was angled out so he was always leaning backwards as he worked with his squeegees nearly ninety metres above the ground.

'That's got to be a stressful job,' Spike said to himself.

They decided to give the window cleaner a cup of tea before they got busy. Spike and Earl had tried waving to him a few times, but he had always looked away, hiding bashfully behind his squeegees. And this was a good time to bring him in.

The first flight of the day, the 747 from Hong Kong, had arrived on time just before five in the morning. Traffic would be light for another hour, and then at six the heavens would open with forty-six planes arriving every hour and another fifty-four departing.

Earl went to get the window cleaner while Spike watched the sky. He kept watching it when he heard the voice from the other side of the podium.

'Make sure your guest keeps his bucket outside,' the voice said drily.

Spike smiled to himself. 'Don't worry about it, Ian,' he said. 'It's cool.'

'Jolly good,' said the dry voice.

Ian was the oldest controller in the tower. Spike, who was twenty-three, and the youngest, although not by much, had no idea exactly how old Ian might be, but he knew it was like forty or fifty or something. That old. Dad old. Ian liked all the old bands like The Smiths.

They would be sharing duties on the watch. Spike would

take care of arrivals on the north runway, while Ian would be taking care of departures on the south runway. So they would be *almost* sharing duties, Spike thought. Nobody liked to admit it, but arrivals were a tougher gig than departures – getting them on the ground needed faster reflexes than getting them in the air. Ian was a good controller, Spike thought. Maybe even a great controller. But he was not twenty-three any more. And if you were an air traffic controller at Heathrow, the world's busiest airport, then you were playing in the Premiership.

Earl appeared with the young window cleaner. The kid had two security clearance cards around his neck – one for cleaning windows airside, and the other for having his cup of tea in the tower. He turned slowly around, taking in the panoramic, 360-degree view of the airfield. Then he looked at them. His mouth fell open.

'I'm Spike. This is Earl.'

The window cleaner stared at them, dumbfounded. Spike and Earl looked at each other and laughed. Because they knew exactly what he was thinking: *Who are these kids?* Spike in his frayed T-shirt and cargo shorts and scuffed Asics, a martial arts tattoo on one arm. And Earl with his shoulder-length hair, sawn-off jeans and bare feet. Oh, they knew what the window cleaner was thinking: *But where are all the grown-ups?*

'Thanks for cleaning our window,' Spike said. 'You're doing an awesome job out there.'

From the outside Spike always thought the control tower looked like an Olympic torch – the long column and then the smoked glass cab on top, tapering out. But when you were going up and down inside, it was like a lighthouse. A long way up. Earl gave the kid a cup of tea. He had earned it.

'I saw that movie,' the window cleaner said. 'That movie about . . . all of this.'

Spike smiled. He knew what he was going to say.

'*Pushing Tin*?' the window cleaner said. 'I saw that movie three times. Did you see it?'

Spike and Earl both nodded, trying not to smirk. They didn't want to hurt the kid's feelings, or to make him think that they were laughing at him. All controllers had seen *Pushing Tin*. It was like people who worked in record shops going to see *High Fidelity*, or gangsters going to see *The Godfather*.

'*Welcome to my sky!*' Spike and Earl quoted in unison, and then they cracked up.

They loved that film in the tower. They thought it was a fantastic comedy. So wonderfully, gloriously, hilariously wrong. The controllers in that film – they have fights, they have mental breakdowns, they sweat, they drool and they sing. Spike had never seen any air traffic controller do any of those things.

But the biggest travesty in *Pushing Tin*, Spike thought, was that all those controllers were just so *old*.

All those geezers with their weekend barbecues and their marital problems and their bald patches and their meetings with teachers about problem children and their potbellies.

Where did all that come from? Air Traffic Control was a young man's game. But Spike couldn't say any of that. Not with Ian on his watch.

Ian was so old he remembered when the tower was actually landside, half the current size and built of red brick, back in ancient history when dinosaurs walked the earth. About, oh, three years ago.

'That film is not *completely* accurate,' Spike said diplomatically. 'I think you'll find that nobody ever raises their voice up here.'

'But it must be so stressful,' the window cleaner said, shaking his head. 'All those lives in your hands . . .'

Spike smiled.

'If it was stressful,' he said calmly, 'you couldn't do it. Excuse me.'

He looked at the screen and at the sky, and he heard the rollers on Earl's chair glide across the carpet and into position.

'BA12, seven miles from marker, maintain three thousand till intercepting the localizer,' said Spike, and his voice was soothing, hypnotic, designed to inspire trust. 'Descend and maintain five thousand. Reduce speed to one hundred and sixty knots. Clear to land . . . and follow the greens.'

He looked again at the young window cleaner.

'There is no stress,' Spike said. 'But there is urgency. Time is everything. You can't occupy the runway too long at Heathrow.'

He looked over at Ian. He was sitting perfectly still in the twilight of the tower, watching the aircraft at their stands. Here was another reason why arrivals were tougher than departures. Noise restrictions meant planes were allowed to land a lot earlier than they were allowed to leave. Ian hadn't even started work yet.

'Follow the greens,' Spike told the flight from Singapore when it was on the ground. 'Turn left on Echo and park on three-two-two.'

A voice crackled over the intercom.

'But our gate's over here,' objected the pilot.

Spike had been expecting a British or possibly an Australian accent, but the voice was American. Spike exchanged a look with Earl. The lighting operator knew how Spike felt about American pilots. They sometimes confused themselves with kings of the wild frontier. *Follow the greens* was such a simple order, and it ensured that everyone was cocooned from harm, with none of the drama and trauma that happened at lesser airports.

'Follow the greens, turn left on Echo and park on three-two-two,' Spike repeated, firmer this time.

'Or you're going to get lost,' Earl muttered.

The sun was up and dazzling now. The window cleaner shielded his eyes as he watched Spike up on the podium, and it was as if the kid was blinded, not by the rising sun, but by the presence of the young air traffic controller. Spike looked down from the podium and spoke in that voice as soft as a prayer.

'What's your name?' he asked.

The window cleaner's cup seemed to tremble. 'Dan,' he said.

'Dan,' Spike repeated. 'And am I right in thinking that you do not want to clean windows for the rest of your life?'

'Not that there's anything wrong with cleaning windows,' Earl said.

'Absolutely,' Spike agreed. 'But I don't think you want to do it forever. Am I right, Dan?'

The window cleaner's voice was barely audible. 'No,' he said.

'What do you want to do with your life, Dan?'

'I want – I want to keep working here at the airport,' he said, and the words tumbled out as Spike smiled and nodded encouragement. 'The airport makes me feel – I don't know how to say it – like I'm connected to the rest of the world.'

'We understand,' Spike said.

'You do?'

'Of course,' Spike said. 'Look – our game is changing. Controllers used to work their way up from the regional airports. Not any more. Air traffic is increasing, the sky is more crowded. You can go from college door to landing seven hundred aircraft in a working day. Excuse me for a moment, Dan.'

It was an Airbus 380 coming in from Dubai – a double-decker, four-engined, wide-bodied liner, the largest passenger aircraft in the world. And when Spike thought about it later, there was no good reason for what happened.

Weather conditions were perfect. Visibility was good. The runway was dry. But the Airbus landed heavily, and Spike heard the plane's twenty-two wheels shriek with protest, and he saw the nose tyres burst in an explosion of rubber.

'That plane!' said the window cleaner.

'Drink your tea,' Spike told him quietly, as he hit the big red crash button connecting Air Traffic Control to the two fire stations, the police and the Star Centre. 'Airbus 380 on north runway with burst nose-wheel tyres,' he said.

His voice betrayed no emotion, but huge chunks of rubber were strewn across the runway and already Spike could see the orange lights of the vehicles from Airside Ops rushing to the scene.

'I'm holding everything at the stand,' Ian said from the other side of the tower. 'Give me everything you've got, Spike.'

And that was how they did it.

Ian immediately stopped all departures from moving. Spike put his arrivals into a holding pattern and then began diverting them to the clear runway where Ian landed them. Although its front wheels were shot, the Airbus still had twenty more and Earl told the pilot to follow the greens as he guided him to an emergency stand.

Airside Ops had men and equipment on the runway in minutes, including a sweeper to clear shards of rubber that could be fatal if sucked into a jet engine at 1000 centigrade. But there was a huge slab of rubber the size of a man that they could not lift. Then, as Spike watched, one of the Airside Ops team slung it over his shoulder and carried it from the runway.

The fire rigs and the ambulances were standing by, but they were not needed. When Airside Ops had the runway clear of foreign object debris, Ian started moving his departures and Spike was ready for arrivals. The entire drama lasted for five minutes. No flights were delayed.

There was an SAS flight coming in from Stockholm that had been circling the airport. Spike could see it lazily drifting across the sky.

'SK525, you are now clear to land,' Spike said. And then – although he hated to digress from the polite efficiency of Air Traffic Control, he felt that he should add something. 'And thank you for your patience, SK525.'

'No problem,' came a woman's voice. Perfect English but with the faintest accent. 'We're just getting some sightseeing up here,' she said. 'It's a beautiful day, isn't it?'

Spike laughed.

'Yes, it is, SK525,' he said. 'A beautiful day.'

And Spike wondered what she looked like.

He glanced over at Ian and watched him effortlessly get a perfect line on departures. One aircraft took off, climbed and banked to the right, then one took off, climbed and flew straight ahead, then one took off, climbed and banked to the left. One right, one straight ahead, one left. One right, one straight ahead, one left. It was lovely work. The calm ordering of the planes gave Spike a warm feeling – like when his pen was parallel to the side of his desk, or when all the cans in the cupboard of his flat were as carefully lined up as tin soldiers.

'Clear for take-off, runway twenty-seven left,' Ian said calmly, and Spike realized that he had learned his tone of chilled serenity from this man.

'Ian?'

'What?'

'Thanks,' Spike said.

Ian smiled. 'It's nothing,' he said. The older man peered at him above his reading glasses. 'I've seen burst nose-wheel tyres a hundred times.'

Spike had seen them once.

And suddenly Spike understood that the biggest problem

of all with *Pushing Tin* was that they were all in their own little worlds – as individual and alone as boxers. But the best watch in ATC would always have a mix of quick-thinking kids and old men who had seen it all and loved all the old bands like The Smiths.

Spike looked at the window cleaner.

'I wouldn't trade what I do for the world,' Spike said, feeling the need for a summing up. 'But this job is not for everyone. Even good controllers don't always settle at Heathrow. They come from some quiet little backwater, like Luton or Stansted, and they just can't stand the pace. But if you're serious, I can tell you how to go about getting a controller licence.'

Dan smiled shyly. 'Actually, what I really want to be is a pilot.'

Spike stared at him. 'A pilot?' he said.

He heard Ian laugh behind him.

'To be up above the clouds, looking down on the world in all its glory,' Dan said, his eyes getting a dreamy, faraway look. 'To walk through the airport in my uniform and have everyone look at me . . .' He held up his teacup. 'Any chance of a biscuit?'

'No,' Spike said, his voice suddenly coated with the thick ice that he used when some American pilot was reluctant to follow the greens. 'No chance of a biscuit.'

When Earl had taken the window cleaner away, Ian came and stood next to Spike. For a while they said nothing, just watched the lights of the aircraft in the distance, and when Ian spoke he did not take his eyes from the sky.

'He would never have made it anyway,' Ian said. 'He was a bit old.'